soft
calls
the
devil

For Emma

softly calls the devil

CHRIS BLAKE

echo
PUBLISHING

Echo Publishing
An imprint of Bonnier Books UK
6/69 Carlton Crescent
Summer Hill NSW 2130
www.echopublishing.com.au

Bonnier Books UK
HYLO, 5th Floor,
103–105 Bunhill Row
London EC1Y 8LZ
www.bonnierbooks.co.uk

Echo Publishing acknowledges the traditional custodians of Country throughout Australia. We recognise their continuing connection to land, sea and waters. We pay our respects to Elders past and present.

First published 2025

Printed and bound in Australia by Opus Group

MIX
Paper | Supporting responsible forestry
FSC® C001695

Editor: Anna Rogers
Page design and typesetting: Shaun Jury
Cover design: Lisa White
Cover image: Haast Pass, New Zealand, by Brayden Stanford/Alamy Stock Photo

A catalogue entry for this book is available from the National Library of Australia

ISBN: 9781786585400 (paperback)
ISBN: 9781786585417 (ebook)

echo_publishing
echopublishingaustralia
echopublishing

PRAISE FOR CHRIS BLAKE

SOFTLY CALLS THE DEVIL
'*Softly Calls the Devil* is a cracking crime tale replete with procedural insight and an engaging, authentic voice. I had no idea where the story was going, but I knew I was in safe hands; I'd follow Chris Blake anywhere.' J. P. POMARE

'Chris Blake harnesses his insider perspective alongside substantial storytelling chops to craft a layered rural noir tale set on Aotearoa's wild West Coast ... A crime novel that is about much more than the investigation of a crime (or crimes), where Blake illustrates the shards of trauma that police absorb over the course of their careers, and the importance of connection and community ... This is world-class crime fiction. Highly recommended.' CRAIG SISTERSON

THE SOUND OF HER VOICE
'Raw, authentic and gripping ... a police procedural with a difference, and a compelling glimpse into the darker side of life.' EMMA VISKIC

'Wow. The pacing is incredible, but more impressive is the gritty authenticity ... like a New Zealand True Detective.' JO SPAIN

'An absorbing novel that ... offers crime readers so much in terms of a strong voice, fascinating and flawed "hero", rich sense of place, and an up-close look at the all-too-real pressures of policing.' CRAIG SISTERSON

ABOUT THE AUTHOR

Chris Blake was born and raised in Auckland. He served briefly in the New Zealand Army's Reserve Force before joining the New Zealand Police in 2006.

His debut novel, *The Sound of Her Voice* (published under the pseudonym Nathan Blackwell), was a double finalist in the 2018 Ngaio Marsh Awards for best novel and best first novel. Chris was an assistant storyboarder for season two of the crime drama television series, *The Gulf*, released in 2021.

A wrong-doer is often a man who has left something undone.

MARCUS AURELIUS

PROLOGUE

January, 2002
Desert Road

Our Holden burned up the long, straight strip of highway that disappeared into heat haze on the horizon. The bitumen was blinding and I was glad of my sunnies. Heading north, we were currently somewhere between the Waiouru army camp and Tūrangi, on the enormous, golden flat plain that was the Central Plateau. Tussock stretched for kilometres in every direction. To our right the brown hills of the Kaimanawa Ranges, and to my left and slightly behind, the three snow-capped mountains of the Tongariro National Park, stood watch. Shihad was blasting out of the speakers, and I was smiling.

Shane was driving. Focused, but with a permanent grin. An experienced detective, he'd been my mentor for a while. The day I'd joined frontline, he'd said that if I ever wanted anything, to let him know. I wasn't sure who he was, but later found out he'd been a friend of my parents when they were younger. Without ever calling in the favour, I'd finally joined CIB and ended up on his team.

We'd been down in Bulls interviewing witnesses for an old mass-allegation child abuse case. We'd made some inroads, and with statements in hand, were heading for our overnight accommodation in Taupō. But I was actually keener to get home. Hailey had just started school, was loving it, and I couldn't have my wife taking all the glory. But it was late, Auckland would be another five hours away and Shane was good company on the piss.

I wasn't green, but I wasn't an old hand either. Having been around long enough to do most things, but not long enough to know if I was doing them right, I drifted somewhere between confident and questioning my ability.

As we approached the end of the plateau, I could see a small white truck, one of those van-height things, pulled over on the left. Beyond it, the land started to duck and dive into wilder green scrubland, as the plain began a steep drop down towards the shores of Lake Taupō.

As we passed, I could see two men in the cab, looking pretty rough. They seemed to be having a heated discussion, and as I came eye to eye with them, they stared, and stared hard. So alert, so aware that they processed the presence of police and that they were being observed. I gave Shane a glance, and saw he'd had the same reaction. He brought the Holden to a stop, swung round and took off back the way we'd come.

As we drew level with the truck, the guys were arguing properly, one of them jabbing a finger at our car. Shane turned again and lined up behind them, twisting on our red and blue flashing lights to legitimise the stop.

I picked up the radio. 'Comms, A-N Charlie, 3T.'

The comms operator came back immediately. 'A-N Charlie, Comms, go ahead.'

'3T State Highway One, northern Desert Road, northbound.'

When the operator asked for the registration, I gave it, and that the vehicle was two-up.

I got a response for a Mitsubishi truck, registered to an address in the South Island. Bit strange.

Shane calmly took everything in, then nodded at me. I got out, retucking my business shirt into my suit pants. I checked my handcuffs were on my belt and cradled my notebook under an arm.

I heard a sharp click-clack of heavy metal on metal as Shane actioned his Glock, then holstered it. This was unusual. Only CIB and the frontline sergeants' cars carried firearms, but we rarely took them out and only had the one. Maybe he was just being cautious on unfamiliar turf.

I approached the driver, pulling out my notebook, unthreatening. I saw a guy in his thirties, long dark hair, unshaven.

He eyed me warily. 'Afternoon, officer. Is there a problem?' He handed me his driver's licence and I glanced at it quickly.

'Not at all. Are you guys alright? Stuck in the middle of nowhere.'

It was then I noticed the front-seat passenger, or, more accurately, his leg, which was jiggling up and down. He was younger, sandy hair long and curly, anxiety on his sweaty face. The leg kept going. But I returned my attention to the driver as he spoke.

'Just taking a rest. Been a long drive. We came over on the ferry this morning, been driving all day.'

That fitted with the South Island origin. I was starting to lose interest, but began copying his licence details into my notebook anyway. I heard movement over in the passenger seat but kept on writing.

But then Shane's voice split the air and my little standard-procedure world turned to shit. 'Stop! Stop! Stop! Drop the gun!'

A loud boom cracked around me and I heard glass shatter. A small spray of red whipped across the inside of the cab windscreen.

I instinctively ducked down and away, moving back towards our car. 'What's happened? Shane!'

I could still hear his voice, but he wasn't talking to me. 'Hands on your head! Get out! Out onto the road! Do it now!' The driver stepped out in front of me, staring across the cab to where Shane must be standing, moving slowly and deliberately onto the ground.

Shane moved in front of the truck, into my line of sight, and I could see he was holding his Glock with two hands, aimed right at the driver's chest.

I got behind the guy, cuffed him and sat him against the tyre. I repeated my question. 'What the fuck just happened?'

'He went for a shotgun.' Shane waved me over to the other side of the vehicle.

I moved around the front of the truck, seeing the blood inside the windscreen and the broken glass where Shane's round must have exited the cab.

The sandy-haired guy was slumped over, blood leaking from his head. There was a bullet hole in the passenger window. I opened the door, dug my fingers into the guy's carotid, felt nothing. Then I saw the shotgun in his lap.

Jesus Christ.

Looking closer, I saw that the pistol round had punched through the edge of his head, taking a large chunk out of the front. I shook my head to regain some clarity, as the realisation that I'd just been involved in a police shooting started to hit me. *Shit.*

I took a few deep breaths, then returned to the roadside. Shane was calm and in control and we had a quick chat. He arrested the driver for unlawful possession of a firearm. I dropped back to our Holden and gave a sitrep.

The comms operator was disbelieving. 'Sorry, Charlie, confirming shots fired by police, one dead, one in custody?'

'Affirm, that's correct. Can we get some units for scene control, local CIB and ambulance?'

Once I was back with Shane, he nodded at the driver. 'Stick with him, Matt, I'm just going to check the back before this whole thing gets locked down.'

He disappeared behind the truck, fucking about with handles and levers, making a racket. I heard the screech and scrape as he got one of the doors open.

I heard a muffled yell, 'Holy fu–', then the sound of retching. He came back towards me, walking fast, shaking his head, then stopped, stared at the ground and threw up on his shoes. Hands on his knees, panting, he stared up at me. 'Go look.'

Before I could even adjust to the dim light, the smell hit me and I began to retch. It was a combination of shit, chemicals and death. I briefly glanced in, took in the buckets, the plastic sheeting.

Then I joined Shane and vomited on the roadside.

1.

Now
Haast

Jimmy Barnes was howling about the rhythm of the highway – I'd cranked the volume as soon as I heard the guitar intro. I was sipping from a thermos as I steered the police four-by-four wagon, bouncing and rocking south along the coastal road between Haast and Jackson Bay.

The sun had just risen clear of the Southern Alps over to my left, and through gaps in the dunes I occasionally caught the sparkle of the Tasman Sea on my right as I burned along the straight road. The rain and the wind were often a given here, but today, Haast had turned it on.

I wriggled to get comfortable. It had taken some getting used to, being back in uniform. The shirt, the pants, the various attachments on the belt of my stab-resistant vest. My baton dug into my hip and the pistol holster attachment into my backside. Speaking of, my coffee tasted like it'd been brewed in a dog's arse. Instant was the same in police muster rooms from Kaitaia to Bluff. I'd probably made around thirty thousand cups over the years and still managed to screw it up at least half the time. I ditched the thermos for the can of V sitting in the door.

I crossed the slow and dark twin rivers, the Turnbull and the Hapuka, both restricted from full flow by the huge sandbar that sat off the coast here. As I rounded a bend and entered another long straight, the land opened up either side where it had been cleared for farming.

Something in a paddock up on the left caught my eye, some sort of machinery. It hadn't been there yesterday. Too late my eyes flicked back to the road. I slammed on the brakes, skidded, heard the thuds, panicked – and then remembered that the ABS would do its thing.

There were two cars parked arse out into the road, looking like they'd pulled over in a hurry. I jolted up behind them onto the grass and yanked on the handbrake.

It was a fucking helicopter. And it had come down hard. The skids were buckled and it was resting on its nose.

I legged it over the fence and headed through the paddock. I could hear yelling and as I got closer saw some familiar faces among those surrounding the wreck.

'Wind your neck in, you big gaping arsehole. Your cows are the least of our flippin' worries!'

'To you maybe, you big bald bastard!'

The bastard in question was Gus McCabe, my predecessor in the sole charge role for two decades before he retired last year. He was a big, solid guy with the heart of a lion and a mouth like a shitter. He was about to swing at his Swanndri-clad provoker as I jogged up and grabbed his shoulder. 'Gus, mate, come on. What's the story?'

I was taking in the rest of the scene. Someone was still in the chopper, being tended to by a girl. Helping her was a guy in his thirties, in jeans and a polar fleece, looking a bit dazed – probably the pilot.

'Matty, my boy, 'bout bloody time! Liam's trapped in there with a broken foot, medic's on the way, pilot's all right… Then this dropkick –' Gus gestured to the guy in the Swanndri who was now standing back, looking sheepish, '– is harpin' on about his cows and can we hurry up?'

I took charge. 'Gus, go grab my radio and tell them I'm off at this crash.' I turned to the farmer. 'Sir, Gus here –' I made sure he was out of earshot '– can get pretty wound up. A spooked herd isn't great. Once the medic's here, we'll get Liam out as quick as we can but I'm afraid his spine takes precedence over your herd until then.'

He put his hands up. 'No arguments, Constable. We all need to take a breath.'

'Brilliant.' I poked my head into the chopper cabin, saw the man trapped inside, another familiar face – Liam Goodhue, the local DOC ranger.

'Mate, I can see Kathy pulling up on the road now, so hopefully we'll have you out of here soon.' I turned to the dark-haired girl who'd been keeping an eye on Liam. 'Hey Tara, are you taking some obs?' The kids around here knew more about first aid than most cops did.

She spoke matter of factly, no bullshit. 'Yeah, his heart's racing, and I can't see how bad his foot is leaking 'cause it's crushed under the fuselage.'

'Ah, I'm right here.' Liam was gritting his teeth.

'We didn't want to move him, in case –' She touched her spine to indicate what she meant.

'Liam, mate,' I said, 'can you move your feet?'

He shook his head. 'My left I can, if you can see that. My right is fucked.'

I leaned in and checked under the instrument panel: his left boot was moving. I grasped his shoulder. 'They'll have some pain relief into you in a sec. Cheers, Tara.'

Kathy had been the local St John volunteer for a decade and because she was the only worker for literally hundreds of kilometres, she had pretty much trained right up to paramedic level. With most things in this part of the world, everyone was sole charge this or lone ranger that. But when things happened, everyone piled in.

She yelled at me before she got anywhere close. 'Bloody hell, and I was counting on some help! Been drinking this morning, Senior Constable?'

I tried to look hurt. 'I don't drink before ten.'

She chuckled, making a beeline for the helicopter cabin.

I kept on her shoulder. 'I could smell fuel, mate, so I'm thinking we should get him out sooner rather than later. His good foot can move, and no sense everyone dying in a ball of flaming Jet A1.'

As she approached Liam, Tara stayed with her, but I took a step back along with the pilot. 'Matt Buchanan.' I figured my uniform needed no introduction.

He shook. 'Phil Stoneham. Westland Helicopters.'

'You okay?'

'Yeah, few sore bits but everything seems to be working.'

'Kathy will check you out.'

I sniffed about, but the fuel smell had gone. Maybe it just got churned up a bit.

It felt like I'd only just used the radio in Kathy's wagon to give an update and clarify our location for the rescue helicopter, when I heard a siren, and eventually the thump of rotor blades coming through one of the valleys until the chopper roared and flared into the paddock next to us. The broken one on the ground didn't explode as we all walked away in slow motion. It wasn't like the movies. Nothing ever was.

2.

Unless you headed inland again, Haast was the last town on the West Coast before Antarctica, but that didn't stop good people, locals and tourists alike, from meeting up at the Hard Antler for a drink or twelve. The background noise was classic Kiwi pub: low chatter, voices raised because booze makes you deaf and the odd roof-lifting yell of laughter as someone enjoyed another's misfortune.

I'd been pretty dark about the posting, in the beginning. As a born-and-bred Aucklander, and a former detective, it wasn't what getting back in should have looked like. But up there, I'd chased a serial killer for two decades, almost getting my daughter killed in the process. I hadn't dealt with the fallout of that too well, and though I'd survived, some others weren't so lucky. The decisions I'd made had really taken their toll. On me. And on the way the department had viewed my application to rejoin.

Now, though, I wouldn't trade Haast for anything. Seated on a stool, back to the wall beside the bar, pint in hand, I surveyed the pissed groups of mates with a grin. I downed the frothy remnants, then passed the glass to Darren. 'One more please, barkeep.'

'You've got a drinking problem. I should cut you off.'

'I've got more than just a drinking problem, and that's exactly why you shouldn't.'

Darren snorted as he swiped a chilled glass from the fridge and pulled the handle on another pint of Monteith's. We'd become good mates since I'd arrived here, probably because he was the guy I saw the most regularly. He was in his late thirties, though the collar-length hair escaping from his beanie helped him to pretend he was younger.

The Antler was the only pub in Haast, but with a population of a few hundred, there wasn't much more the town needed. Dining and seated tables in the back half, sports bar in front, it was legendary.

I heard bustling in the kitchen area. 'Uh oh, you're in trouble now, Daz. Best start polishing those glasses before the Dragon figures you've been pissing about.'

Jodie cast me a look as she started placing bottles in the fridge. 'Matt, stop distracting him, he can't do two things at once.'

Darren couldn't help himself. 'Not what the girls in Dunedin used to say.'

She came straight back. 'They were probably from Auckland, weren't they? Wouldn't've known a real man if he sat on them.'

'Whoa, whoa, Jodes,' I cut in. 'Present company and all that.'

She started to grin, unable to keep up the charade. 'You might be the only okay Aucklander I've met since I came here as a teenager in the eighties, but hey, jury's still out.'

Darren was on a roll, wiping a tear from his eye. 'A teenager in the eighties? Thought you knitted socks for the Anzacs.'

An apple came flying out of the kitchen, clipped the bench next to Darren's elbow and smashed against the taps in front of him. A few punters looked up. Darren grinned and raised his hand in apology.

The door was pushed open with force and in sauntered the big guy, broad shouldered and bald, eyeing up the place. He waved happily at a few folk before setting his sights on me, grunting with effort as he hauled himself onto the stool next to mine.

'What'll it be, Gus? Beer or liquor?'

'Liquor please, Daz. How are you both?'

'Things are good, mate,' I replied. 'Still feel like I've stolen a dream.'

'Well, you have, but don't tell anyone. Rest of the world goes bloody crazy and Haast is insulated from all that. Just remember that if you ever think about heading back to the big smoke.'

He was watching Liam, who was at a table under the TV, chatting with a few locals, his crutches propped against the wall.

I followed his gaze. 'He got off lucky.'

Gus made a noise I couldn't place. 'Yeah, well, everyone down here lends a hand when needed. But we've all got skeletons. Him more than most.' He downed his rum and Coke and signalled Darren for another.

Jodie appeared, saw Gus and feigned shock, jabbing a thumb at me. 'Oh great, if this guy wasn't bad enough, now we've really killed the vibe.'

Gus slapped my shoulder. 'I'll take my dues, but Jodes, you're forgetting Matt here is the best copper south of the equator. Leave him out of it. Shit at de-escalating a fight, mind. If it wasn't for him I'd never have had a go at that knob in the Swannie.'

She rolled her eyes. 'That your third, Matt? You driving?'

It was the best part of the place. My home, and the local station, were a two-minute walk around the corner.

3.

My headlights lit only the road, nothing but blackness either side. It was something I still found claustrophobic. In the big cities there was light pollution everywhere, letting you get your bearings. Here, even though I knew there was nothing between me and the ocean on my right, and nothing but swamp under the mountains on my left, it felt like a tunnel.

It was a different type of policing here. In a year I'd attended a handful of domestics and a couple of crashes. The community did a good job of policing itself, and because everybody knew everybody, there wasn't a lot of room to make enemies. If some of my old CIB colleagues could see me now, they'd describe me in a single word: soft.

My lights swept the vegetation lining the gravel entrance as I turned into the refuse station. The padlock had been cut and the gates swung wide. I drove through mānuka scrub and swamp rushes on both sides, right into the scrap yard that was almost entirely hidden from the main road by trees.

There was a small fire burning down the far end. I couldn't

see much else, so I rolled the vehicle slowly, eyes searching left and right, mentally taking note of where the pepper spray and taser were on my belt. With my windows down I could hear bass pumping and my headlights finally washed over a couple of cars and a group of teenagers beside the flames. 'Oh shit,' said one of the girls. 'Matt's here.' She stubbed something into the ground, which did nothing to hide the obvious smell lingering in the cold night air.

A skinny lad on a folding deckchair turned and gave me a shaka. A couple were standing, drunkenly in love, the guy holding her from behind. I knew most of the group. They were all kids of locals, would have grown up together, all attending the same tiny primary school, and were now boarders at more distant high schools because there wasn't one here in Haast. Must be school holidays.

The guy in the deckchair, Harry I think his name was, stood and came toward me. 'Sorry, Matt. Look, we'll pack this in …'

I held up my hand. 'Nah, nah. If you guys want to freeze your arses off out here, hey, who am I to judge.'

My torch beam landed on the girl with the joint. 'Tara, you can retrieve that if you want. I'm not going to be taking it off you. Shit'll be legal in no time anyway.'

She scrabbled in the stones. 'Thanks, Matt.'

'Cheers for your help the other day.'

She nodded like it was nothing.

I turned to go. 'Look, I only got called 'cause someone wanted to make sure nobody was getting hurt. Flames from the road and all that. Surprised you even got the fire going in this weather. Just tell me, who cut the lock?'

They all dropped their eyes except Tara, who put up her hand. No hesitation, no fear. 'I did.'

'Right. Before Monday, a replacement. Solid one. Drop it in to me. It's not always just you locals round here, you know.'

She stood there, taking it in. She was wearing a hei matau, a fish-hook pendant carved from bone. People around here had an affinity with the land and the sea that went right back, to way before Jackson Bay was settled by immigrants. The bountiful Haast coastline had always been a top food source and it kept the area alive. I pointed at the necklace. 'For luck, right?'

She nodded. 'My grandad was Ngāi Tahu.'

Harry piped up again. 'Vinnie should get one for his fishing boat 'cause he catches fuck all.'

4.

The morning was a real shitter. The wind off the Tasman was blowing the rain near horizontal as I slowed to enter the long single-lane bridge above the swollen Haast River.

I was heading north to see what was up on the state highway.

I couldn't see too far, with the rain and the spray swallowing everything up, but I spotted headlights ahead, in one of the passing bays. Getting alongside, I could see a figure in a dark green raincoat, hauling a tyre out of the boot. After stopping in the bay on my side, I jumped out, pulling on my police fluoro. I was soaked before I even got my first arm in.

'Hey, like a hand?' I yelled.

A pale face turned, squinted against the rain. 'Hi! Oh my God, yes please. Oh, you're police?'

I grinned through the rain lashing my face. 'Apparently so.'

She stood and passed me her tyre iron. 'This thing is buggered.'

I checked the inside grip of the tool and saw it was worn smooth. 'Where you heading? Haast?'

'Yeah, staying at a B&B tonight before heading to Hāwea.'

'Hold on.'

I tried my tyre iron, which worked great, probably because it got stuff-all use.

'Wait on.' She opened her front passenger door and returned with a can. After a burst of oil under the nuts, things got much easier. I got a couple off, then passed the iron to her. 'Here, do the rest while I jack this thing up.'

She got the other nuts off, no trouble, while I was still stuffing about on my back, searching for where to put the jack, and then using the tool to twist and raise it. By the time I'd slid back out, she'd pulled off the old tyre and was seating the new one.

I chucked the nuts on, made sure they were tight, then extended my hand. 'Matt Buchanan, Haast Police. Sorry this didn't happen faster or drier for you.'

She shook my hand and laughed. 'Anna Travers. Thanks so much.'

'If you're staying, the local pub is all there is. The Hard Antler. The whole town will be there. It's karaoke night.'

Her eyes widened as if she'd just won the lottery. 'Count me in. And thanks.'

Once she'd started up and driven away, I continued north over the bridge, humming something by Split Enz and smiling for no reason at all.

5.

The Antler was pumping. Even in the wake of the tourism hit from Covid, there were probably forty people there, locals and visitors, and though the vibe was cheery they'd darkened the place to try and coax up a few people with stage fright.

Right now Gus was up the front belting out Springsteen, not too horribly, while Darren and I lounged at a high table and raised our beers to him. He delivered an impressive finish, down on one knee, arse end of the microphone pointing to the ceiling, head tilted back, throwing out the final lines with his gut hanging out the bottom of his shirt and a full sweat on. It was beautiful.

As he stumbled back up to us, he threw me the microphone to a chorus of cheers from the audience.

Normally I'd rather cut my nuts off, but tonight, I was well on my way to being solidly pissed, and inhibitions were out the door. But when the opening notes of 'Heavenly Pop Hit' rang out I knew I was in trouble. Still, I gave it death.

Right then, the door swung open and in walked a woman

of about thirty, her hair blowing about her face as the wind followed her in. She headed for the bar, then looked across at me, staring, before breaking into a laugh.

After making a shambles of the end of the song, I ducked out humbly, to pats from some locals and a whisky pushed across the bar by Jodie. 'You know, you sound as shit as you look, Matt.'

'Tell me something I don't know.'

'Bollocks, Jodes, voice of an angel Matty has.' Darren was thoroughly enjoying himself.

'And what moves! I thought I was at Eurovision.' The voice was light, unforced.

Darren spoke up. 'You've met already, Anna tells me.'

I almost choked on my drink. Out of the storm, she looked different – dry clothes, lighter hair, beaming from ear to ear.

The uniform could be a bit of a barrier to recognition, yet she'd picked me out in nanoseconds. 'So … you're on holiday here?'

'Sort of. Born and bred in Canterbury but I'm taking a yoga course in Hāwea. It's the new Bali, hadn't you heard?'

'Not in this fucking climate it's not.'

She grinned and sipped her drink. 'And what about you? You're not a local. Where are you from?' Darren started smirking like an idiot. 'I probably shouldn't say.'

She grinned. 'So you're an Aucklander?'

Darren couldn't resist dropping me in it further. 'Hey now, he may be an import from Auckland, but Matt here isn't any old local cop. He used to be murder police.'

Anna showed some surprise. I could see assumptions, thoughts, prejudices even, all churning through her mind.

As we chatted, I picked up a hippie vibe and a positivity that could have been mistaken for naivety, but I was getting the feeling she was razor sharp. She turned me down when I offered to buy her another drink. 'I'm actually heading through the pass early tomorrow. I shouldn't have another or you'll be locking me up for drink driving at 8 a.m. I'll have a lemon, lime and bitters, though.'

My eyes followed her as she headed for the bathroom.

Darren punched me in the arm. He was pissing himself. 'What the hell was that about, Matty? Someone's got to you. I've never seen that before. I thought you were all business. You're a bloody flower.'

6.

It was midday and I was hungover. Eyes barely open, I was impressed with my coffee-making efforts, despite my wish to sleep.

I was in the police station, conveniently part of the same property as my house. Both were red-brick and grey-roofed places, the larger one kitted out as a home and separated by a couple of trees from the smaller building.

I was eyeing up the coffee tin on the bench, already thinking about cup number four, when there was a knock at the door and Tara and her mother Sheryl walked in. There was no doubt that they were related – same hair, though Sheryl wore hers short, same face shape and slim build.

Tara dropped a plastic-wrapped padlock on the muster room table. It would do the job well. 'Great, thanks. I'll chuck it on later today. That was quick.'

Something unsaid passed between mother and daughter before Sheryl said, 'I didn't even have to remind her. She was out to Reece's first thing.' Reece Mackie had run the service station for donkey's years, and had a few other businesses dotted around too.

Tara was looking at a map of the region on the wall, then started reading a poster with the police's strategic objectives plastered all over it. 'I've never been in here.'

'Well, that's probably a good thing.'

'You've thought about the police, though, haven't you?' said Sheryl.

'It's something I'd really like to be able to do, yeah,' said Tara. 'But there are parts I think I'd be into, and bits I just wouldn't be right for.'

'When I joined, I wasn't sure it was for me. But you get taught everything you need to know. If you're healthy, then it's doable. How old are you?'

'Eighteen. It's the deaths and the child abuse . . . I . . . I don't know if I have it in me.'

'Well, I can't speak for other cops, but I've always taken the "Well, if I'm not going to do it, who the hell is?" approach with those situations. Public expectation gives you the balls to do your job, I guess. No one's born with what it takes. Most of it you make up as you go along.'

'And you have guns in your cars now, right? Something else I'm not so sure about.'

'The training's better. A lot better. As for the guns in the cars, all that's really changed is that we can now deal with problems quicker. Makes sense to me. Anyway, I'd definitely head to uni, or travel around or something first.'

'Why?'

'Well, I didn't do either, but the job sucks you in, so you don't think about that until later. Do it first. The police will always be around.'

7.

Joe's place was out off the Haast–Jackson Bay Road, past the refuse station. A long stretch of not much, besides swamp on the inland side of the road and dunes and harsh coast on the other. Houses were few and far between.

And when I say 'Joe's place' – well, it wasn't exactly prime real estate.

I trudged through the mud in my boots, water around my ankles. Sometimes it was knee deep, depending on the rains off the mountains, and how much filtered into the swamps. But it was always freezing. I used the plastic storage box I was carrying to help push the reeds aside as I made my way through the bog.

A couple of hundred metres from where I left the car, I found the piece of driftwood, carefully attached to two posts, that formed a little footbridge over a deeper part of the water. It was so narrow you could only put one foot in front of the other, and it wobbled the whole way.

I dropped into the reeds at the other end and followed the worn pathway that wound through more sludge towards a little corrugated shack, almost enclosed by taller, white-trunked trees rising behind and around it.

'Joe, you big raging alcoholic! Get a shirt on and get out here!'

I paused, listening for movement. Nothing. Strange as it may sound, it didn't smell like shit. I'd holidayed in Aussie, and Louisiana, and seen parts of South East Asia where swamps are loud, hot, steaming, stinking places. The swamps here, though, were dark and cold. Decomposition didn't take hold like it would north of here. But the water looked the part and swarms of sandflies kept me company.

'Joe, put the sheep down and get out here. I'm not coming into that rat-infested home of yours.'

I heard him then. A small giggle emerged from the shack, and the muffled sounds of someone pulling on clothes. I heard him mumble something and giggle again. Then he stumbled out, with a big toothy grin, wearing a heavy Swannie, gumboots and no pants.

'Up early to get your ticket quota, were you? Be in the running for that meat pack I hear they give out end of every month?' More laughter.

'It's ten o'clock, Joe.' But I was grinning too.

First time I'd met him he was sitting on a dead tree trunk down at the beach, halfway through a twenty-four-pack of Double Brown, yelling at the waves. We'd crossed paths quite a few times since I'd been here, and always for stuff I'd have considered pretty minor – drinking, weed, wrong-place-wrong-time. He always seemed happy with himself. He'd never caused me any actual trouble. Always complied. And always, always, gave me shit. Either about my Auckland heritage, the police or some part of my appearance. No doubt he appreciated the ribbing he got back from me.

I liked the guy. I saw some of myself in him. I could have gone there, quite easily.

'Hmm, the law brought presents, eh?' He was eyeing up the box of Heineken I had under my arm. Then his face fell. 'Fuck.' He looked up at me questioningly though he was still grinning. 'The good stuff? What've I gone and done now?'

I put the box down, pulled two out, popped the caps on the metal frame of the rusted, half-sunken tractor that'd been here probably since before Joe had and passed one over. 'Got a warrant again, Joe. For your plants. Sorry, mate.' I touched my bottle to his.

He just laughed. 'Goddamn. Do ya know how long it takes me to get a crop going? Just when I'm 'bout to harvest too. Can't you wait a couple weeks?'

'There's a limit to this small town copper act you know, Joe. This is the … what, sixth time since I've been here? And I brought beer. You should be flipping grateful.'

Foam burst from his nose as he cackled. 'How'd you even know? How'd you get the warrant?'

I looked sideways at him and he erupted into laughter again.

I reckoned Joe had been growing weed since before he could walk. He constantly had thirty-odd plants on the go, usually in different stages so he never had to wait. And he was hardly Mr Asia. He smoked it all away, kept to himself most of the time. But the law was the law, and after several warnings, I'd executed a warrant a few months back and he'd put his head down, taken the home detention.

But he'd told me then he'd always grow, no matter what. To help him forget. When I'd asked the obvious question, he'd said, 'Everything.' But he'd also told everyone at the Hard Antler on karaoke night that he was harvesting in a week.

'C'mon, Joe, let's have these, then you can help me pull 'em out. I'm not doing the hard work by myself.'

'Ya know, you're all right, Buchanan. Cut from different cloth to some of the pigs I've seen.'

'Yeah well. The pigs are changing.'

'I hear you, bloody oath.'

'Well, unless of course you're the sole charge cop at Haast, unsupervised, and make it what you want it to be.'

He grinned and drank.

'But still. Blabbing all over town is kinda taking the piss, mate.'

We hauled his plants out and dropped the filled rubbish sacks onto the grass. Then he held his arms out, wrists ready for the cuffs.

I shook my head. 'What's the point? It's just screwing you over. This is a warning.'

I wasn't being lazy. It was that I just didn't care. There's a very fine, but very important, difference between the two.

And Joe was alright. He kicked the Heineken box. 'One more?' I shook my head. 'And hey, thanks for helpin' out old Liam the other day, Jafa.'

'You know Liam?'

He wheezed. 'It's Haast, you cabbage, everyone knows everyone. How old do I look to you?'

'A hundred and six?'

'Get fucked.' He took another beer from the box, then looked out across the lagoon. 'You know who Liam was, right?'

I shook my head.

'Before he worked for the Department of Conservation, he was with the Forest Service – as a ranger. Ask him. Few beers and he'll chat to you, I'm sure.'

I'd known Liam was a bushman, but not for how long.

'Pissed old bastard likes Lion Red, though.' He coughed into his beer.

'Says the guy who drinks dog piss like it's nectar.'

'You hasslin' my favourite cans? You've got no taste, Buchanan.'

And he turned away, dropped his jocks and pissed, right there on the ground. 'See? Your green-bottled shit might be four times the price, but end of the day, it comes out the same bloody colour.'

8.

Like pretty much everything round here, Liam's place was also out between Haast and Jackson Bay, along that same stretch of road. It was a small A-frame among a dozen houses and baches on a triangle of land that jutted out into the Okuru River mouth.

I was down the far end of the houses, near the gravel strip that ran down to the stony riverbed. Opposite Liam's, a stack of cray pots was sitting ready for shifting. A guy came out and waved. I recognised Vinnie's dad – they fished together – and raised my hand. No degrees of separation around here.

It reminded me a bit of Omaha Beach back home, though without the three-million dollar price tag. Beyond Liam's place, I could see the Alps rising above the bush beyond the main road. To the right, out over the rivermouth towards the ocean, I could see the huge sandbar formed from the collision of the Okuru and the Turnbull rivers terminating together and getting smashed back by the Tasman Sea.

Liam, on crutches, opened with a smile. 'Good to see you,

Matt. Thanks for your help that day. I mean it. Come on in. Coffee?'

'Absolutely.' I grinned and shook his hand.

While he got busy in the kitchen I pretended not to be too nosy about his lounge. There were a few faded photos on the walls of him standing triumphantly in front of Forest Service huts in his shorts, hair to his shoulders. 'Hard man, I see.'

He laughed. 'Hard-ly. It was labour, but it was outside. Couldn't complain. It still felt like a hobby.'

The man handing me my coffee was very different from the one in the photos. In his sixties, hair gone, a life lived. In another frame, Liam was standing with a group of guys in jeans and leather jackets, with long hair. I remembered Gus's words, thought about the jackets.

'I think I'm the opposite. Not so much in love with the outdoors, but I joined the army to prove a point to myself, I think. See what I was capable of and all that. Hated nearly every minute of it.'

'The yelling and the telling, huh?'

'Bit like that, yeah.'

'Cheers.' Liam touched his mug to mine. 'So, any more fallout from the shambles that gave me this?' He indicated his cast.

'Nope. Civil Aviation Authority is investigating – looks like power loss. What was the flight about anyway?'

His pause made me look at him. 'A hunting recce. I'm heading into the backblocks in a few weeks maybe. I was just checking out the rivers and some landing sites with Phil.' He smiled. 'Bloody hell, Gus is a loose unit. It's a wonder he survived in the force for so long.'

'He's from a different era.'

'I must say, Matt, I was impressed by how calm you were. I

remember thinking that you can switch it on when you need to.'

'Well, it wasn't my first rodeo.'

He grimaced. 'I know. We all looked you up before you arrived. You're no tyre-kicker. You've done some things.' He meant it as a compliment.

'And fucked up a few others.'

'You can't think of it like that. You're still in. You're doing this, down here. If you truly felt like that you'd be growing kiwifruit in Motueka – lifestyle block, beer and not much else.'

'You're probably right.'

'You had to see people die, Matt?'

Friends. Strangers. A few that fell into neither category. I was able to accept the memories now, didn't try and bury them as I'd done in the past.

'A couple. Mostly dead when I got there.' *Mostly.*

'True, true. Sorry.' He put his mug down. 'Been meaning to ask. If someone I know . . . had information – like, I don't mean rats and mice stuff, something serious – can the cops look after them?'

'Keep it confidential? Of course. I mean, depending on who you tell. It's the early stages that matter, so there isn't a chain of loose lips. The police aren't great at dealing with information well, on the whole. But within police, there are some who are top notch at it. Find one of them and you're okay.'

'And which are you?'

'I'd like to think of myself as the latter, but time will tell. I guess.'

As he opened the door for me, he said, 'Great to see you, Matt. And I'll let my mate know they could be in safe hands.'

9.

I kept the inflatable straight, hand on the tiller, aiming for the wide, empty boat ramp. It was sunny and clear, Jackson Bay sparkled a little and the gulls wheeled.

With the ocean behind us, to our left stretched the wharf, the small and striking blue-topped bright orange building that was the Craypot, the famous fish and chippery at the arse end of nowhere, and the road disappearing back along the lowlands towards Haast.

The water stopped churning and began to glide gently past as I backed off the throttle, the whine of the motor changing to a gentle putt-putt as I aimed for the right side of the ramp. I lifted the engine, slowing us right down so Darren could jump out into thigh-deep water and bring us to a stop. A few minutes later we had the boat up on his trailer, no worries.

Now that I could stare without losing concentration and writing off Darren's boat on the concrete, I could see north all the way along the coast to the Haast River mouth. The forest crept up the hills behind, and beyond them, the dark shards of the Alps were crowned with more snow – a reminder that it wasn't summer.

It had been a good day. Darren lifted the chilly bins full of crays onto the tray of his Ranger and we bungied it all up. Just as we were setting off, someone from the Craypot waved me over. 'Matt! Hailey's on the phone.'

Because cell-phone reception was mostly non-existent in these parts, Hailey had the numbers for the station, the Antler, the cafe and here – places I frequented and where people could track me down.

'Hey, Dad. Happy birthday. Got your gold card in the mail?' She was obviously in good spirits.

I gave her one back. 'Who's this?'

She laughed. 'What have you been doing?'

I gave in. 'It's been great, actually. Just got in from a dive with Darren ... he says hi. Beers soon, with crayfish on the barbie. Lemon butter or garlic, that's the question.'

'Man, I wish I was joining you.'

Hailey was living in Wellington now, having landed a high-flying job working for the Ministry of Foreign Affairs. She'd joined as part of their new graduate program. Whenever we were together I told people she worked for the foreign service, but always followed it up with a whispered, 'I think she's a spy.' She'd been eye-rolling at me since she was an infant, so why stop now?

'Hey, you're living the dream in the capital, remember. Don't worry, there'll be plenty more birthdays for me.'

'Not at your age.'

'You still coming down next week?'

She'd booked some leave to take a long weekend, let me show her the best the wild West Coast had to offer.

'Of course, it's just crap it couldn't have been over your birthday. By the way, did you get anything in the mail?'

'Shit, you sent me something?'

'Sure did. Go check – you're gonna like it.'

I grinned. 'I'll check soon as we get back into town. What is it?'

'Uh-uh. Wait and see.'

'Hey, thanks. Big-time government wage going to your head?'

'I said you'd like it, not that it was expensive.'

As I hauled myself into the ute I asked Darren if we could swing by my place to see if anything had been dropped off.

And there was a parcel sitting on the station porch. It was a big square, hard and flat. I opened it and drew a decorated card sleeve from the thicker cardboard protectors. 'Holy shit.' I turned it over, checked the track listing, turned it back. The gold silhouettes and painted galaxy cover art jumped out: it was the fiftieth anniversary edition of *The Piper at the Gates of Dawn*, the first album by one of my favourite bands.

Darren was also a fan. 'Shit indeed, Matty. You've raised her right. Let's whack it on when we get to mine: my turntable's in the garage. Have a listen while we get the coals going. I'm always up for some Floyd.'

10.

The barbie was lit and we were ready to go. Darren was OC tongs, and my job was to keep a supply of cold beer heading his way.

'Jodes will be by shortly,' said Darren, 'once she's handed over. And Gus should be here any minute.'

Speaking of the devil, the gate into Darren's backyard swung open and in came Gus, puffer jacket on, a box of beer under each arm.

'Bloody hell, Gus. It's not O-Week, mate.'

'What're you on about? These are for me. You can both get fucked.'

He cracked open a can and took a swig before marching over to check Darren's cooking technique. 'Did Matt tell you how I almost got clobbered by a nutcase farmer?'

'No, he didn't actually. You were telling me how you thought Gus was a wanker, weren't you, Matt?'

'The only one out of control was this guy.' I thumbed at Gus, who started laughing.

'Bollocks! That guy needed some sense knocked into him, he did. Flippin' cows. There were people hurt, mate. Shoulda hit him harder.'

When Darren disappeared inside to find something to shake onto the cray tails, Gus lifted his beer can to me. 'You know, Matt, I was meaning to have a word with you – about Liam and something I've been looking into for a while. Might be right up your alley, and it is a local case after all.'

I raised my eyebrows.

'And fishy as fuck. An old one, real old: 1978. Family went missing in Haast Pass, right up in the saddle. They found the car, empty, a few days later.'

He paused to take a pull from his can and I jumped in. 'What, no trace?'

He burped and wiped his face on his sleeve. 'Oh, there was a trace all right – found the bodies in the bush. Murder–suicide. Bloke killed his wife and daughter, then himself. But I tell you what, there's more to it, much more, and some of the folk round here know a bit more than the files record, know what I'm saying? And Liam, he was right in the thick of it . . .' He trailed off as Darren came back out, with a handful of chopped coriander. 'I'll come see you at the station and we can chat more about it. It'd be nice to pass the torch, now that you've settled in.'

I was well into my third beer when Jodie came through the gate with some bags and wine. 'Look who I found standing all lovely and bright outside –' She gestured as Anna breezed in behind her. I gave her a kiss on the cheek, and immediately sent daggers at Darren, who was laughing his arse off behind the barbie.

Anna caught my look and filled me in. 'Darren ran into me

yesterday at the cafe. Couldn't resist inviting me here so that we could catch you unprepared.'

'You're both nuts.'

I took Anna aside to catch up on how the yoga and green tea were going. As we chatted and drank, I was drawn in by everything about her, from her content, happy-with-life vibe to her quick wit. She seemed to belong here, fitting in without effort. I think that's what was intriguing me. I'd always placed the health and wellness camp in with the anti-vaxxers – people who saw conspiracy in everything and ignored science mainly because they weren't the ones doing the experiments. But Anna wasn't in that camp at all.

She touched my hand lightly. 'Time to tell me your story. How'd you end up down here?'

'Well, I was a cop in Auckland for more than twenty years. Now I'm a cop in Haast.'

She laughed. 'I'd like the long version, thanks.'

Holding up a finger for a pause, I swallowed some beer. 'I worked murders and rapes, and the rest, for most of that. I quit twice, once because a mate got shot, another time … I was in a pretty dark spot. But I came back twice. The second time, I didn't get to choose where I went.'

'Jesus, okay. Was it … something you did?'

'Yes and no. I guess you could say I rubbed a few people up the wrong way. Lucky for me, there were still a few I'd rubbed the *right* way, and the result was I got back into the police, but ended up here as Gus's replacement.'

'And you love it here.' It was a statement, not a question.

'It's nice, it's different.'

'Probably less violent, a bit less visceral.'

'That's … yep, that'd be spot on. Doesn't matter what the

bosses or the politicians want, the world keeps on spinning. There are some great people down here who are good company.'

'You aren't chasing the bad guys anymore?'

I finished my can, reached into the chilly bin and cracked another. 'Someone else can do that. People do dumb and stupid things. People panic and they live complicated lives. No effort from on high is ever going to change that. We'd probably all do ourselves a favour by just letting stuff happen and dealing with it afterwards. Down here I get to do that.'

You don't believe all that, though, do you.

'Mmm.' She was thinking about something, but I didn't probe.

I changed the subject. 'So why are you here, chatting up the local cop?'

'I'm not chatting you up.'

'Yes, you are.'

'You're chatting *me* up. Ask Darren.'

He could hear most of our conversation and decided now would be a good time. 'You're chatting her up, Matt.'

Eventually I just took the direct approach and walked Anna the few hundred metres around the corner to my place. We were both quite smashed but not to the point where I wasn't aware that I was pretty happy.

When I finally got the door open, she propelled me inside and kissed me against the wall. She gripped the back of my head and pushed herself into me, feeling me against her, before shoving me off and ahead of her through to the bedroom. She started laughing as I began a slow strip.

11.

I wasn't too bad the next day. Anna was up early, feeling right as rain and wanting to hit the markets in Wānaka. I made my apologies for not joining her, but it was a work day for me and I'd had a call from the owners of the Makarora Lodge about some found property.

As I drove inland, the road rose up, out of the cabbage trees and bogs, and into the foothills of the Alps. The Haast River grew faster and narrower beside the road, and the steep, sheer rock appeared on the other side as the highway climbed and twisted. When it eventually began to flatten out as I neared the saddle in Haast Pass proper, the beech forests closed in on both sides. They weren't like the forests up north, all light greens and browns and tumbled together. These forests were like something out of Tolkien – soft edges, lots of moss and vines, dark but welcoming.

In the pass the forest closed over the top of the road, forming a dark green tunnel. I drove through the DOC carpark area where walking tracks offered options on both sides of the highway.

Two huge rivers came pouring off the mountains here: the Haast, rushing towards the coast behind me, and the Makarora, which came from more or less the same place, but flowed in the direction I was heading. It parallelled the highway now, and would eventually terminate at the head of Lake Wānaka.

I was spat out of the beech forest into the flats, a series of clearings formed originally by the Makarora flooding and receding, its braided path feeling its way through what had long since become agricultural land. If I kept going, I'd eventually end up in Hāwea and then Wānaka, but I wasn't going that far.

The lodge, on the left side of the highway, was a long log building with a green angled roof, like something you'd see in Yellowstone National Park. The vacancy sign was lit red and a couple of cars were parked out front.

Technically this was Otago's patch, and therefore a Wānaka officer's job, but Marilyn Chambers was Haast born and bred and this was a little closer to me. She and her husband had owned this place for years, and now, in their late sixties, kept it running because they loved it.

'Matthew, thanks for coming out. It's really good to see you.'

I perked up immediately. Everyone was 'Senior Constable this' or 'Officer that' until I really got to know them. I'd met Marilyn before but didn't know her well, so to have her use my name was refreshing and told me I'd been accepted into the inner circle.

'Not a problem. How's Ivan?'

Her husband appeared and took up station at the reception desk. 'Just fine thanks, Matt. It's good to see you.' We shook hands, the strength in his at odds with his skinny frame.

Marilyn smiled and ushered me back into the staffroom where I sat on a couch while she mucked about with a coffee machine. 'It's nothing much, I'm afraid. I just thought I'd better hand it in in case someone was looking for it. I know the police have better things to do.'

'Hey, I'm free today and happy to help.'

While I sipped at the froth on my cup, she disappeared briefly and returned with a paper bag. 'It was on the roadside, back up towards Cameron Flat.'

Inside was a smartphone. I noted the model, then popped the cover and wrote down the IMEI number.

Marilyn looked out through the bay window. 'Mist is rolling in. Gets creepy out here.'

'Creepy? It's Otago. Heartland.'

'Well, this place has its own kind of history. Murders before the British arrived. Some horrors not so long ago. It's been a while since anything happened, but we keep our fingers crossed it stays that way.'

I remembered what Gus had mentioned at Darren's.

'Guests used to say they'd seen people run across the roads, in the mist, in the night. People made up urban legends about old car crashes, and the valley holding onto them, but it would've often just been campers.'

'Mmmm.' I decided I had nothing to lose. 'I heard about the family who died in the pass, if that counts.'

'Oh, the Fawkes – that was awful. Major story back then. I was in my twenties but I remember it like it was yesterday. That poor girl.'

I looked interested so she gave me a bit more of a rundown than Gus had.

'It was in there.' She gestured back north up the road, towards the pass and the bush. He'd led them in, they reckoned, off a trail, and then . . .'

'How'd he kill himself?'

'Blew his own head off with a gun. At least he got his comeuppance. But what a tragedy.'

* * *

Even at the slow speed I was going, the wagon rocked and kicked over the uneven surface of the gravel path that wound through thick scrub and bush towards the river. Back in Haast, Sheryl had been on me before I'd even stepped out of the wagon. 'Matt, everyone's looking for you. Get down to the rivermouth. Reece is down there – the track just before the hotel, by the bridge. He found something. He was white as a sheet, wouldn't tell me anything.'

As I rounded the bends, looking for the opening at the end, scrubland crowded in. It was mainly cabbage trees and mānuka, all that could grow in the alluvial deposits of the riverbed, but it rose up well above the wagon. A couple of hundred metres in I finally popped out of the bush into more open, stony ground, with a tendril of river gliding past, aiming for the sea.

Reece's tall, red-headed frame jumped out of nowhere, arms raised, bringing me to a stop. I pushed my door open. 'Jesus Christ, man, what's going on?'

'Matt, I can't, I can't . . .' He was pale, almost hyperventilating.

I tried to calm him. 'Whoa, Reece, hold on. Are you okay? Sorry, fucking phone system. Breathe, just breathe, and then we'll talk.'

He nodded and put his hands on his knees, sucking in air. When he was calmer, he pointed further down, to where the track met the riverbed. 'I saw it from the bridge, coming back south . . . I thought, What the fuck is that? I drove my car down –' he pointed behind me and I saw his red ute nosed into the brush, '– and took a look. He's dead. He's been fucking shot, Matt.'

'Who?'

Reece was starting to wheeze, and I realised a serious panic attack was setting in. I needed to focus his brain on something, stop the cycle.

I gave him my keys. 'Can I give you a job?' He nodded, gasping. 'In the boot there's a roll of red and white crime scene tape. Get back to where this track comes off the road and tape the entrance, right across, chest height. Nobody comes in. Wait there for me. I'm afraid you're going to have to leave your ute in here for the time being because it's part of the scene now. With me?'

It felt like walking on sand. My boots crunched as the smooth, rounded riverbed stones compacted beneath me. Now that I was out of my vehicle and away from the trees, the wind cut through my jacket, making me shiver.

The body was right near the water, down by a long, low protruding wall of rock the locals had bulldozed to prevent the makeshift boat ramp from being washed away in a flood. I checked the ground, looking for anything obvious I might destroy by treading on it. There was nothing. The surface wasn't helpful for footprints. Even my boots just left depressions in the pebbles.

As I stepped closer, peering over the back of the large bald head, recognition dawned. I pulled back, exhaled hard through the fist I'd raised to my mouth, staring across the river, seeing nothing. I approached the body again.

Gus's eyes stared vacantly at the sky. And there was no mistaking the bullet hole through his forehead.

12.

Freeze, control, preserve. That's all I had to achieve and then I'd just be holding the fort until CIB arrived. Greymouth was the nearest lot in my district, but Wānaka, over the Otago border, was actually closer.

With Reece manning the cordon up by the road, things were pretty secure already. Before I did anything else, I found the orange tough-case in the boot of the wagon, extracted the camera and started snapping away at everything: body, wider scene, the two vehicles . . . all of it.

Then I jogged back up the track to Reece. 'Mate, just make sure no vehicles pull in here.' I pointed down to the mud and grit. 'These tyre tracks may be all we get.'

He gave the scene tape he'd erected an even wider berth.

I snapped away up here too, getting some close-ups of all the vehicle tracks. It looked like a mess, but you never know.

Then I wandered over to the Heritage Hotel and dialled Hokitika station, got the sergeant, Will, my boss for admin purposes. 'Hey, Will. Little bit of a shitter down here.' I rattled off the basics, asked for CIB.

'Jeeze, Matt. Hang on, Brent's here with some of his guys. They did a warrant this morning.'

Brent Donovan I knew. He was ex-Christchurch; we'd done courses together. He was one of the detective sergeants up there and would quite possibly land this case.

'Matt, what you got?'

'Body in the riverbed. Shot in the head. It's Gus, mate.'

He went quiet as he processed it. 'What?'

'Gus. He's dead. Shot in the head and dumped by the Haast River.' I swallowed. 'Right by the bridge. I've contained it but I need to know what you want done about the body. It's okay for now, but it might piss down soon.'

In the city everyone would be here in no time. CIB, the guys from Environmental Science and Research, the undertaker, the pathologist if need be – sorting the body and whisking it away. But this was the West Coast.

Brent took some notes, then started making decisions. 'You got a tent?'

'Nope. Fire volunteers do, though. Can't guarantee it being sterile. I'll chuck a sheet over him, then their tent over the top?'

'Yeah, that sounds good. That's all, I reckon. There's not much more you can do, mate. We're on our way down.'

I gave him the finer scene details: exactly where the body was, where the outer cordon was, where he could meet Reece.

'Thanks, Matt. I'll get hold of Wānaka, see if they can get a uniform car to you. Help with scene management. They're less than two hours away. Beats three and a half.'

Back up at the outer cordon again, where a bunch of people had gathered with Reece, I made some requests. 'Can somebody get the fire tent? I need it brought here.' There was no full-time fire service, but half the town acted as a volunteer brigade and had access to the facilities. 'Reece, let me know when it arrives. Come down and find me. Nobody else past this tape.' I continued. 'Cavalry's coming from Hokitika. Maybe some more uniforms from Wānaka. In the meantime, we're all cops today. I'm gonna need a hand. If someone can maybe man the landline in the service station over there to update Hokitika Police every once in a while, that'd be grand. You'll be able to relay me updates from their end too, through Reece.'

At the scene, I grabbed another roll of crime scene tape and wrapped it around a cabbage tree in the bush to the right, then out behind Reece's ute, across to the other side of the track, then down as far as the brush went before tying it around some mānuka. I'd basically created an inner cordon around the body, in case somebody did manage to stumble in here. I doubted anyone would wander in from the sea or the river, so I ignored that direction.

Only one thing made sense: someone had driven in, dumped the body and driven out. It would've been nice to know that before I added my tyres to the mix. *Stuff it. It is what it is.*

Head in the boot again, I pulled one of the white plastic sheets from its packet, got it down and over Gus to keep anything forensic in and laid a heavier tarp over the lot. Then I lifted my notebook off the passenger seat, opened it and, like a good old detective, I started writing.

13.

They had a full police service up in Nelson for Gus. Flag, dogs, bagpipes, the lot. It wasn't something every retired cop would have got, but given he'd only retired a year ago, and due to his length of service, he'd been bestowed the honour.

I'd flown up, along with quite a few from the community, and the days since had been pretty sobering, especially because a killer had walked among us. The homicide team had set up in my tiny station, packing themselves into the place. I didn't envy them. They were all from either Otago or Greymouth CIB, had no idea how long they'd be here.

I checked in on Brent, who had indeed ended up in charge, and was dealing with all the incoming information from his team and firing the tasks out. 'You off for Gus's wake at the Antler, Matt?'

'Yeah, if that's okay. Local crowd and all.'

'Of course. I'm not your boss.' He grinned.

'I know. But, you know, host and all that.' I dropped the

keys on the desk. 'Just gimme a bell at the Antler if you need anything.'

They were working their arses off with local inquiries, but I'd had the message from the top loud and clear: I was only to be involved in the homicide as community liaison. Which suited me fine. Watching them churn through reams of paper and carry bagged exhibits all over the place didn't get my pulse racing. But I knew they'd get the job done.

Gus's words came back to me as I made the short walk to the bar: *Fishy as fuck. Some of the folk round here know a bit more than the files record.*

I couldn't believe it was a local, but I needed to find out more about whatever Gus knew. I'd given a full statement, of course – we all had, all of us who'd seen Gus at the barbie that night. I just wasn't sure if they'd found or pulled the old file yet.

* * *

The Antler was quieter than usual, but it was packed, and everyone was several drinks down. I managed to gulp the pint Jodie pushed across the bar to me without talking to anyone, but it didn't last.

Reece had stood up near the TV and was getting everyone's attention. 'Right, everyone. We're here to remember the rock of this community that was Gus McCabe. There isn't much that needs to be said. We're all shaken. We're all stunned. We're all angry. There's a group of men and women in Matt's place, working day and night to get some answers, and we're thankful for that, but it won't bring Gus back. Tonight we remember him in his own style: beer, and laughter. To Gus.'

He raised his glass and we all followed suit. 'Matt, if you have something, everyone would be grateful, I think.'

Oh fuck, thanks, mate.

I got off my stool and addressed the turned faces. 'I've only known Gus this last year and a bit. Far less than anyone else here. It didn't take me long to realise I had huge shoes to fill. And I know that the warm response and welcome I got from all of you was down to Gus, and the manner in which he went about his job. Speaking for the police, I know the inquiry will do what it can as fast as it can. My role hasn't changed. If anyone's struggling, hears any bullshit, wants anything, talk to me. We'll sort it out. Let's not dwell on the bad stuff tonight, though. Let's remember him as Reece said. To Gus.'

As I took my stool again, I was ambushed by Anna, who appeared out of the crowd in jeans and a zipped black jacket, her light brown hair tucked under a soft blue merino beanie. We hadn't spoken since the morning after the barbecue.

'Shit, I didn't know you were coming.'

'I know, I know, I only just made it. I couldn't miss it. Jesus, Matt.' She threw her arms around me.

'I know. It's fucking nuts. He didn't have any enemies.'

'How come you aren't on the inquiry? I would've thought they'd nab you, with your background.'

'Still gotta be a community cop here. Can't do two things at once. The higher-ups don't want blurred lines. They see me as a local, so it's good to get some external perspective in here.'

'So you can't follow your nose with this one.'

'Didn't say that, now.'

She frowned. 'You're not going to get yourself in the shit, are you?'

'Nope. But I'm community liaison –' I took a long gulp, cutting my sentence in half '– and this whole place and everything in it is the community, far as I can bloody tell.'

14.

I drove out along the coast road toward Okuru, taking a right at the hall and down into the seaside collection of houses. Liam hadn't showed at the send-off for Gus and the homicide team hadn't caught up with him either, so after speaking with Brent I got permission to do them a favour.

I could hear the booming waves, unseen over the sandbank. I thought of Tekapo, with the white river pebbles crunching underfoot and the cold, clear sky. Nobody was about. Vinnie and his old man must have been out on the boat; the stack of pots down the end of the road were half gone.

I knocked on Liam's door and waited. A minute later I knocked again, harder. *If he's taking a dump on crutches he'll be a while.* Still nothing. I went up the river side, then onto his back lawn. I peered through his windows into the kitchen and lounge. No movement. But his car was in the drive.

When I rapped on the neighbour's door an elderly woman opened it with a smile. I'd only seen her once or twice but she clearly knew who I was. 'Constable Buchanan, good morning! Is anything the matter?'

I smiled back. 'No, just trying to reach Liam. He isn't answering. Have you seen him today?'

She seemed puzzled. 'He's there. He went for a walk on his crutches down to the river earlier and came back not so long ago. He's definitely home. Look, I'll come with you.'

Before I could politely decline, she had closed the door and was at my side. We crushed the pebbles together back around to his rear doors. The large glass windows offered the best view of inside. We banged again.

'Liam? It's Nora. I'm with Constable Buchanan.'

I went to the side closest to the river and called up at the windows. 'Liam! Are you home?'

Nora could see the concern on my face. She said what I was thinking. 'You don't think he could have had a fall?'

Decision made. Her reassurance that my concern was legitimate sealed the deal. I worked my way around the house, but everything was locked. I finished back where I started and was surprised to find that Nora had the back door open. 'Hey, nice work. You didn't smash it, did you?'

She looked at me in horror. 'My goodness, no. It was open.'

'Liam!' I called. 'It's Matt, and Nora from next door. We're just worried, mate. Don't want to scare you.' *Why am I trying to make myself feel better about this?* There were dishes in the sink. A newspaper lay open on the kitchen bench.

Nora stayed put, but I went for the stairs. Nothing up there.

As I reappeared, Nora pointed. 'I haven't checked the bathroom.'

I grabbed the handle and turned. It budged a little but met resistance. Something was propped against it. I shoved harder.

Then I looked through the gap. I could see the trouser leg sticking out oddly, but not him. He had his back to the door on the other side. *Oh shit.* My heart sank. I'd seen this before. Many times.

Nora had noticed me freeze. 'What is it?' She knew something was wrong.

'Nora, could you do me a favour? Head back to your place, get on the phone and call Kathy, the medic. I need her here. With her wagon and radio.'

'Is Liam ...'

'I don't know. Please just do that for me?'

But I did know. I put my weight behind my shoulder and pushed Liam's lifeless body out of the way, making a space just big enough to squeeze through. I turned and squatted. 'Fuck, mate.'

I checked his carotid, pushing in beside his Adam's apple, under the thin rope digging into his neck. Nothing. His face was purple. His tongue was out far further than you would have thought it could go. His eyes were open and yellowed.

I went back outside and sat at the front door, waiting for Kathy, staring out at the sky and hearing the sound of the ocean. *Didn't I leave this shit behind?*

15.

The whole town came to Liam's funeral, on the stony beach at Okuru, with the waves crashing in just down from us and the wind whipping through our coats.

Standing protectively at my side was Hailey, her wild, dark curls belying her strenuous hair-straightening efforts. Just that morning she had flown into Queenstown, picked up her rental and driven through the Central Otago valleys and then up through the pass ... smack bang into a funeral.

She hadn't said a word when I gave her the news minutes after she arrived, and now she stood there silently, thinking God knows what. I could tell her brain was in overdrive, and I hoped she wasn't remembering all the shit I'd been through in Auckland, and how all this kind of stuff had burnt me out.

When I gave her a nudge, she turned her head. 'Hey,' I whispered. 'I'm okay.' She searched my face, then smiled.

Liam's community spirit. That's what the service concentrated on. He'd never married or had kids, but extended family had travelled to the Coast for the service.

I had a few words with Liam's sister, Helen, the executor of his will, who lived in Christchurch. She was looking for legal documents and I passed her the number for the Greymouth detectives who'd done the full examination of the house. She'd had a few questions about his death that the inquest officer up in headquarters had been vague about. I told her everything I could.

* * *

I initially didn't notice him slumped against the driver's door of my wagon, but I heard the words drifting over. He was singing something about fate, and even with all his well-placed additional swear words I could tell it was Iron Maiden. I hadn't spied him in the crowd down on the beach, but he must have walked here.

When he saw us coming, he stopped singing. He looked at me, looked at Hailey, back at me.

The first thing he did was apologise, standing up straight, Jim Beam can clutched to his chest. 'My apologies, young lady. I was after a word with your old man. I didn't mean to interrupt any father–daughter time.'

Then he resumed some level of normality for Joe, grinning, despite the mood of the day. 'Makin' your escape, eh Buchanan?' A cackle and a swig from the can. A look at his bulging pockets told me he'd stashed a few more.

'Joe, how're you keeping your pants up with all that piss in them?'

He grinned, downed his can, squashed it, put it in a pocket I couldn't see and ripped the top off another. 'Magic.'

I could see Sheryl looking towards us over some heads in the crowd.

'Jafa.' He clicked his fingers. 'Don't you go listening to what that town mother's gonna tell you. She's been at me for years.'

'Sheryl?'

'Yeah. Look, this town's like any other in this fine country. Better than most. But you've been here, what, a year? And what have you found out?'

I paused.

'Look I'll frame it for you, city head. How long were you up in the big smoke?'

'Forty something years.'

'And how much d'you know about all of it?'

'It's a big place. Not much.'

'Not the whole place. I mean where you grew up. Glenfield, wasn't it?'

That shook me. I stared at him. He was grinning again, but there was something behind it that I couldn't quite place.

'Nah, don't get your little panties twisted up there, Jafa. We just do our fuckin' homework down here.' He took a gulp, turned to Hailey again. 'Apologies for the language.'

When I glanced back, I saw that Sheryl had disappeared.

'Oi.' The finger snap brought me back.

'I know, Joe, I know. Everyone here does their research. I know.'

'Yeah. This big-time detective comes swanning in here, in his twilight years maybe, to give up the hard graft, come do something useful, help kids cross the road, help old folk find their missing dog . . . Am I right?'

I started to open my mouth but he kept talking.

'But hey, from what I've seen, that isn't you. Unless you've all of a sudden got your shit together.'

'I do have my shit together.'

He extricated another can. 'What I'm saying is, Buchanan, is this place could use a guy with a little of your now-forgotten enthusiasm.'

I wasn't sure what to say. 'It's shit what happened with Liam and Gus, mate. It's gonna be hard.'

'Liam was a casualty.' Joe drank deeply. 'What I'm sayin' is, there needs to be accountability. Two deaths one after another? I hope you're not just gonna melt back into this community and leave those suited-up boys from out of town to it.'

I wasn't planning on just leaving them to it, but then I also wasn't going to make promises I mightn't be able to keep.

'It's not really my choice, Joe. Bosses want me in blue. Doing the rounds. No suicides or murders for me.'

He paused mid-sip. 'Is your direct boss here?'

'He's in Hokitika.'

'Right.' He waved his hands. 'Anyone else floatin' about who's gonna tell you what to do?'

'No. The homicide team aren't part of my command chain.'

'Huh. Well. Seems to me like you do have a choice then, don't you.'

He bowed slightly to Hailey, then headed for the road that would take him out onto the main.

16.

The time with Hailey was brilliant. We hiked to Lake Ellery in the hills behind Jackson Bay. She met most of my mates again, through regular brews at the Antler, and we went both north, to check out some rustic West Coast heritage, and inland to the Otago wineries. But the four days went quickly, and before I knew it I was giving her a hug on the driveway.

'Dad, you don't need to worry what I think. Anna's great. Whatever happens, I'm really happy for you.'

'It's pretty casual, Hailes.'

She chuckled. 'Maybe don't tell her that.'

I gave her a questioning look, but she just smirked. 'Bye Dad, take care. It was awesome. I'm gonna call you tonight.'

'Okay. I love you.'

'I love you too.'

She went to open the door of her car but stopped. 'I know you and Gus were close, but don't chase that just because you feel obliged. Leave it to homicide.'

Several years ago a victim I'd helped had said something

similar. I'd remembered it ever since. *Don't go back to something just because you're good at it.* Hailey's words were an eerie echo. All I said, though, was, 'We'll see.'

She'd always looked after me. Saved my life, twice. Once without her knowing she even had, when I'd been at my lowest. How she'd ended up so grounded I had no idea.

***

I was sitting in the cafe with a large flat white, thumbing through the paper on the table, when he appeared at my side. 'Senior Constable Buchanan?'

I looked up at a young guy in his mid-twenties, dark blond hair long and short in all the right places, chinos and a navy jersey. He looked like life was great and he knew it. Good for him.

'Yeah, how could you tell?' I was in uniform and delivered it deadpan.

He laughed. 'Mind if I sit? I'm a journalist, from Queenstown.'

Ah, shit.

I indicated the seat opposite. 'Want anything? Sheryl's a legend with the coffee art.'

After ordering, he sat down. 'Sorry. Alec, Alec Robertson. I'm here because a murder and then a suicide are two pretty significant stories. I'm looking at examining the impact of trauma on a small town.'

Been done before.

I gave him the time of day, though. Mainly because I had nowhere else to be. 'I could probably save your bosses a few headaches but until the coroner reveals what may or may not have led to Liam's death, I couldn't really help you any further. And you wouldn't draw any conclusion either, I'm sure.'

He shook his head. 'Course not. This isn't a who-gets-in-first piece. It's more of a people story. Time is on my side.'

'Well, fill your boots, champ. Long as you explain yourself to whoever you chat to, I guess. Be full and frank, and be okay with being told to piss off. But if you treat people right and you're honest, then I'm sure you'll get everything you need.'

'Thanks. I just wanted to touch base, you being tapped into the community here. People get word of a reporter nosing about and prejudices come out. I'm not looking to shine a spotlight. I'm just pursuing something that may help people out.'

I turned my palms out. 'Hey, shine away. It's a free country and the people here are pretty straight up and down.'

'I thought so, yeah. Look, there's going to be some heat down here, from the media. Not from me, I mean from all quarters. The town's recently retired cop murdered? That's huge. If there's anything I can do, any trouble, I'd be happy to help. My outfit has good relations with most of the big companies.'

'Right. Actually, there *is* something you can help me out with.'

That perked him up a bit.

'Look, I'm all for media articles about trauma. It's been closed doors for far too long, and I'd know. I'll smooth any troubled waters you encounter with the people here, as long as you do two things.' I counted on my fingers. 'One, you don't act like a wanker and two, you don't ever mention or quote me.'

His teeth said it was a deal.

17.

I didn't have long to wait before Alec's bosses obviously decided they needed to get in first. When I checked the online news for the South Island, there was a piece on Liam Goodhue. Very wholesome, very nice.

Or so I'd thought.

I was woken from my caffeine-induced haze by a banging on my door. I could tell it was Jodie from the hollering.

By the time I opened up she was mid-sentence. '… pissing everyone off round the Antler with his questions. It wasn't even the fact he was asking, it was that it was so close to the funeral. Everyone feels bad talking to a reporter, right? Apparently you told him he had a free pass.'

I got her inside. 'No, that's not what I said. I told him I didn't have a problem with him being here, but I told him not to be a dickhead.'

'He was asking who'd lived here longest, who'd left Haast but been back in the last few years, who had records, like criminal records …'

'Leave it with me.'

It only took me half an hour to find him. He was staying at the little stone-clad B&B cottage out on the southern side of Okuru, across the rivermouth from Liam's. I spoke with Glen, the manager of the place, who was trimming plants along the edge of the manicured lawn. A few minutes later Alec walked out, Glen following behind.

I waited until he was well within earshot. 'Get in the car.' He slowly opened the front door, trust still in place. 'Not there. The back.'

'Eh?'

'I'm not asking, Alec.'

He obeyed. I started the car so Glen could never be accused of knowledge, and moved off down the gravel drive before stopping.

'Mate, you wanted my help and you've just shat on me with your talk at the Antler last night. It doesn't sound much like a trauma piece to me. Sounds investigative. I might seem a bit of an idiot but I've been around the block when it comes to journalists, death and sniffing out horse shit. So I'm gonna give you this one opportunity to tell me what the fuck you're actually up to, and if it doesn't float my boat, then I'll personally make sure your stay here is limited.'

He shifted. Looked out the window, then back at me through the mirror. 'Matt, I don't think you're an idiot. I didn't mean to piss anyone off. I was trying to cover the community feeling, because that'll fuel the later piece about –'

I cut him off. 'Alec, what are you investigating? Is it Gus? What about it?'

He paused, thought about it, then went for the easy question. 'Sorry?'

It was time to stop the pissing about.

'Mate, last chance. What the hell is your actual task here? 'Cause they don't send their star investigative journo, a guy who's eyeing up a TV slot, someone from solid Dunedin heritage, to write a trauma piece.'

That made him sit up.

'Yeah, I can use Google too. Look, I've never been good at explaining myself to people when I'm pissed off, but I'll give it a go. I used to work murders in Auckland, and now I work flat tyres and lost cats down here for a couple of reasons. I'm not working on Gus's case, and I didn't look into Liam's death beyond finding him. There are other cops you can talk to about those. But as the local guy in uniform, if there's something you can tell me, then I probably need to know. What are you looking at?'

'I can't say.'

'For fuck's sake.' I mimed banging my head against the window.

'No, I mean, it's my livelihood, Matt. I've signed a non-disclosure agreement. I actually can't. Not right now anyway.'

I'd expected it.

I reversed back up to the cottage. 'Okay, get out.'

'Does –'

'I'm glad you have employment policies and stick by them. But I've got a town here that expects me to take care of this. So if you aren't gonna help me with that, get out of my car.'

18.

There I was, Sheriff of Fucking Nottingham, leaning back in my chair in the station with a cup of instant. I was watching the homicide team nut things out and tap away on the computers they'd brought with them from Greymouth.

But my thoughts were still on Alec. *Little piss-taker.* I'd been pretty welcoming, I thought, and he'd given me nothing. *Non-disclosure. What bollocks.* It had come back to me that Liam had known something. *Before* Gus was murdered. Then in walks Alec.

I signalled Brent over for a chat. 'What's happening?' he asked.

'Hopefully nothing, mate, to be honest. But I've got a journalist sniffing around about both Gus and Liam, and I don't quite know why. There's more to it. And I've remembered something: Liam asked me about providing information. My fault. I'll get a jobsheet through to you.'

'When was this?'

'A couple of weeks before he died.'

'Did he tell you anything?'

'No. He made out it was a friend, but I'm pretty sure he was asking for himself.'

'The coroner will want that. Probably a lot weighing on his mind.'

'Absolutely. Hey, who would I need to talk to about a look through his stuff?'

Brent had dealt with all of it after the suicide. He'd have spoken with Liam's family and friends.

'His sister. She's in Christchurch. I'll email you her details. She's good as gold.'

'Great, cheers. If that's Helen, I've spoken with her before.'

***

Minutes later an email came through. Helen Corrigan. Merivale. A cell and a landline. I picked up the phone, introduced myself to the voice at the other end.

'You knew him quite well, Matt?'

'I wouldn't say well, no. But you get to know almost everyone, of course, just by being out and about. Everyone uses the same dairy, same bar, same petrol station. There's only one or two of everything.'

'He called me about you.'

'After the crash?'

'I … no, no … well, he did call me that day, but no, the day after you went to see him. He was grateful.'

I filled her in on what Liam had said. 'I just wondered if you might be able to send me in the right direction. It seems like you and your brother were close.'

The pause could have been thought, but her voice told me

I was missing something. 'Matt, you have a lot of Liam's police history on record, right?'

'Police history? He didn't have a record.'

'No, no, not a criminal record – the rest.'

'How long ago are we talking? All convictions are in the system. When they moved from paper to computers it all went in but without the detail. But there's nothing for Liam.'

'So if he just witnessed something a long time ago it wouldn't be in there?'

'Probably not, not if we're talking –'

She cut in. 'Nineteen seventy-eight?'

I stopped and stared at the wall. 'Sure, yeah. Too long ago. A conviction would be in there. Nothing else.'

'Matt, it's about the pass, it's got to be.' She started murmuring to herself. It was muffled, she'd turned away from the phone. Then she was back. 'The family that went missing in '78 over there, there was a big search for them...'

'Yeah, the Fawkes. What does –'

She interrupted again. 'Matt, Liam found the bodies.'

19.

To be fair, I hadn't expected much, not for a case from 1978. The NIA, or the National Intelligence Application, our police database, held pretty much everything. Not only convictions, or matters going before court, but every interaction the police had with anyone. Traffic stops, domestics, lost property – it all went in. But it was only as good as the info that cops entered into it, so I was pushing shit uphill if I wanted to know about something from forty-odd years back.

I was shivering, despite the heat pump. I briefly had the station to myself: the homicide team were out shaking trees and revisiting parts of the scene. What sounded like a hurricane was barrelling in straight off the Tasman and smashing the walls of my little building, providing an appropriately moody background track to investigating the past.

And I had the deep feeling that the past was the key. Gus hadn't died through some random encounter. It was planned, deliberate. It had to be, for a gun to be used in Haast.

I couldn't find the case at all initially. It was only linked to the father, Michael Fawkes, and from there I found the other family members. Michael was listed deceased as of '78. So was his wife, Lynn, and their fifteen-year-old daughter, Casey.

I'd seen *The Blair Witch Project.* Deaths in a forest generally wind people up, so I was intrigued that I'd never heard of this case. There was nothing in the narrative. No actual information at all. The case had been hauled through the whole paper-to-digital nightmare, and then multiple system upgrades. It was simply coded 1110. Homicide. A sub-entry was coded 1X. Suicide.

And that's all I got.

But the one thing I did have now was clarity about what Alec was probably poking his nose into. Maybe the media had a lead or something, but he'd clearly been interested in both Gus, who'd been looking hard at this for years, and Liam, who apparently had a starring role. It could have been a mystery. But mysteries, I'd found, were the domain of TV and literature. Generally, the logical answer won out, time and time again.

I'd spent years digging into deaths. For the most part, they'd been recent ones, ones where someone was responsible, and most of the time, was still alive. There was purpose, there was pressure, there were consequences.

But I'd ended up in Haast for a very good reason, something I couldn't overlook. They'd wanted me back, but not in the state I'd been in. So I'd gone 'Sure, great' and given a thumbs up. I'd been burnt out, and I'd known it. Here, I was stress-free and a whole pile of worries had evaporated. My brain was ninety-nine per cent worry-free, as Hailey had noticed.

So if you had any brain cells left, you'd take all that to heart, accept the insight into your character and shove this murder to the side.

I stared out the window at the rain falling in sheets over the ring road. Then I rang district headquarters in Nelson and asked for the records section.

20.

While the boxes of files were flying down by carrier pigeon, I carried out my search of Liam's home, with his sister's blessing.

Although I'd developed a sound approach to life which usually worked for me, that it's easier to receive forgiveness than permission, I'd gone against my programming and talked to Brent. He'd attached a couple of his guys to help me out, because while he was in no way pursuing any solid link between Gus's death and Liam's, he saw value in any activity in the town.

This would be a methodical search, forensically aware even, but practical. The place had already been given a once-over after his suicide. The D's were happy to search the downstairs for me. I wasn't expecting to find much there, and after all, they were helping out, not doing the donkey work for me.

The place had been tidied up, probably by Liam's family. I knew they were still in the process of working out his will, though, so nothing had been removed. I checked the garage, but it merely confirmed his interests: diving gear, hiking equipment, quad bike maintenance stuff. Cray pots and a small dinghy.

His bedroom was sparse – a bit of outdoor clothing in the wardrobe, books, the usual stuff. But then I spotted the safe. The safe that wouldn't have been searched because it was locked, deemed unimportant for a straightforward hanging, when no one was looking for evidence of a crime.

I phoned Helen from Liam's landline.

'Oh hi, Matt. Find anything that makes sense?'

'Not yet. But the safe in his bedroom, do you know where he kept the key?'

She thought. 'Kitchen. Top of the pantry there's a row of baking tins. Under there somewhere. I've seen him grab it before.'

Inside the safe I found house documents, a title, some old photos from his DOC days, his passport and some financial crap.

Two things lifted my heart rate slightly. The first was one of the black and white photos. Liam was facing the camera, long hair and younger face, and three other guys had their backs to it. This time, I could see the patches on their leather vests. Patches that contained the skull and the hangman's noose. The Epitaph Riders.

I was pretty sure Epitaph had been Christchurch based. I knew they'd spread and gained a reputation. They'd overthrown several other South Island gangs since the late sixties. But I was fairly certain they were long gone. Defunct. The players were getting old, and the younger guys were joining the flashier, richer clubs.

So Liam had moved in those circles. Maybe. Perhaps just a mate or two. He was born in Christchurch, so that made sense.

Towards the bottom of the safe I found some yellowed paper.

When I unfolded it, I could see that most of the writing was faded or illegible, but it had clearly been ripped from a kid's journal or diary. There was some doodling and abstract drawings. But I managed three lines:

We leave on the fifteenth.

He's not going to stop.

I think I could die.

21.

I stepped onto the creaking, bone-white planks. The water beneath was black and the swamp was eerily silent. On the sodden ground beyond, the reeds, soaked by rain, offloaded moisture onto me as I trudged and brushed through them. I was glad, for once, of my wet-weather pants.

I rapped on the door. 'Joe, I need to pick your brain! What's left of it anyway.'

Usually I could hear him, or the other way round. But there wasn't a sound.

Boots saturated, pants muddied and wet up to my nuts, I retraced my steps through the reeds, over the planks and back to the solidness of the road. I crossed over into the dunes on the other side, then up and through a cutting in the marram grass and onto the beach. Waves crashing in front of me, I peered in both directions. Driftwood, curved and twisted like deer antlers, marked the high-tide line.

I caught the figure on the log a couple of hundred metres away, playing an air guitar. As I got closer I caught the liberties he was taking with the lyrics, adding curses every few lines. I came up behind him. 'Hey, Joe. Nice additions, Hendrix would've been proud.'

He looked me up and down. 'Well, shit on my dick, that what they teach you at detective school, huh?'

'What, how to take the piss?'

He was staring at my muddied wet weathers. 'Nah, how to dress like a tosser.'

'Fine, I'll have both of these.' I pulled the Heinekens from my pockets. 'Looks like you don't need any extra help.' I popped a cap on the edge of his log and sat down beside him.

He reached over and helped himself to the other bottle. 'Whatcha want?'

'Chat. Few things going on.'

He lifted his beer to the ocean, giving it a toast. 'Shit, you know you ain't as dumb as you look.'

'Joe, I need to talk about Liam.'

He took a long pull. 'Uh-huh.'

I pulled my coat tighter around me. 'What the fuck are you doing out here anyway? It's howling.'

'What're you talkin' about? It's beautiful out here. That angry or that glimmering sea.' He zoned out temporarily, eyes unfocused. Then, 'You wanna talk or not?'

I did. 'Seems like this town did more research on me than I did on it, before I got posted here.'

He just looked across the water, a tiny smile playing at the corners of his mouth. 'Locals here, they give a shit, y'know. Town's small enough to give a shit about. Not like where you come from. And it's small enough that everyone can be on the same page 'bout some things.'

'And are you on that same page, Joe?'

He kept watching the waves, thinking about his answer. 'I'd say so.'

I cut to the chase. 'I didn't know about '78. Not until Gus told me about it. About the Fawkes family. And I only just discovered that Liam found them.'

His face didn't even twitch. He mouthed one word, still staring across the grey water towards the horizon. 'And?'

I pulled out the piece of yellowed paper I'd found. 'Liam was probing, wanting to know if I could keep mum about something. Something from long ago. He never told me what it was about. But then I discover that he found those three bodies. So I'm rethinking his suicide. Had he been struggling for a long time? Long before the chopper crash?'

Joe was listening properly now. Even if his eyes were locked on the waves.

'You knew him, Joe. I know you did. You need to tell me what the fuck this is all about. Gus was shot dead because he went looking into something. Like a warning. But a warning to who, Joe? And now we've lost Liam as well. There's a journalist snooping around. I need to stay ahead of him too.'

I held the paper out to him. He twisted his head down slightly to look, then took it. As he unfolded it his eyebrows went up.

Recognition? No. Fear.

I didn't know how much he could read, but he knew what it was, that I'd stake my career on.

He got it together pretty quickly. Took another long drink. 'Well?'

'I need a hand, mate. Some advice, where to direct my time.'

'With what? They're both dead. So are that family. I'm no Sherlock. But something tells me it's all kinda fucked.'

'I'm just talking about the truth. I've got some questions about '78, about the impact on Liam.'

Joe grunted.

I closed my eyes briefly. It had been a while since my brain kicked into this gear.

We sat in silence for a few minutes before he spoke again. 'All I know for sure is, you're wrong about a couple of things.' He eyed me with something between mild acknowledgement and approval. As though he'd been proved right about something.

'First thing is, there's much, much hairier things than Liam out there. Things that'd scare the shit out of Jesus Christ himself. So you leave him be, and let him rest. Yeah, he might've been strugglin' for a while. But it'd be a shame to let the family know and put that burden onto them.

'And second thing is –' he burped and wiped his mouth on his sleeve '– he didn't find *all* of their bodies.'

I glanced sideways at him. He didn't meet my eyes, but carried on.

'He found two of 'em.' Joe got up and dropped the empty bottle at my feet. 'They never found the girl. So get your facts right, ex-detective.'

Then he staggered off down the beach, navigating the driftwood and shell piles as he went.

22.

The boxes arrived more quickly than I'd expected. The files were old, typewritten, the paper discoloured. The photos were real prints, all the colour drained into pale yellows and browns and reds.

I skimmed the overview, then turned to the witnesses folder. The extended Fawkes family consisted of parents on one side, living in Nelson at the time. The other side were already dead. No other family in Haast itself.

I found a statement taken from Fiona Abraham, Lynn Fawkes' mother.

We saw them a few times a year. They always came up for Christmas and then often during each school holidays. Casey loved it up here in summer, we'd often go up to Kaiteriteri or Golden Bay …

I can't say I saw it coming, not at all. Michael was often short with Lynn, and Casey, but fatherhood is hard, and so is being a husband. I understood all that, I didn't think anything of it. Looking back now, though, I guess there was an undertone of abuse that I just didn't see ...

I'd seen that a hundred times: the living always trying to take some blame for the dead.

I flicked and flicked, looking for the one I was most interested in. I found it a third of the way through the pile. *My full name is Liam Henry Goodhue. I am making this statement to Constable Benjamin Neeson of the Wanaka Police ...*

I sipped from my mug and bit into a gingernut.

Around the tree I could smell it. It smelled like compost. I came around and saw a male body on the ground. I think I called out, but it was pretty clear he'd been there a while. There was leaf litter and he was soaked. I could see a dark purple hole in the side of his head. I looked around the forest floor and saw a rifle about a metre from him. I didn't touch it, but it had a wooden stock and a scope. I couldn't tell what calibre it was ...

I blinked and kept reading. *I was about to leave to report back to search HQ without contaminating the area, but then I saw her. She was lying on her back, several metres from the man. She was pale, very pale ...*

I read through all the Search and Rescue jobsheets, saw just how enormous and sweeping the search had been. And Joe was right. They hadn't found Casey Fawkes.

I found the ring-binder containing all the scene documentation, removed a scene diagram done in pen and pencil and found the scene photos. The prints were curled at the edges, still glued onto card. As I went through them, I glanced every so often at the diagram. As it all joined together in my head I started to see the three-dimensional scene.

There was no mistaking the Haast Pass beech forest in the photos. The trees and the moss-covered ground looked the same as it did now.

Michael Fawkes stared lifeless at the sky, a rifle at his feet. A closer shot of the exit wound revealed that half the back of his head was missing. Lynn was on her back in the moss. Eyes closed. Deep purple marks on her neck.

I turned to the officer jobsheets, discoloured pages in difficult handwriting, and began reading. Or deciphering. I found the one for the scene. Things among the list of seized items jumped out at me.

0001 Located beside body of Michael Fawkes. 1 × rifle .303 calibre.

0002 Located 2.5 metres from item 0001. 1 × spent cartridge .303 calibre.

The jobsheet, and the item list, continued on over a couple of pages. Anything not natural had been seized by the cops. I kept scanning.

0012 Located inside chamber of item 0001. 1 × spent cartridge .303 calibre.

So two shots. Two shots, the second through Michael Fawkes' own head. That casing, obviously, hadn't been ejected because he'd died. Fair to say, then, that the first shot had been for Casey.

The officers had taken everything: the rifle, the casings, the various other random things that mattered to the reconstruction. Like item 0042: *Located beside Lynn Fawkes' left hand. 1 × button. Appears to match those on Michael Fawkes' jacket.*

I pored over various parts of the file, but I was satisfied – the rumours I was hearing matched the work that had been done. And Casey's disappearance mattered not. The coroner's report was thorough. Excluding alien abduction, the report concluded that Casey died 'between the 15th and at the most the 18th of July 1978, in the area of Haast Pass'. The winter conditions at the time meant a healthy adult would have been unlikely to survive even a night in the bush. And Casey had been fifteen, alone, with no equipment and nowhere to go. The only options were unscalable snow-capped mountains, freezing rivers and cold, wet forest.

And that was if she hadn't been shot by her father and then scattered by animals.

In the witness folder, a folded scrap of paper was Sellotaped to one of the pages. It was a receipt, almost completely illegible. Assuming it related to a statement before or after it, I turned the pages back and found exactly that. There were only several lines, a vague recollection, no heavy detail, but then it didn't need much.

> *On the fifteenth of July I was working at the pumps. I don't know what time it was, all I could say was it wasn't at the start or the end of my shift. But a family I recognised as the Fawkes pulled up in their brown station wagon, a Holden, and filled up. I knew the family from just generally seeing them in Haast these last few months. The father did the pumping and he paid for the petrol with a twenty-dollar note. I gave him change. I don't remember anything about the conversation, it was really*

brief. I saw his wife in the front passenger seat, and I saw their daughter in the back. She must have been about fourteen or fifteen. The car was full of stuff...

I reread the first line, the date.

We leave on the fifteenth. He's not going to stop. I think I could die. Casey might never have been found. But something she'd written had ended up in Liam's safe.

23.

If I wanted to know about Liam, all I had to do was ask the locals. But ideally, I wanted people who'd known him back in the day, people who'd been in Haast their whole lives.

Their house was in Hannah's Clearing, near the school. Sheryl ushered me inside. 'Tara's back at school, so it's just me. Coffee?'

'Please. Which school is she at?'

'Dunstan, in Alexandra.'

'Why does everyone end up there?'

'Closest really. The college in Wānaka doesn't take boarders. And that's a two-hour drive. So Alexandra is next closest. Some kids even go to Dunedin.'

As she disappeared into the kitchen, I called out, 'Hey, what's Joe got against you anyway?'

Her voice carried. 'Joe? Against me?' She said nothing more until she returned with two mugs, handing me one and indicating the couch. 'Well?'

'Nothing really. He just mentioned that you gave him a hard time for a while.'

She rolled her eyes. 'Me? Me giving *him* a hard time?' She laughed. 'Joe wasn't always an alcoholic and he was a good guy. He's only about fifteen years older than me, but he looks another fifty. He's just wasting away and I don't get it.'

'Right, so it's a concern then?'

'Of course. But he won't give me the time of day anymore.'

I understood. People move on and life changes. But I got the feeling I should change the subject. 'Anyway I was just going to ask a bit more about Liam.'

She sighed. 'Of course. What a time for him to go. Right after Gus. Almost like it ... drowned Liam out, you know. Gus is all over the news, Liam is just ... gone.'

I hadn't actually thought about it like that.

When I explained that I'd only just discovered that Liam had found the bodies, something like a shudder washed over Sheryl. 'Well, that's obviously where it all started for him. I ... I can't imagine something that horrible.'

She was really struggling with something, but she hadn't asked me to leave. It was for her to tell me, not for me to ask. But shit, I hated awkwardness.

'Hey look, I'm really sorry, we can do this some other time.'

'No, no, Matt, this is ... good, it is. I'm ... I'm just feeling a lot of things right now. Go on.' She made a waving motion.

'That trauma will be an important part of the inquest into his suicide, however long ago he experienced it. Did he ever talk about it?'

She was trying not to cry. 'Not really, no. After all that happened, he left. Moved on with his job, I think. I heard he'd shifted to Christchurch for a while. He'd float back to Haast every now and then, but he was never the same. He was sad. Depressed. For a long time. Much later, probably fifteen years later, I heard he'd been in hospital. For head stuff –' she tapped her forehead '– but then later he moved back here. He was still sad, but I thought he was also just the same old Liam too. A good guy.'

She was isolating some blame, forcing herself to feel guilt where she shouldn't.

'Look, I don't know if this is going to be helpful, probably not right now. But for every recollection of signposts and red flags, there's another story about how someone could never imagine their friend or son or cousin doing it. Hindsight is a disease. If you seriously thought at the time something was wrong, or more recently, you would have acted.' I raised my mug to her. 'The signs weren't there, mate. Don't try to hunt them down now.'

She wiped away tears.

I fumbled in my pocket. 'Look, I wondered if this meant anything to you, if you maybe knew the Fawkes.' She sat up straighter at hearing the family name again, blinked and waited. I pulled out the note in its plastic ziplock bag and passed it to her.

Sheryl stared at it, then began, once more, to weep.

24.

Sheryl gulped half the port I'd found in a cupboard and splashed into a glass, then sat back. 'That's from Casey's diary, absolutely.'

'You were friends.'

She smiled. 'The best.'

'So where's the rest of the diary, do you think? Did she always keep it with her?'

'I'm not sure. I mean I assume she took it with her. I never saw it anywhere afterwards, if that's what you mean – not that I remember.' She was turning the note over and over. 'Where did you get this?'

I kept my face neutral. 'It was at Liam's. Locked inside a safe in his bedroom.'

A look of disbelief crossed her face. She swallowed some more port. I gave her a minute, then mentioned the rest.

'Before he died, Liam wanted to tell me something, but he never got the chance.'

Sheryl had arrived at some sort of conclusion in her head.

'It all kinda makes sense.' Then she asked, 'How did you end up here, Matt?'

'What, Haast?' I gave it to her straight, omitting the detail. 'When I rejoined they weren't going to send me where I wanted. I wasn't exactly flavour of the month, despite what court reporters might say about me.'

She smiled slightly. 'I can't at all see how you'd rub brass up the wrong way.'

I grinned. 'I was CIB through and through. I never thought I would, but I enjoy this type of work – the people here mean something to me. I only learned about Casey and her parents because people here want to talk.'

Sheryl took a deep breath. 'Me and Casey, we grew up together, until they all buggered off that July. At the time I had no idea why. Later I found out neighbours had been hearing the domestics, and Michael had shifted them, found a new job.' She was thinking hard. 'The last time I saw Casey was a couple of days before they left. She snuck over to say goodbye.'

I felt an odd sensation come over me. The past, till now seen only in faded files, coming to life in someone's words. It had happened to me before, and it brought with it another feeling, a chillier one. *Don't make old mistakes.*

'This must have been written not long before they left, right? I mean, it all made sense later – that Michael killed them. And himself. But Matt, I think Casey had a boyfriend.'

I almost choked on the brew. 'Here? Slim pickings surely?'

Her face was drawn, her eyes staring at nothing. 'Maybe ... that's what I'm now thinking ... Haast is small, right, and it was the seventies. Weed. Booze. Looking back, there was a lot going on.'

'You've got someone in mind. Who?'

'She never told me his name, just said he was older – nothing else. I assumed she didn't want him to get in trouble, you know. If he was . . . much older. But now I think –'

I was nodding before she finished.

'I think Casey and Liam might have been together.'

25.

I'd grabbed the ring-binder that contained all the scene information from the eerie murder–suicide, measured some distances on Google maps and thrown it into a daypack along with some warm gear. On both sides of the road, spindly trunks rose out of the scrub. Ahead, the mountains loomed. I'd taken this route countless times to get somewhere, but this time I was going to be stopping. To see where this all started.

The rock of the Alps towered above me as I wound inland once again, following the Haast River and leaving the water-logged plains behind. As I climbed higher, the dark, twisted greens of the beech forest slowly appeared. Eventually, I left the river behind as the winding road turned south, deeper into the mountains. When it flattened into the saddle between the peaks, and the trees closed in, I slowed, not wanting to miss the parking area.

I parked by the Haast Pass DOC signage, pointing visitors to the tracks that led into the bush. The highway, which split the forest in a straight line, dropped around a bend back the way I'd come. In the other direction, it disappeared south, over the saddle, down towards Cameron Flat and on to Hāwea and Wānaka.

Feeling the cool air on my face, I opened the ring-binder on the bonnet of the wagon and started to re-examine the scene diagrams. This carpark wasn't here in '78, but otherwise the landscape hadn't changed drastically. The scene area was on the eastern side, the same side I was parked on but further into the forest. There were coordinates. I fucked about with a topo map I'd brought from the station, drawing lines and checking directions. Satisfied, I stuffed the ring-binder back into the daypack, shouldered it and took a bearing with a compass. I'd need to use some good old pace checking. GPS wasn't a friend out here, not with the forest, the mountains, the weather and the lack of cell coverage to help close that margin of error. But any sort of old-school navigation through close country was also fraught with its own accuracy problems.

Although I wasn't hoping to nail the exact spot – I just wanted a rough idea – I needed to go in a few hundred metres. I knew that seventy-five of my right feet equalled a hundred metres, so trying to concentrate without getting distracted by nature, I kept on the bearing and went in under the canopy.

My extremities pretty quickly started to freeze, and then burn, as my warm blood tried to fight the lowered temperature. The opposite started happening inside my clothes. My nuts were beginning to itch as sweat gathered and clothing rubbed. I crossed over the marked trail and headed directly into the forest, following the little red compass needle and knowing to trust it, and not my senses, which would quickly get disorientated without a horizon or any reference point in the wall of green.

It wasn't dark here. The high canopy was sparse enough that

sunlight could pierce it and illuminate the greenery, yet dense enough that a feeling of claustrophobia still existed. Bushes and trees at eye level stopped you seeing too far.

Most forests smell a bit like mud and shit, but this one didn't. I guessed that the crisp mountain air kept everything pretty fresh. And everything – the ground, the tree trunks, the rocks, all of it – was carpeted in dense, spongy, light green moss. And it wasn't just a thin layer, it was like a shagpile rug. I wouldn't have looked twice if I'd caught one of Frodo's mates pissing against a tree.

I did get distracted as I counted my paces. Not by the scenery, but by my brain. I ran through the statements I'd read, the summary I'd pieced together. The Fawkes' brown Holden was found pretty much back where I'd parked, but on this side of the road. Give or take. Complete with food, wallets, everything. The search had fanned out from there, covering the tracks first and then more of a grid search later.

Besides my brain chatting away, there wasn't much to hear apart from trickling water. No birds or insects. Again probably something to do with the climate. Too cold. Too wet.

Something broke through my inner monologue and tried to tell me something. I was almost a couple of hundred metres in now, and it hadn't been easy. The moss underfoot hid branches, rocks and logs, and the smaller trees reached out, grabbed and tugged. Either Fawkes had convinced his family to walk in here – a gun would certainly have done that – or he'd dragged them in. But that would've been hard. It wasn't tropical jungle thick, but it was still slow going. He couldn't control his wife and Casey together in here. Maybe that's why Casey wasn't found. Maybe she ran.

But the gun bothered me too. Why not just kill them both

near the car? He was going to kill himself anyway.

But there was no point trying to nut it out. That's why cop shows on TV were bollocks. No rational mind can ever know what a killer was thinking. Irrational people do irrational things. That's all I could rely on.

***

I got to where I thought I should be, and it was unremarkable, like every other part of the forest. Sitting on a rock, I tried to match the scene photos to something, to anything, here, but nothing looked the same. The trees had grown; some had fallen. Moss had covered everything, died and spread again.

The rage that must've been coursing through Michael Fawkes' veins when he killed his wife would've been over relatively quickly. Plenty of gruesome killings aren't what they seem. Rage might deal the death blow, but panic is what leads people to do batshit crazy stuff like sinking bodies off boats, cutting them up and dumping them in the bush, dissolving them in acid or setting them on fire.

But Fawkes didn't panic. He methodically killed his wife by strangling her, and then probably his daughter with a round from his rifle, or inadvertently sent her fleeing into the wilderness. Then he killed himself.

There was some raised, moss-covered ground out to my left. I checked the photos again. The hump could possibly be the one in the photos. Maybe I was in the right spot, maybe I wasn't. I sat and let my brain drift.

If Casey had made it out of here, wouldn't she have been found? Even if she'd fallen into a river, surely the body would have turned up somewhere. Could a fleeing fifteen-year-old get far enough to avoid the sweeps by Search and Rescue?

It had happened before, though. Many times. A famous double murder in the Coromandel Ranges had yielded only one body several years after the event; the other had never been found. And SAR had been through that place with a fine tooth comb.

This area would be paradise for many, Kiwis and tourists alike. Nobody and nothing for ever. But right here, right now, it scared the shit out of me. What a fucking lonely place to die.

26.

I knocked on the heavy aluminium and glass door. I was in one of Queenstown's newer and quieter suburbs, out near the airport.

After leaving the forest I'd sat in my wagon, thinking hard, before deciding what the hell, it was the weekend, and stuff it, let's give him a crack. I'd driven the two hours without stopping. Out of the beech forest of the pass, through Hāwea along the edge of the lake, then out the back of Wānaka into the Cardrona Valley and over the Crown Range to Queenstown. It was a stunning journey. On any other day, I'd have paused to take in the breathtaking scenery we had in our own backyard.

Alec was cheerful as ever, despite how we'd last parted. Faded jeans this time, Nikes and a hoodie. 'Matt, what brings you here?' He was smiling, genuine, with more than a hint of interest.

I looked him up and down. 'How the hell do you afford this place?'

'Emily's a lawyer. She's always working overtime, and I reap the rewards.'

The wow factor didn't let up as I followed him inside. Open-plan lounge and kitchen, polished stone benchtops, soft lighting and digitally controlled everything. He opened the fridge, grabbed two beers and headed for the leather couch and chairs positioned in front of a huge picture window.

'Fuck me days.' I didn't even consider Alec's appetite for language, but felt he deserved whatever he got from me. The cold blue sky reached across a view to die for. The sun glinted off Lake Wakatipu, bare willow trees lining its edges. And with the jagged snow-covered peaks of The Remarkables over to the left, there wasn't much to bitch about.

I wanted to come at him open and honest. 'Alec, I need to know why you're looking into Haast.' He went to speak, but I held up my hand. 'Just hang on, I know, I know. But I've uncovered some things. Some you may well already know. Others maybe not. I've got to be careful. Can't just pass every official piece of information to media. But maybe a bit of give and take should see us both right, know what I'm saying?' I took a sip, watching the lake. 'I know Liam found Michael and Lynn, and I know Casey was never found. You're probably all over those facts, hence your interest when Liam died.'

'Yeah, I received a partial file, after making an Official Information Act request.'

Good. They'll have given him a lot, but not everything.

'There's a possibility, too, that Casey may have had an older boyfriend. As in much older.'

He spluttered through his mouthful of beer. 'Seriously?'

'I said possibility. It's been reported as an opinion, but there's nothing else yet to confirm.' I'd keep the diary page to myself for now.

Alec was getting animated. 'Okay, okay. Well, that actually

sews up a very large hole, Matt. Pulls a whole lot of threads together.' He finished his beer in one gulp. 'Another?'

When he returned, he started talking about a call, more than a year ago, from a guy who said his mother used to work as a nurse with the Canterbury District Health Board. 'Early nineties. Community and mental health outreach. It wasn't what it is now, it was piss poor, but it existed.'

'I can imagine.'

'So apparently his mum often mentioned a patient she'd had who'd confessed to burying a body.'

'Police involved?'

'That's the thing. He never knew. He said the way his mother talked about it, the family assumed she *must* have gone to the police back then.'

'Did she?'

'It seems not. I believe he's since told the police but there's not much they can do without more details. And the mother died some years back.'

'Okay,' I said, 'so somebody buried someone, somewhere. What's that got to do with Haast Pass? Pretty large leap.'

'Exactly. But I did some digging into missing people in the South Island. As I'm sure you'd know, it's no small number. But the Fawkes did come up. It was nothing more than a lead to run down, absolutely no indication it was linked.'

'So how did you link a call about a body that may or may not exist with Haast?'

Alec was thinking about his words. 'It wasn't my guess. But apparently some locals in Haast had caught the attention of the law with this already, and so we managed to focus in on Liam, given he'd found Michael and Lynn back in '78. And there were other discrepancies . . .'

Something was confusing the shit out of me. 'Hang on, who's we? I thought *you* got the call. And what do you mean, catching the attention of Haast police? Hang on a fucking second . . .'

'Yeah, he was like a dog with a bone, wouldn't tell me everything he was doing. It was Gus, Matt. I was working with Gus.'

27.

I put my dad face on. 'You need to get your arse in to the homicide inquiry and tell them that, mate. Quick smart, before they come knocking and you're in the firing line. Jesus fucked, I should be calling them right now, letting them know …'

Reception was okay here so I could use my mobile. I spoke briefly with Brent, who sounded as though he'd launched himself off his chair at the news.

'He's on his way? Good, and where's that file? Nelson?'

'No, that's the good news, it's right there under your nose, I got it out a few weeks back. It's just missing a scene folder, which I've got.'

Alec spoke. 'I was about to call them, Matt, I was. I've got an apology to make. When Gus was killed, I … I flipped out. I raced over to Haast, and I pissed a few people off. I'm sorry. I was trying to make some sense out of it and I felt bulletproof at the time. I was angry.'

I got it. 'It's okay, mate, but why the fuck didn't you speak to the inquiry?'

'Because now I've had time to think about it, I'm scared shitless. I know Liam's probably the one who did it, but did he have people with him? Did you see the cameras over my drive? They're new. I wouldn't have opened the door if I hadn't seen you on them first, I'm worried about Emily –'

'You think *Liam* killed Gus?'

I'd been harbouring thoughts, too, but when it came down to it, there wasn't even what you'd call circumstantial evidence. There was a link to Casey, and the link to Epitaph, but on their own they made no sense.

When I told Alec what Liam had asked me, he said, 'Maybe he wanted to confess.'

'No, it was *before* Gus died.'

'Well, maybe he'd figured out his own solution.'

'But why kill someone who's onto you, then kill yourself? One or the other would make more sense. Doesn't add up, Alec.'

I was ready to leave. Sure, the case had been blown wide open, but maybe I'd said too much. I didn't want to be accused of leaking to the media. But then how long would Alec have waited to tell the inquiry?

'Well,' Alec replied, 'Liam had a lot to hide. Especially now that you've mentioned the possibility of an underage relationship. Come inside. I've got something for you to read.'

He ushered me down the hall and into his study. He had a laptop plugged in, beside bundles of documents and notebooks. Shelves covered a whole wall, with books I didn't get the chance to look at.

'Here.' He'd dug something out of a ring-binder on the desk and handed it to me.

'What's this?'

'It's part of a second Official Information filing I did recently.

I'd asked for Tasman District information from the late seventies. Most of it's redacted.'

As part of the OIA response, someone from HQ had scanned in an old police jobsheet. The whole top part was redacted, probably the names and something else deemed too private. I checked the bottom footer for the author's name: Detective R. Boyd, 4th September 1978.

I read what I could below the blacked-out redaction.

The cannabis is grown in the hills around Nelson. I can identify a few areas for you, but really that's our bread and butter so you'll understand if that stays mum. But we run it down the coast, then it goes all the way south and into Queenstown. Epitaph do the runs from about Greymouth, we don't move that far past there, so we meet up and do a handover to them. They take it the rest of the way. Ecstasy comes back the other way. Back up here.

I looked up at Alec. 'This is an informant report. Even redacted, even from '78, you shouldn't have this.'

'Yeah, I figured. But keep reading.'

There were details about how the Epitaph bikers concealed the drugs in satchels they could ditch if they came across any cops. Towards the bottom there was a section that didn't make much sense initially, because the bit immediately before it was blacked out. It must have been a response to a question from Detective Boyd. *Yeah they do, they have a guy in Haast who works for DOC. He stockpiles some of it in places where he has access. Well out of the way. They meet up with him when they come through …*

'Jesus. Liam was running drugs.'

28.

I wasn't that far from home, but as I entered Hāwea, I realised that coffee was needed. As I left with my takeaway flat white I almost knocked her over. 'Shit, I'm so sorry . . .'

She collected herself and pushed her hood back. 'No, no I should've seen the door . . .'

It was Anna.

'Matt? What brings you over here? Is it the case?' She was beaming, but worried for me too.

'Not really, more work avoidance.'

'Ah.'

'And what brings you to the Hāwea corner store?'

'Green tea.'

I made a face. She rolled her eyes and deepened her voice. 'Beer, coffee, steak, potatoes . . . Am I getting warm?'

'Yep. You missed white bread, full-cream milk and bourbon. And you'll be off to your sixth meditation session for the day?'

'I am.'

'Are you down by the lake?'

She pointed further east along the lake shore, away from the shop. 'That way. Holistic Health.'

'You walked?'

'Yeah, it's not far.'

'Well, let me give you a lift back anyway.'

As we drove, brown hills rising in the near distance, Anna tried to wind me up. 'So I couldn't interest you in a yoga session while you're visiting?'

I kept my face straight. 'I'd rather wipe my arse with a handful of stinging nettles.'

She closed her eyes in mock horror but was trying not to laugh. We were soon at a little place that Anna told me was called Gladstone. The hippie end, the Byron Bay of Hāwea's Surfers Paradise. Not that either came remotely close.

The centre was a collection of buildings clustered around the main hut, sheltered by trees and reached by a few stone steps, that doubled as reception and a small shop selling everything from bread made of insects to ointments made from tree bark.

A smiling woman of about forty, with a long plait and wearing a loose linen dress and sandals, approached. 'Ursula, this is Matt. He's the one who gave me a hand changing the tyre.'

I shook Ursula's hand. 'So has Anna sparked your interest in some wellbeing, Constable? Don't judge us before you try us.'

'I wouldn't go that far, no. People with doctorates in psychology have tried and failed.'

'Nonsense, I can see there's a bit of an athlete under there. You cops are all the same, always putting yourselves down. You never know, a bit of time focusing on yourself might ease that load I know you'll be under. Your job isn't easy.'

I shrugged. 'Hey, maybe you're right, I'll try anything once.'

But the best I could do was to buy some green tea and make

a hasty exit, taking Anna by the hand. 'You're all the same, you wellbeing lot. Full of praise for everybody. It's unhealthy.'

'Hey, Ursula and I are quite different. First off, she's not into you.'

I tried to look offended. 'How do you know?'

'She's into girls.'

'Right. Well, then she and I still have something in common.'

Anna stood on tiptoe so we could kiss.

'See you for a hike soon?'

She grinned. 'Sold. I'll come over Friday afternoon. I might even bring a friend.'

'Are you sure you want to inflict Darren on anyone you know?'

'Are you kidding? It's you I'm worried about.'

29.

The Antler wasn't busy. A few tourists, the regular locals. As usual, I was drinking with Darren, who'd worked the day shift and knocked off, handing over to Jodie and others for the evening. He was talking a big game. 'If you can get someone like Anna interested, then surely it's time my number came up. I mean look at you. You're a shambles of a man, Matty.'

I finished my pint. 'Totally agree with you, mate. But ours is not to reason why.'

'Maybe Anna's got glaucoma.'

'Fuck off.'

The doors opened and Anna came in, more dressed up than usual in boots and a floral skirt. Her mate had Darren's eye immediately. Taller and blonder than Anna, but with the same happiness oozing everywhere. I nudged him. 'Daz, I know nothing much happens around here for you, but for the sake of the community, can you not fuck things up for me tonight?'

He was chuckling before I'd even finished. 'Matty, it's me.'

He was out the gate before they'd even sat down. 'Hey again,

Anna, and … Imogen, lovely to meet you. Imi, you say? Great. Sorry, Matt here was just telling me how he doesn't agree with women in the workplace. That's a shocking thing to say in this day and age, don't you think?'

I closed my eyes and pinched the bridge of my nose. The guy wouldn't survive anywhere else.

My turn. 'Imi, I'm going to warn you, this guy here has a problem. He's just incapable of telling the truth. Everything that comes out his mouth is bollocks.'

Anna leapt to Darren's defence. 'Are you serious, Matt? I haven't heard anything other than bollocks from you since the day we met.'

I've lost already.

As Darren and Imogen got chatting, I was able to ask Anna a personal question. 'You never got the chance to tell me how you ended up here.'

'You finally want my life story?'

'Always did, never got the chance.'

She sipped her cider. 'I've got a big family. Went to Otago, that's where I got my BCom. Fat lot of good that did me, though it got me to London for my OE. I realised the world wasn't that awesome and came back to concentrate a little on myself.'

I bit my lip. 'Seems like you've got to the end of the knowing yourself book. I'm still reading.' I signalled Jodie and indicated another pint. 'There may be a slight hint of jealousy involved in why I like you so much.'

She tilted her head, feigning seriousness. 'Come on, former-Detective-now-Senior-Constable Buchanan, you're saying you haven't seen enough of the world, of the people that occupy it?'

I shook my head. 'I've seen bloody plenty. I'm just saying I haven't figured out where I fit into it all.'

'You don't. That's the key. You aren't supposed to, and you don't.'

'What does that mean?'

'It means you don't matter.'

'Sounds nihilistic. What happened to happy?'

'It's being comfortable with it, that's the difference. Do you think I'd hook up with any old cop who helped change my tyre?'

'If he was as fit and good looking as me, then obviously.'

She punched my arm gently, then finished her glass. Jodie, grinning to herself behind the taps, started pouring another.

'If you're happy, keep doing it. If it would make you happy, do it. Don't think too hard about it. That's all there is.'

'What about if it doesn't necessarily make you *happy* ... but you think it matters just as much.'

Anna took the glass Jodie pushed toward her. 'Well, if it matters to you, then it's worth doing, I reckon.'

My head swam with images of Gus, of Liam, of the dead bodies in the pass. They were a certainty. But like the last case that had broken me, it was the sense of something left unfinished that I couldn't shake. Though at least I could recognise that now, and make a call either way.

Darren snapped me out of my daydream with a slap to my back and an arm around my shoulder. 'You've got your thinking face on, Matty. You stop that now, there's a good lad ...'

30.

A week later I was still squashed into a corner of my station, and the homicide team from Greymouth were still doing their thing, but not as energetically as when it all kicked off. They'd settled into Haast life and Brent was running the ship pretty well.

As far as I knew they were following all lines of inquiry, including those pointing in Liam's direction, but with the added workload of reviewing the entire Fawkes file properly, they'd certainly dropped a few gears in speed.

I was reading online about a police raid in Timaru. They'd gone through the gates of the Road Knights pad with a goddamn digger. There was a video taken by some neighbour on their phone, of an Armed Offenders Squad member in all his black kit driving it up to the gate and taking to it, before the rest of the squad flooded in through the gap. I scrolled through the standard police commentary: 'It dealt a significant blow to organised crime groups and the harm they cause to local communities.' Give me strength.

'Seen the news in Timaru?' It was Alec on the phone.

'The Road Knights? Sure. I'm reading it now.'

'Mind if I swing over your way? Something to show you.'

'I reckon I could fit you in.'

I had time for a run, a shower and a first coffee before he showed up.

He perched on a stool near the kitchen bench while I dealt with the coffee machine. 'I've been looking into the gang make-up around these parts, historically, right? As part of all this.'

I handed him a mug. 'Because of Liam's links to Epitaph. Sure.'

'You got it. But that informant report, it's talking about drug running down the West Coast. Epitaph are from Christchurch. This was a thriving business at the time right? In 1978, drugs were big money and competition was thin on the ground. And yet, there's a big gaping hole in all of it.'

'How's that then?'

He talked about his far-reaching OIA requests, the drug statistics he'd sourced, the research into homicide cases, all pointing towards a thriving drug market running up the entire South Island. Gangs partnering up, getting it into the different areas where there was increasing demand.

I've fucking nailed this brew. Coffee amount, milk quantity ...

Then Alec got to the problem he'd found.

'It doesn't make sense. The Road Knights had more to do with Queenstown than Epitaph ever did, and yet Epitaph were running weed all the way down there from the gangs up in Nelson. They had a huge market share, somehow managed to muscle the Knights out.'

'Epitaph have a reputation.'

'Don't they all, though?'

'Well,' I said, 'maybe everyone was in on it. The others probably left it alone 'cause they got paid a tax for it happening on their turf. Just a business deal, nothing more.'

'Maybe. But then right in the middle of all this –' he went over to a huge map of the South Island I had pinned to the wall, '– weed coming south –' he traced a finger down the West Coast, '– market in Queenstown –' he drew his other finger up from there, '– and then Epitaph from Canterbury.' He drew his first finger from Christchurch, south-west through Tekapo and into the same area where his fingers met up. Haast.

'So what? That's how business works.'

'It's not just the where, Matt, it's what's *happened here*. There's something going on here. Somehow Epitaph gained control right here, and it makes no sense. But then there are these odd coincidences, odd collisions. Maybe they did indeed have that reputation you're talking about.'

I let him hold my attention.

'Right when the Epitaph weed business was booming, the Fawkes family died in the pass. Then all of a sudden, decades later, Gus is murdered for looking into it all, and within days Liam, with Epitaph links from way back then, kills himself. There's more to this. There's got to be.'

He was starting to lose me. This all seemed like a rehash of what we knew. A history lesson with no answers.

'And then there's this.' He slapped down a thick file of paper punched at the top left and clipped together. He gave me a summary. 'You remember that French girl who went missing back in 1991?'

'Yeah, I recall that on the news, though I can't say I know the details. What was her name?'

'Nadine Ruyer.'

My eyes found the name in the file and into my head came a distant image of a brunette girl smiling, wearing a backpack.

Alec continued. 'She was backpacking her way through the country – confident solo hiker. She'd been fruit picking in Tauranga and had just finished up working at the Cardrona skifield. The official line is she died by accident, lost in a ravine somewhere, fallen off a cliff, who knows.'

'And?'

'Guess what I find in there? In the days before she goes on her hike, a witness sees her chatting to a guy. He isn't named in the pages, but there's a mention of a patch, with a skull. Doesn't narrow it down, but it's there.'

'What, you think she was offed by Epitaph for some reason?'

He shrugged. 'I'm not saying that's what happened, but there's more to it, right?' He indicated Haast on the map again. 'That guy, the patched member seen with Ruyer, never came forward and said his piece. I'm just saying, it's odd. All this is odd. Gangs cropping up all through what have otherwise been open and shut events, right in the middle of major drug activity. A lot of effort was being put in, right here, despite it being the arse end of nowhere.'

He was losing me again. 'You could find that shit anywhere, Alec. Take a look at any Auckland missing person or unsolved murder and you'll find mention of a gang somewhere. Mostly it's bollocks. Society has a lot to answer for. They think gang members are what goes bump in the night, the root of all evil. They aren't. They capitalise on what's otherwise a bunch of social issues, but they aren't the cause of them. For the young and forgotten they actually fill a gap that society should be filling, but fails to do. I don't agree with crime but I don't judge people for joining these clubs. What you're talking about might be a knowledge gap for us, but these gangs aren't the devil.'

He looked up, questioning. 'But you agree, we're looking for a devil.'

'Alec, look, I agree that there are unanswered questions. No shit, we're a few decades late to the party. But is all this related? Doubtful. Please don't go drawing lines where there aren't any, mate. Haast is quiet. It's peaceful. It relies a lot on tourism. Can you bloody leave it that way? My focus is Gus. I know yours is too. But the homicide team are all over that. Let's not complicate the shit out of it with a history lesson on the few criminals who ever walked through here. The answers are in the Fawkes file, somewhere, and the homicide team will find them.'

But there was something else. 'The witness who saw Nadine Ruyer speaking with the patched member. Who was it? Is the name redacted?'

'No ... Sandra. Sandra Adams.'

'Date of birth in there?' I was writing on a pad, having left my notebook over in the station.

'No, but she was twenty-two when her statement was taken in '91.'

As we parted, I offered some advice. 'It's not going to be complicated, mate. The obvious answer always wins out.'

He forced his lips together. 'We'll see.'

In the station, I sat at my screen again and did a quick NIA check, but couldn't find any Sandra Adams born in 1969. I sent out a few official requests – Births, Deaths and Marriages, Internal Affairs – knowing it'd take an aeon.

31.

Boyd, the detective from Nelson. The name alone didn't help. There was nothing in our system, but then again I didn't expect him to still be working. He could be in his eighties. Or dead.

I phoned Nelson HQ and asked who the longest serving officer there was. In ten more minutes I had the name: Chris Shelton, former detective sergeant, now non-sworn file briefer, raking in some extra cash in his retirement years to supplement his nice police superannuation. I phoned his private mobile, apology ready to go. But he was happy to help.

'You worked Tasman longer than anyone, I hear. How's your memory of the late seventies?'

'The seventies? Oh Jesus, here we go. What's happening, another royal commission?'

I chuckled. 'Not at all, I'm trying to track down a D who was working back then. Don't know his full name – first initial R, last name Boyd?'

A pause. 'Boyd, did you say? Boydie? Hell, yeah. Richie Boyd served longer than me. I was his boss but he'd been in way longer. What are you after him for now?'

'Just some information. He worked on something years back, something that –'

'This about Gus? I knew him well.'

There was no reason to hide stuff from this guy. We were all on the same team. 'Yeah. Gus was looking into a case from '78 before he was shot. It's who he last spoke to or why that they're interested in, but Boyd ran a source that had access to some of this 1978 stuff. Am I making sense?'

'Yes, yes, of course. Look, Boydie and I go way back. He lives in Christchurch now, but we catch up. I'll give you his number, but do you mind if I call him first? Grease the wheels? He'll appreciate it. And he's the nicest guy in the world. He'll do whatever you need, and he'll make a real go of helping you out.'

***

I was balls deep in some low-level paperwork when my landline rang not fifteen minutes later and it was the guy himself.

'You need to pick my brain?'

'Yeah, going back quite a way.'

'Late seventies, he said. The murdered ex-cop was looking into something? Would have been the Fawkes, then.' He said it matter of factly, not even questioning it.

'It was. You worked on it?'

'Me? No. Greymouth did. Some of the guys from Nelson got sent down to help in the early days. Not me, though. I got stuck chasing local burglars.'

'Ain't that always the way. Look, Richard, bear with me.' I

told him about Liam's suicide and how Alec had managed to get hold of the redacted jobsheet.

'He bloody what now?'

'I know. Someone fucked up his OIA request. This jobsheet, though, it mentioned some weed being trafficked down from Nelson towards Queenstown. Ring a bell?'

A deep breath. 'Yeah, the informant was a local guy I locked up several times. Not so bad, mixed up, but always respectful, which is ironic given where he ended up. He was hanging around the Lost Breed at the time.'

Nelson bikies. Makes sense.

'I'm wondering if that informant is still around.'

I could almost hear him racking his brain. Then he started to laugh. 'Back then, he was a small player. Low-hanging fruit. And yeah, he's alive all right. But good fucking luck.'

'How's that?'

'Well, back then he might've just been a hang-around in a now collapsed gang, but after what the AOS lads did to that pad in Timaru, I'd say you'd be pushing shit uphill.'

'You're saying he's now a member of the Road Knights?'

He coughed out another laugh. 'Member? A member? No, shit, no. He's their bloody president.'

32.

Reefton sat in a river valley, way up the Coast and then inland up the Grey River. Nestled among green hills, with the Alps lurking behind, the little town had been forged in the gold rush and kept the look going today. Although I'd left Haast at dawn's crack, I still didn't arrive until lunchtime.

My request had actually come up with the goods – a married name for the witness from 1991. She ran a souvenir shop in Reefton.

Charmed turned out to be a small store with a maroon timber frontage, right down the far end of Broadway, the main street, past all the similar shops and buildings with 'Cottage' this and 'Est.' that prominently displayed.

Sandra Morrison, nee Adams, intercepted me as soon as I strode in beneath the jangling beads at the entrance. She had short greying hair, looked somewhere over fifty and was beaming, genuinely delighted to have someone to talk to who wasn't a local. 'Constable! A pleasure. How was the drive?'

'Long and miserable, but that's how I like 'em.'

'Rain the whole way?'

'Nope. Became a bit of sleet around Franz Josef.'

She laughed. 'Come on back. I'll boil the jug and I've got scones.' I followed her between shelves of crystals and gem-trees, carved bone necklaces and herbal remedies and ducked through the doorway to the staff only section, beneath a large print of a faun playing a flute in a forest that reminded me of the pass.

Sandra took my jacket and hung it over a chair. 'Now, I don't know exactly what you want to see me about, but I think you all do a bloody fantastic job. I know it so often mustn't be good news. Always been only one officer down in Haast, and what a terrible, terrible thing. I didn't know him, but my condolences for one of yours.'

'You used to live in Hāwea?'

'Sure did, for a time. You aren't local either, are you? Too clean. What were you, something else before coming down here?'

I confessed.

'Well, crap on my kitchen bench, CIB. Who'd you piss off? A friend of mine, her dad was a detective, over in Blenheim, long time ago, when that young couple got murdered in the Sounds. Kept me awake at night, that case did.'

'Piss off is probably an understatement. You sussed me out in seconds. You're pretty switched on.'

'Have to be. I've got a shop to run and some grandkids to spoil.'

'You've lived on the West Coast your whole life?'

'My whole life. Hāwea, like I said, then Greymouth, then settled in Reefton. The Coast is home, yeah.'

Through a mouthful of scone, jam and cream, I asked, 'How'd you end up owning this place?'

'I bought it for a dime in the late nineties. This type of stuff went out of fashion in the eighties, completely tanked, but I thought it'd bounce back and it did.'

'The eighties. Must have been the satanic panic?'

She looked me up and down. 'You're smarter than you pretend, Constable, has anyone ever told you that? But yeah, you're right. Goddamn United States panic sent everything into a tailspin.'

West Memphis popped into my head. 'Not much in common, though, is there? Crystals and dream catchers – pagans and satanism? They aren't cut from the same cloth. Why even the implied connection?'

She rolled her eyes in agreement. 'Why, indeed? Depends who you ask. Ask the goddamn Christians, they're the ones who made the link. Threaten the church, and all of a sudden respecting the earth and sky becomes devil worship.'

It was time to be straight up about why I was here. 'Mrs Morrison.'

'Sandra, please.'

'Well then, it's Matt, not constable.'

'Of course. You're going to tell me what this is about?'

'Yeah. Now, I apologise for what this might bring up. A long time ago, you helped the police out with something, and I'm hoping to ask you about that all over again. It's nothing new, nothing to be concerned about now.' She looked uncertain. 'In 1991 you gave a statement about a tourist who went missing. Nadine Ruyer.'

It was as if someone had turned the lights out. She went still; even her eyes didn't move. 'Jesus wept, Matt.'

I couldn't help but notice that the mug in her hand had begun to shake. She put it on the table.

'I'm really sorry. I don't want to go over it all. I know you saw Nadine, but it's the man she was talking to I wanted to ask about.'

She went white.

'I'm asking because I think I might know who that man was. But let me clarify a couple of things. First, what you're telling me isn't going in any statement, not at this stage. Second, I'm going to show you a photo, and … none of this would hold water in court, but it doesn't matter because the guy in the photo is dead now. You with me?'

'I get it – it can't go to court.'

'That's right. Possibly a coroner's inquest, but that's dreamland right now. And if that happens it isn't like a trial. We'd just recount this meeting like it is.' I pulled out a photocopy of her statement, flicked through to my highlights. 'Now you described the guy as tall, weather-beaten, about forty, hair below his ears. You said it was light brown. The face you haven't described too well, but you did get a brief look, long enough to know you'd seen him a few times before, around the place. Now I'm going to show you the photo. Remember, this ID won't stack up. But showing you eight photos isn't going to get us anywhere fast … it was a long time ago.'

I pulled out the black and white photo of Liam standing with the Epitaph members.

Sandra squinted for a while, then turned her palms out. 'It could be him? I can't remember the face. Does it match the description? Maybe a little?'

'Basically, yeah, though this man has darker hair than you described.'

'I do … I do remember the hair being lighter, but now I've got an image of her, of that girl, and it's a sunny day …'

I decided to leave the ID in the inconclusive pile. 'Do you remember anything else about the man?'

She took a ragged breath. 'I knew of him, he was a local. I didn't know his name, not then, not now. But he was a gang member all right. You'd hear whispers every time he walked past. This was a lot earlier than this French girl, though – would have been late seventies. I guess I probably only laid eyes on him a couple of times, but through others I knew who he was.'

'When was the last time you saw him?'

'Probably then. And I wouldn't have seen him for more than a decade before that. That lot disappeared in the early eighties, there was nothing for a while. Seeing him again in '91 and talking to Nadine, that made me go to the police. It was odd.'

'Did you ever hear about him working for DOC? A bushman?'

'This guy? No, not that I recall.'

I decided to let it rest. But as I stood, she gripped my forearm. When she spoke her voice had lowered. 'Matt, this doesn't have anything to do with that other girl who went missing, does it?'

'What makes you say that?'

'A teenager went missing in the seventies. The rumours were rife. Nadine went just over a decade after her.'

I placed my hand over hers. 'You know something?'

'Those bikers, there were rumours they were mixed up in something.' Her gaze rested on the faun playing his flute. 'I … I don't know.'

'They were supplying drugs, Sandra. From Nelson into Queenstown, most likely. It's what they did.'

Her eyes filled as faded memories were wrenched back into the present. 'This hasn't all come out of the blue, has it? It must be all related to your predecessor, what he'd found out?'

'That's the thing,' I replied. 'I have no idea.'

'Well, if you get anywhere with this, Matt, with these girls, you tread carefully. Those bikers didn't go gently. But if you tore them limb from limb I'd say you'd have the backing of the whole Coast. It's not something we let go, our own going missing.'

I managed to calm her and asked if she'd have some company that afternoon. 'Yes, yes, a couple of friends will pop in for tea. I'm sorry, Matt. Don't take what I say to heart. You do your job the way you know how.'

To our right a door banged open and a pale guy wearing a green cheese-cutter stepped in from outside, holding a couple of boxes. 'Sandra, where shall I put it?' He was softly spoken, but to the point. Then he saw me. 'Oh, sorry to interrupt. Sandra been tempting you to buy some of her knickknacks? Load of old shite. Bloody crystals.'

I grinned. 'I'm probably in that camp too.'

Sandra pretended to slap me. 'Stop insulting your host. David, this is Constable Matt Buchanan, he's Haast Police. Matt, this is David Williams. You should catch up with him some time. I'm sure you two could get a lot done together.'

'Indeed.' He lifted his cap. 'Pleasure, Constable, but I won't bother you now. Cheerio.'

Sandra turned back to me in explanation. 'David's the school counsellor. Has the most amazing garden, drops me off something every few days. Lots to go round. But he works with kids all the way down the Coast, the high-riskers, the sad, the ones into booze and drugs. Terrible stories, some of them. They need all the help they can get.'

* * *

As I headed for my car, I passed David, head inside the boot of a Mazda station wagon. He saw me and called out. 'Time for a cold one after all, Constable?'

I paused. *You do your job the way you know how.* When you were introduced as a cop, in a small town, you felt obliged to follow things up. I strolled over, extended my hand and five minutes later we were chatting over pints at the hotel. Given his role, I wanted to know more about the landscape in which I worked. The kids there weren't around much, so there wasn't really an undertow for them to fall into. But I knew that these more northern parts, Westport, Reefton and certainly Nelson, had their issues. Could things up here affect Haast?

'So it's meth around here?' I asked. 'I've read the news articles, but haven't heard much inside the organisation.'

'It's like a last bastion of homebake and amateur meth labs. Bit different, no doubt, from what you'd have been used to up in Auckland.'

He was correct. The meth industry had grown wings and taken flight. Garage meth labs were almost a thing of the past, given the amount of the finished drug now imported by sea. A few years ago it was rare to nab a kilo in Auckland. But now, the drug squad turned up their nose at anything less than half a tonne. If the finished product was flooding in, the fuck-around involved in clandestine cooking made little sense. The West Coast, though, was a long way from a metropolis, however you measured one.

I laid it out for him. 'It's just distance, right? The big international supply gets sold long before it'd ever wind up here. So cooking still makes sense. That breeds a whole lot of issues around the gathering of ingredients and paying for them: burglary, robbery, assault, rape ... How am I doing?'

'You know it – that's the sad fact. And look, the kids here, they're like the kids up north. They just want a good time. Weed's plentiful, and hey, they'd use pills if they could, but they just aren't easy to come by. So it's garage drugs, and all that goes with that. Bloody sad.'

'So what do you do?' I asked. 'Encourage them to move away? From home?'

'Sort of. Education is the answer, right, and hey, there's Christchurch, and Dunedin – best education in the country. Or, for those who don't get seasick, Sealord have great opportunities on their fishing fleet out of Nelson for people wanting to get into the industry. Woodbourne isn't far, so the air force is another option. But it's like anything. They gotta want to do it. And sometimes they're too far down the rabbit hole.'

'So what then?'

He took a gulp of beer. 'Everyone's got their part to play. Nobody should be lost.'

'Do you see anything growing legs further south? I don't have many local issues like that, but will it spread?'

'No. I've lived around the West Coast a long time and I don't think so. Too close to the bright lights of Queenstown and Wānaka – it's cleaner over there. I don't think Haast is gonna change. I'd sleep easy if I were you.'

I've still got a dead ex-cop on my hands, though.

33.

'Oi, Joe! It's the law, mate. Get your hand off it.'

I heard chuckling and stumbling and out he came, in a singlet and shorts. It was blowing a gale, even in the confined clearing in the swampland. Rain wasn't far off. It was about three degrees. I looked him up and down. 'What's wrong with you? It's bloody freezing. Every time.'

He spat. 'Just like you to come here, to my house, and then start judgin' me.' He grinned, spat again and made an effort to check what was in my hands. 'Where's the beer?'

I rolled my eyes. 'You aren't in trouble, Joe. Need to pick your brain. Again.'

'Jesus.'

'I know.'

'Take you all of thirty seconds.'

'I don't doubt it.'

I followed him into his shack, took a seat on a wooden table crowded with books and not much else. A volume titled *Classical Myth* was sitting on a crate.

He caught me staring. 'What you lookin' at?'

'Nothing. Didn't pick you for a classics buff. If you'd had to suckle on the she-wolf's tit, you'd be asking where the beer was.'

He gave me the fingers. 'Thought you were gonna make a crack about me not being able to read.'

'Yeah well, that too.'

'Fuck you, Buchanan.'

Joe grabbed himself a beer but I shook my head, dived straight into my reason for visiting. 'What do you know about drug running through here back in the seventies, through to the nineties?'

He didn't bat an eyelid. 'Lots. What d'you wanna know?'

'Police raided a gang pad in Timaru recently.'

'The Knights.' He grimaced. 'They're just old men. Never came over here.' He watched me, trying to suss me out. 'Who do you really wanna know about?'

'I . . . this journalist is digging up the past. Thinks Liam was running drugs with Epitaph, way back when the Fawkes family went missing.'

Joe spent a good minute without sending any beer down his throat. I'd never seen him with such a grip on reality. 'And what d'you think about that?'

'I don't know. I mean the drug supply was happening, but I don't think . . . fuck, I don't know what I think. Why would Liam – yeah, that's it. Why would Liam, is what I'm asking.'

'What, weed? It's bloody *weed*, Jafa. Plenty worse than that. You gonna hang him out to dry over a bit of green? It was the seventies. Shit was like bread back then. Come on, you're better than that.'

'It's not the weed I care about, mate. It's the people involved, the gang, the money. How much it was all worth. And what happened around the outside of it.' He didn't answer, so I changed topic – mentioned Nadine Ruyer.

Again, a sharp moment of clarity on his face. He met my gaze. 'Ruyer.' He pronounced it correctly. 'Yeah, I remember that. Poor girl went hikin' and never came back. Is that fuckin' journalist stirring that up too? Haast doesn't need conspiracies, Jafa. You might need to sort him out.'

You're telling me.

'So was Liam the sergeant at arms for Epitaph?'

Joe coughed and spluttered. 'Liam? You kiddin'?' He cackled and some brightness returned to his eyes. 'You been sippin' diesel out of your bloody fuel tank?'

'What did he do, Joe? I need you to tell me.'

'Liam was salt of the fuckin' earth. Nothing he ever did came anywhere near to wrong. Stuff you, Jafa. I had high hopes about you coming down here, but I'm startin' to think ...' He drank from his can, then slammed it onto a crate so that beer fizzed out the top. 'The fuck has the French girl got to do with it all anyway?'

'I think they're linked. The gang, the weed, the Fawkes, Nadine Ruyer.'

'Well, now you sound like the one that's nuts.'

He cracked another can, downed half of it, then pointed his finger at me. 'You think if there was somethin' going on, the people round here would let that in? Think they'd stomach that? You're shittin' me. Locals here been battlin' for decades. And the town is still pristine. You remember that. Before you start swingin' your dick around.'

'You knew him, Joe. That's all. Whatever this is, it's to do with Liam. I thought he was a good guy too, but some questions have come up and I've got to ask them.'

'Well, I'm tellin' you straight up. He was a good guy. Next question.'

'This isn't an interrogation, mate, I just want ...'

'It sure feels like it is.'

I closed my eyes, thought hard before I said any more, not wanting to piss him off.

But he spoke first. Gently. 'Why'd he die?'

'What do you mean? He was dealing with a lot.'

'He was dealing ... with bloody everything. Ev ... er ... ry ... thing. You ever wonder what that was? What might push a man to do that?'

My burning house. Hailey screaming at me, dragging me out.

'Look, I can't say I watch much telly but I read, and much as it might offend you, Constable, for me to say so, I reckon if you peel us back enough, we're not too different, you and me. So when you're pushed into a corner, do you give up, or do you shake every tree, and then set 'em all on fire? I know what I'd do.'

Flicking that lighter in the meth lab in West Auckland. What I'd said to the guy before letting him burn.

He searched my face. 'Liam was no tree shaker, no fighter. Had a heart of bleedin' gold. So at the end, he had only one other option, didn't he?'

I sat there, insight hitting me hard. But what had Liam been dealing with?

Joe snapped me back to the present. He'd been searching my face again, and he'd found what he was looking for. 'There he is.' Joe's teeth appeared in a wider smile. 'Saw him clear as day just now.'

'Saw who, Joe?'

'That other guy.'

34.

The rain splattered the road and my vision was restricted to the fall of my feet on the wet tarmac. Beanie on, jacket hood up, I'd chosen a shit time for a jog, but truth be told, the thought was worse than the act and I enjoyed submitting briefly to the weather. It made the warmth of the station afterwards so much better.

So far I'd jogged up to Haast junction and then out along the road to Jackson Bay, heading past the service station towards Okuru. Every so often I'd raise my head to check for traffic, and all I got was grey, and wind, and rain lashing my face. I was breathing hard, mouth open, spitting rainwater when I exhaled.

Running cleared my head. Always had. It didn't let my mind do anything but keep the body going. I'd never been the fittest guy around, but I certainly held my own at my age, and it gave me a break – from brain stuff, from painful thinking. But I knew my subconscious was hard at work, and I was grateful for that too.

My thoughts had been going in circles. I was worried that

some of the things I was doing, some of the people I was talking to, might fuck up the homicide inquiry. I'd generally kept Brent in the loop, and told myself I was working on historic cases, not Gus's murder. But really, at the moment, they seemed to be one and the same.

Thing was, I didn't quite know why it was stressing me out. The prime suspect had killed himself. So I'd never be getting a bollocking from a Crown prosecutor or be ripped to shreds on the witness stand by a defence KC.

So what is it, dickhead?

I spat more rain out of my mouth and kept huffing along.

Maybe some boss will do a case review one day, make some assessments and guesses.

But it wouldn't change the outcome.

A car thundered past, showering me in its cast-off water, red tail lights briefly adding a new colour to the haze in front of me before they, too, disappeared into the grey.

I turned around at Okuru and headed back, on the coast side of the road, wondering why the hell the wind was still blowing rain straight into my face. I puffed on up to my front door, freezing fingers clutching the keys. Before entering I kicked off my soaked shoes, then shook out my jacket, hanging it on a hook just inside. I relished the immediate warmth of the heat pump, then a quick but hot shower.

The phone went just as I came back out. 'Matt, Boydie here. I managed to get hold of him.'

It took me a minute for my brain to fire up. 'The source? Really? Good shit, mate. How the hell did you do that?'

He elaborated on his long-winded contact attempt, claiming association with the team that had hit the Road Knights pad, wanting to return seized property, before the president finally gave him a call to tell him to piss off and leave the club alone, then realised who was on the other end. Another better-timed call later, and Boydie had had a good, long chat.

'Are you sitting down?'

'Yep, go, what could he say?'

'Well, a lot of what he was getting off his chest was the warrant. He wasn't pissed off about the reasoning – he accepts guns and drugs and the guys will bring their business in there, fair play to the cops and all that – but he did have something to offer. He reckons you're on the right track with Epitaph.

'Matt, you need to get your arse to Oamaru by tomorrow night. I'm heading down there now. I'll call you in the morning, give you the details. He has something else, but he won't do it over the phone. He wants to meet you.'

35.

Oamaru hadn't changed much since I'd visited as a kid. I was there in darkness, but there was enough light from the period streetlamps to see the massive old Victorian buildings, cream stone, huge wooden doors.

He hadn't wanted to meet anywhere near his own town and club, so Boydie had suggested the next biggest place going south. It wasn't too bad for me. Other side of the South Island, sure, but I just had to go through the pass, out the arse of Wanaka, head around towards Twizel and take a valley road straight east towards Oamaru.

I pulled my coat around me as I sat in my car waiting for Boydie's call. I was parked up by a service station, just as he'd asked me to. And at exactly 7 p.m. my phone rang.

'Hey, Matt. Go straight across the road, look for the hospital driveway that says ambulances only. Walk down between the bollards.' I followed Boydie's voice on the phone as I crossed Severn Street and found the driveway.

I didn't bother looking for Boydie. He was old school – I

knew he'd be watching me somewhere. 'See the building on your left, keep it there, hug it close. Look straight ahead now – see an alleyway with a couple more bollards to keep cars out? Head for that. You'll pop out onto Thames Street. Then go left. Second building along is Fat Sally's. We'll be in the back. Order yourself a beer and join us. See you soon, mate.'

I stopped at the entrance of what looked like an old bank building. With a bit of mist hanging around already, it wasn't hard to conjure up thoughts of Jack the Ripper. What the fuck was I getting into here?

As I went up to order at the bar I didn't look around like a cop normally would, but there was a good buzz. I took my foaming glass up one step into the darker, more private rear area.

The voice came strong and firm from a table beside me. 'I should've shouted that pint, in return for you being yoinked around like a donkey, but Boydie here said you deserved to get your own 'cause we're doin' you the favour.' The broad-shouldered, bald hulk of Vaughan Stammers, Road Knights president, stood and shook my hand.

I couldn't help myself. 'Well then, you can get the next one.'

He wheezed. He wasn't wearing his colours, but red still shone through in his T-shirt beneath his dark hoodie.

Richard Boyd was as I'd pictured him, tall, a shock of white hair, confident after a lifetime of catching crooks. He greeted me with a cheeky old grin and we all sat down.

Vaughan was staring at me. 'I know you from the telly. Put away that paedo ring up north.'

'Took me long enough.' *Best part of twenty years.*

'It's funny this, meeting the opposition. But then, the subject matter ain't exactly what I'd call the normal rivalry.'

'I haven't worked organised crime for a long time. I think we have similar views on more than you'd expect.'

Vaughan glanced at Boyd, who gave an encouraging look. Then he continued. 'And for the record I said opposition, not enemy. As in you're the only people that can lock me up. Doesn't necessarily mean you're gonna.'

Boyd cut in with some admin. 'This is a business meeting, craft brewing, should anyone see Vaughan with us. I've never been here, and neither have you, so we shouldn't have a problem. Worst case scenario, you're a bent cop, which isn't a hard story to spin either.'

He was right. It was important to have something ready to go, in case someone fronted any one of us at a later date.

It was clear that Boyd had given Vaughan quite the rundown, so I didn't have to explain much.

'Well, I told Boydie that I might have a smokin' gun for you – literally.' He sat back, then looked under the table at the daypack I'd brought with me. 'You bring the file? Photos?' I nodded. 'Okay. Look, I did the product handover so many times I couldn't put a number on it. Sometimes Reefton, sometimes Greymouth, sometimes further. It wasn't Liam very often who took it from me – usually it was their patched guys. He had a rifle he carried everywhere. Used it for both huntin' and to look after himself. You know, pigs out there in South Westland, they'll run you through if you do the wrong thing. I remember it plain as day. Walnut stock, scratched up to buggery – he liked it that way he said. A .303. Always called it the three-o.'

I knew already, but I pulled out a clearfile, then laid down copies of the photos of Michael Fawkes and the rifle.

Vaughan studied them. 'What did I tell you – scratched up walnut stock, .303.' Boyd and I looked at each other. 'Gettin' back to the beginning, though, in the late seventies I was hangin' around the Lost Breed. You familiar, Matthew?'

'Old school. Absorbed into the Angels?'

He swore. 'Those fuckers. But change is life. And that was long after I'd gone down to Canterbury.' He signalled the passing barman for another beer. 'I was a little bitch, just ask this guy –' he elbowed Boydie '– but I was trusted to sling. We grew, we harvested and ran it down the Coast. Epitaph would hook up with us near Greymouth, then they'd run it all the way south. Bit of tit for tat: we sent the weed south, they had sources of ecstasy down there. Weed down, pills back. Both clubs sold the product and both made a lot of coin.'

'Where were the pills sourced? Queenstown?'

'Don't really know. Some little hippie joint down there, a community, one of the weed customers, I assume. They had hook-ups for the happy pills. I didn't get involved in all that, I just did what I was told, met up with whoever, handed over, took back.'

When Boyd went for a piss, Vaughan said, 'Did Boydie say why I trusted him? Why I told him anything?' I shook my head. 'He'd been at me for years 'cause I was the local dealer. One afternoon, back when I was a total piece of shit, I was down the road drinkin', left my older boy in charge. Eight. Would you believe it? Anyway the kids were fuckin' about in the kitchen and the stove caught fire. The place went up like kindling.'

'Holy shit.'

'Boydie was cruisin' the suburb on shift. He was the first one there. Smashed a window to get in. Cut himself badly. Grabbed the two kids, threw them both out, then burned himself gettin' out through the front door. He was in hospital for two weeks for smoke inhalation and the rest. Saved my kids' lives. Really made me think. But I couldn't break away.'

He looked down at the table, then back at me. 'So I'm no snitch, and never fuckin' have been. It wasn't a debt. I genuinely respect the man, and what he's done for me. There's this sweet spot where I don't see any problem in passin' on facts. And I've been askin' 'bout you and seems like you may be cut from a similar sort of cloth to him. What's right, first. What's allowed, a distant bloody second.'

I kept very still.

'And if Boydie entrusted you with the knowledge of me, then hell, he must think you're all right. 'Cause he's never told anyone anythin' 'bout us.'

When Boyd returned, zipping his fly up as an afterthought when he was almost at the table, Vaughan clapped him on the shoulder and kept talking. 'So 1978 shook a few things up. That family wasn't supposed to end like that. Boydie came and saw me. He thought somethin' was up, knew about the drugs, brushed over that for stuff about the dead family. At the time, I was just thinkin' business. I thought, What if Epitaph killed that family? Saw somethin' they shouldn't? Hell, that's on them. Maybe my lot could've taken a bigger chunk of the business with a little competition removed. That's how I thought, back then. But Liam was a town hero, seemed like, so he wasn't put under the microscope. Nothin' happened.'

'And now?'

'Now? Well, for a while I never thought anythin' of it. I tried stitchin' up that Epitaph crew by feedin' Boydie here, like the piece of shit I was. That was the end of it, I never once tried anythin' again. But then I get this call.' He grinned flatly at me, eyes drilling in. 'Hear some shit-hot ex-detective from the big smoke is lookin' into it all ...' He glanced from me to Boydie and back again. 'I never did think Liam was that way inclined. Even lookin' at these photos. He wasn't the guy with the stones for that. Epitaph maybe, but not Liam.'

I was listening intently.

'Liam was helpin' his best mate out, part time – worked well with his ranger job. But it was the friend who was the real muscle, he was the Epitaph sergeant.'

The enforcer.

'He put me and Liam in touch. Sometimes, the Breed would run it all the way into Haast, when Epitaph had business back in their real patch, Christchurch. Liam would step up, 'cause he stockpiled it for them. I never did that long run, though.'

'But why now?' I asked. 'Why tell the cops anything at all?'

Two more beers appeared and an odd expression came over his face. 'As time drags on I've come to see that we occupy an even more fucked-up position in this life than I ever thought. Everyone's done bad, Matthew, but for all the bad I've done, there's still bad that I don't agree with. Guess I reconnected with Boydie 'cause I realised that, maybe one day, some smartarse will come knockin'. I could've snuck through life with no one bein' any the wiser, but here's a chance for me to start clearin' my conscience, so to speak, without any debt owed.'

He raised his pint to me. 'And in you stroll, motherfucker, like the angel of death himself. More than four decades later, dredgin' it up. I don't agree with what happened to that family, and I don't know it all either. But I do know that there's someone out there needs a fuckin' noose.'

'The Epitaph sergeant.'

He landed his beer on the table a bit too hard. 'Bingo. Give yourself a pat.'

'He alive?'

His words carried more than a hint of warning. 'Right under your nose. He dropped off the radar in the eighties, apparently. Liam went AWOL too – that whole crew sort of fragmented. Epitaph disappeared back over the hill. But he's been out your way for a long time now, livin' the hermit life, pullin' the wool over a lot of people's eyes. Thing is, Matthew, he's sharp as a fuckin' razor. And a mean motherfucker, as ruthless a guy as I ever met. And believe me, I've met a few.'

I began to go cold – there was only one person this could be. *You've always known. It's why you hassle him.*

'And so I apologise, Matthew, that this is all happenin' too late, too late for your brother in blue, over there in Haast. Sorry for sayin' so, but trust me, if someone went pokin' his nose into *this* guy's business, he was always gonna get what was comin' to him.'

I looked up at the ceiling.

'Guy's name was Joseph. Ring any bells?'

36.

I stepped cautiously this time, across the driftwood bridge and into the swamp beyond. My right hand rested on the pistol grip of my M4 rifle, thumb dancing on the safety. I carried it across my body horizontally. Not the police way, but when you're walking for a while, army habits are hard to break.

Joe had been Joe for as long as I'd been here, and the locals all knew him, and though they talked fondly of him, they seemed to avoid him too. But sergeant of a gang of bikers? Didn't seem like Joe at all.

But I'm carrying this rifle so I must think something.

The cold water rose above my boots, chilling my lower legs as I trudged on, looking over the reeds. It had just been background noise before, but now I could hear a frog croaking somewhere right in front of me. As I kept moving forward it went silent, but with the reeds, algae and dark water it didn't need to move to remain hidden. Once I passed, it stepped up the croaking again behind me, and was joined by some of its mates.

I spotted the half-sunken tractor, the rusted machinery

perched at its odd angle. Joe's corrugated iron and wooden shack beyond, a hermit's last stand.

Training started to kick in. *He's a suspect. Don't go in underprepared.*

I paused, scanned the waist-high field of reeds spread out before me, hiding the water beneath. The shack dead ahead, on the higher, drier ground. Bush rising up beyond on nearly all sides.

The trees to my left offered concealment, and maybe some cover, and so I struck out for them. I figured I'd box around the shack, come down from the trees in towards the rear, so I could at least get a view along three whole sides before I announced my presence. That'd satisfy my inner alarm bell. And it would be a hell of a lot better than striding on up to the front, totally exposed.

But you've been here before.

I had. And had never had any issues with Joe.

But you know different now.

Did I? I had third-hand information from a source. A source I personally knew nothing about, a source who was definitely involved themselves somewhere along that supply line back in '78.

I pushed all doubts away. I'd get to the back door, call out and knock, then ask Joe what the fuck was up.

As I lifted another mud-caked foot, I heard a scratching sound, then a hiss. My brain processed it. Matches? Fireworks? The hiss suddenly lowered in volume, stifled.

An ear-splitting explosion kicked off out in front of me, blowing out my hearing. I felt the thump as the shockwave passed through the ground. It sent me to my knees, then to my stomach, as I dropped low into the cold water to try and gather my senses. My ears started ringing. I jammed a finger into each and wiggled them about. Putting my head up, I saw a puff of black smoke drifting over the reeds. I ducked back down.

A thunderflash. Military grade equipment. Black powder, to simulate a grenade during field training. Why the hell would Joe have a thundie? They were harmless at any significant distance, but could blow your hand up if you held onto one.

I had to move. Things had changed. Unless he was playing a joke on me, cackling away to himself, watching me squirm while sipping his can of shit beer.

I pushed through the swamp to where the trees overhung the reeds, then waded through the sludge until I could stand on the brush without sinking. Soon the spindly, skeletal forest began and the ground got a bit firmer, meaning I could move quicker. I hugged the trees, keeping eyes on the shack, circling it. I couldn't see a thing.

I lifted my boot to take another step. And my heart went into my mouth as I heard it: the click of metal on metal.

The words were right beside my left ear. 'You just hold on there now, Jafa.'

The voice was his but the delivery was different – calm, deliberate, in control. I turned slowly, placing my hands on top of my head, because I knew what I'd see. Coming out of my periphery, into focus, Joe, sighting over the top of an automatic rifle, aimed at my chest.

'You just get onto your knees, so I can keep control a little better. Listen to my voice, comply with my instructions and everything will be fine.'

It was a version of a phrase we were taught at training. A phrase used by tactical units to keep people calm.

But I had to speak. 'Joe, think about the consequences here.

Just place the weapon on the ground, and we can talk. Nothing's a done deal yet.' He was holding what I could see now was a semi-auto .223, maybe a Mini 14. My stomach tensed, subconsciously preparing to take a round.

Is this really it? Squatting in a swamp in Haast, after a stupid decision to come out alone. I'm gonna cark it out here because I'm a moron?

'Shut the fuck up and get on your knees.'

I did what he asked. Well, half of it. 'Joe, I need to talk. I don't care what you've done, I need to know some things.'

He kept the weapon on me. 'I haven't done a fuckin' thing, but that's all gotta change.'

'Talk to me.'

'No, not here, not now. Things have been in motion a long time. What's triggered you? Why the change?'

'Change?'

'Caught you skulkin' in way up by the bridge. Carryin' your rifle. Normally you just stroll on up.'

This was a Joe I wasn't familiar with. *Tactically aware. Precise.*

'I . . . I know about Epitaph, Joe. I know what position you held.'

He lowered the rifle slightly. 'That it? Epitaph?'

'No. Fuck the drugs, Joe. I know about Casey. And Nadine in '91.'

'They're both dead.' The words were low but they echoed around the swamp, locked me in place.

'Joe, be smart about this. You're fucked, mate – take it head on. Come on, you were patched, you know what's going to happen. You're a smart guy. New Zealand's too small to run. Come on, you know I'm telling it like it is.'

He listened but he'd already made decisions. 'You aren't

wrong, Buchanan, but I've got somethin' on the boil.' He opened his hands, causing the rifle to tip briefly up to the sky. 'After that I'm yours, I'll tell all. Because then, yeah, then I may just have some explainin' to do on the other side of an interview desk. But not yet.'

'On the boil?'

He took a deep breath. 'You aren't chasin' what I'm chasin', and that's good, 'cause if you were, I was gonna tell you to butt out right now.'

'What *are* you chasing? Tell me.'

'Doubt you'd believe me if I did. But there's some things worth protectin'.'

'Joe, I need ...'

'No.' He started walking backwards, rifle still on me.

'Joe!'

'You stay there, you stay and count to five hundred, Buchanan. I'll be keepin' an eye for as long as I can. But I'm runnin'. You stay for five hundred and then you can make it back to your wagon, nothin' to fear from me. Got it?'

'Joe ...'

He raised his voice, cutting over me. 'If I don't make it back for that interview with you, Jafa –' He backed up, keeping me in sight with his rifle aimed.

'What?'

He stopped, lowered the rifle to point it at the ground. 'The town's gonna need you back, but not just the new guy. Some of him. But also some of the guy you used to be.'

Then I lost him in the foliage.

37.

I was outside the Armed Offenders Squad command truck on the Jackson Bay Road. It was late, the light was fading over the Tasman and an icy wind was kicking spray over us.

Come on, he'll be long gone.

But I couldn't wade back in, lone ranger, like they would on TV. I'd radioed for back-up, finally got hold of Hokitika and AOS had been paged. A dozen members were checking their kit and moving off. They wore their standard black, with some disruptive pattern or green role gear in the mix – a helmet here, webbed vest there, in army greens and browns. I spotted a couple of marksmen off to the side, bits of leaf and shit hanging off their weapons. They all moved away into the long grass, heading for the marsh and Joe's shack.

I didn't expect to hear much through the reeds and trees. At most AOS warrants there was the entry team symphony – dogs barking, glass breaking, yelling, more things breaking – and when things went really tits up, flashbangs going off as distractions. But not for this.

I peeked in the sliding door of the command truck. Zero Alpha, the boss, was in there on a headset, forehead creased with worry, but in control. He was receiving comms feeds and waiting for a moment to speak with whoever was in forward command out in the swamp.

You don't ask Zero Alpha what's going on. He doesn't care about you. His team is out there and he needs to keep them alive. But I knew enough about the job, and about AOS tactics, to absorb what was happening if I just watched and listened.

They would approach the shack, appeal it with voice and then probably launch gas into it. And after a while I heard the loudhailer drift over the trees out of the mire, though I couldn't make out the words.

We waited. And waited some more. Then came the boss's clipped voice as he chatted to his forward commander.

'One one Zero Alpha.'

'Zero Alpha one one.'

'One one at your leisure.'

The gas must be going in. They'd let it do its thing, then assume he wasn't in there and clear it carefully.

After what seemed an age, leaning against the truck, alternating feet, I got a tap on the shoulder. Zero Alpha was looking at me. 'Matt?' He spoke into his comms set once again, then murmured to me, 'All yours. Someone's coming out to take you in.'

In minutes a green-and-black-clad operator emerged from the reeds and stood on the road. He mumbled something through his balaclava that sounded like 'Follow me', so I did.

We made it across the driftwood and dropped, knee high this time, into water on the other side. *Why have a bridge at all, Joe.* The numbness set in pretty quickly. It was getting colder and the wind was up. Freezing my nuts off, I waded like a crab several metres before rising on the other side.

I was starting to enter a denial stage. Denial that Joe, Joe who I'd spoken to so many times, was prime suspect for killing Gus ... plus God knows what else. But I was also pissed off. With myself. *Right under my nose.*

AOS members were propped outside the shack and the guy who'd led me in indicated that I could head in. I waited for my eyes to adjust to the dim interior.

I'd been in here a few times, but only ever in what I guess you'd call the lounge. What did I want here? Other than the crime of getting me at gunpoint, there'd be wider evidence we'd need to pull. I decided on a recce, see what was here for the immediate offence of sticking a rifle in my face, then back out and return later with a warrant if I had to for the rest. The Search and Surveillance Act probably allowed me to take it all anyway, but I'd figure that out in a minute. Initially I just needed to look through his life.

The *Classical Myth* book was still there, open this time to where he'd been reading: 'Pan and the Pastoral Tradition.' A little faun stared out at me, playing a flute. There was some underlining: 'incorrectly explained that Pan was in fact the totality of nature.' And 'Pastoral tradition ... antidote to the refined but corrupt ways of the city.' Had Joe been researching the benefits of the quieter life? He didn't really need any help there. I turned the page. Above a discussion about the root of the word 'Pan', Joe had scrawled, 'The Feeder'. No answers that I could see there.

A door I hadn't noticed on my previous visits led to what looked like a study. There was a desk, and some photos on the wall. In one of them a group in leather vests faced the camera.

I knew what would be on their backs: the skull and noose of Epitaph.

I picked Joe out, even though he was in his distant youth. His hair was the same length, and though his face carried a calm seriousness, there was no mistaking the ears and the nose. His appearance matched Sandra Morrison's 1991 description to the letter.

There was no other gang memorabilia – not in a brief scan of the room anyway. It was when I turned to go back to the lounge that I saw more possessions hanging on the wall, just inside the door.

There was a framed group shot, of about twenty men, dressed in olive fatigues, hands on their knees. The names were written underneath. *Joseph Kranz.* He was harder to identify than he'd been in the Epitaph photo. His hair was shorter. His eyes were bright. But they had the same focus, the same determination.

Glancing left, I spotted the sand-coloured cloth draped over a hook and realised it was a beret. *Surely not.* I turned it over in my hands, saw the cap badge. The dagger and the little wings.

I must have gone pale, because the AOS member who'd followed me in grabbed my shoulder. 'You okay, Matt?'

He looked at the beret in my hand and his eyes widened beneath the balaclava. I looked again at the photo, and the board sitting on the ground in front of the men. I read the inscription: 'Papakura Camp. 1983.'

38.

While Brent's team hunted Joe in a physical sense, I found myself wanting to understand the guy. He wasn't who I thought he'd been. Not just once, *but twice.* But a murderer?

My guess was he'd long since left Haast, had gapped it from the entire region. He wouldn't risk a ferry or a plane, but he had the whole South Island to play with, and though I believed what I'd said to him about not being able to run, someone with his background would certainly give the police a good go for their money.

On the phone I started on a series of hops, skips and jumps from Defence Headquarters to various departments and numerous people. Yes, Joseph Kranz had served. No, they couldn't tell me much over the phone. Yes, they could send me more with a court-approved production order. Maybe someone still serving could talk to me.

Eventually I was put in touch with Terry Moffatt, a civilian employee at Burnham Camp just outside Christchurch. He looked after their range and their urban clearance site. Apparently he'd been in the SAS in the early eighties.

When I mentioned Joe, there was a huge pause. 'Kranz, you say.'

'Yep.'

'He was one of the hardest bastards we had, and that's bloody saying something, you understand.'

I did.

'But he was a guy with something ... kind, dead centre, you know. He wasn't an aggressive guy, didn't have any issues. His thing was focus, determination. I don't remember him being anything other than a solid operator.

'Look, there's another good rooster you need to call. Chap called Billy Wikaira, lives out in Luggate, between Wānaka and Queenstown. Billy and Kranz were tight. I can't promise he'll help with your hunt, but I think he'll be honest about the past. If that's what you want to know. I can get in touch with him?' I politely accepted. 'I'll call you back, or you'll hear from him.'

Not ten minutes later the phone rang. It was Billy. *Shit, they move fast.*

He was happy to talk about Joe, but not on the phone. 'I'll see you here tomorrow, if you have the time. Luggate pub, eleven hundred.'

39.

I'd met a few SAS over the years, and Billy was exactly as I'd pictured him. A small, wiry guy in his sixties, with searching eyes, a few tight grey curls hugging his head and a warm, rubbery grin that only hinted at the mischief he clearly placed high on his list of priorities.

I wanted to front this quickly so he didn't get the wrong idea. 'Billy, can I start by saying that I liked Joe, I really did, and we got on great. I thought he'd had a rough life, but I enjoyed his company, and I guess on some sort of level I'd say we could've been mates . . .'

He eyed me, took a sip from his beer.

'These latest events, and what I've learned, just doesn't gel with the guy I thought I knew.'

The grin appeared. 'Kranz was one of the smartest blokes we ever had. I'm not talking degrees, I'm talking system smart, street smarts, you know. He knew how to get what he wanted and he didn't care what anyone thought about that.' He downed some more of his pint. 'He'd come for selection from 2nd/1st

Battalion. He had a good rep. He hadn't been in too long, but he'd joined the army later in life than most, and he was spoken of highly. I was a ... what was I, probably a lance corporal back then, and I still remember him. He had that look, that focus. You can't really pick 'em, the ones that get through, but if ever there was a way to do it, it's that look, where they have the goal sitting there a few feet in front of their eyes and they close out the rest of the world. That was him.'

'When he made it in, and got badged, did you find out much about his past?'

'Yep, sure did. Boy, did he have me in stitches. Some of his stories with the bikies ... Apparently he got the nickname "Elephant Man" quite early on. When the cops were looking to lock him up, he'd just strip off, get naked right in front of 'em and invite 'em to cuff him. Every time.' He started giggling.

That sounds more like the Joe I know.

'But there was this dark streak he never talked about. He'd definitely fought some demons to make it into the army and then the unit. He had something to prove. I knew he must've done some bad stuff, or seen it, there was this air of ... what would you call it, atonement, about the bugger. Like he really had it in for himself, you know? But there's lotsa guys like that in the unit. You know, the unrelenting pursuit of excellence.'

'How long did he last?'

'He could've been a lifer. He became a corporal and was on the training wing for a bit. By that time, the guy he must've been before he joined up, I couldn't see him anymore. He'd changed. Kranz was a bright fella, determined. He'd put his demons to bed and come out the other side.'

'Why did he leave?'

Billy shrugged. 'The guys don't talk too much if they go.

They just go. Many different reasons. With him, though, it wasn't planned, or not to my knowledge. It was like a bolt from the blue. One day, he comes up to me, he's in his civvies, and he just gives me a hug, says something like, "Billy, I'm gone. Something I need to do. See you round maybe."' Billy snapped his fingers. 'And he went, just like that. I never saw the guy again.'

'Would that have been around 1991 by any chance?'

He thought for a bit. 'Yeah, I'd say so. We were all fixed to the news, you know, the Gulf was happening, I remember that, late '90, early '91. Kranz was there with us for some of that. And not long after that he left. So yeah, it would have been about then.

Something pulled him back here. Then he was talking to Nadine Ruyer.

'Look, Matt, I've known a lot of the boys in blue, you understand. As a kid I saw a mixed bag. Then in the unit we sometimes worked a bit with them, and I always respected the coppers once I was in the army.' He was doing his best to tell me what he thought of the police, while trying his hardest not to offend me. 'I've seen plenty bad guys, but Kranz wasn't one of them. So I'm wondering, do you think you could maybe … divulge some more of the story – help me to help you, if you know what I mean?'

So I did. I spoke slowly, not rushing, letting it sink in for Billy.

Billy watched his pint for a long time. When he spoke it was in a calmer tone, with an acceptance that maybe the world wasn't the way he'd seen it. 'That's some dark recent history. Makes you wonder how many times we go around.' He picked a spot outside to stare at as he talked. 'See, up by the pass there, near where you're talking about, there's a long history of bad things happening up there. My family are Ngāi Tahu. You know the background?'

'Some of the locals in Haast are Ngāi Tahu. I know it was rough in the early days.'

Billy continued. 'You've described some things that kind of make my blood run cold, you know. That area, that's always been like that. You know, back in – what the hell was it? – the 1830s, there was a massacre right there, in the flats. Two children were murdered, by invaders from the north.'

My face must have given me away, because Billy tapped my shoulder to check I was with it. 'The world's full of darkness, Matt, and it just keeps cycling. It's up to some of us to sort it out however we can.

'I don't think I know much about the world. I'm just a humble fella from Harihari who didn't have too many options in life. But I know people – I've seen the best and I've seen the worst. And I'm telling you, if Kranz is running, it isn't 'cause he's running *from* something.'

I watched his expression as he spoke.

'Only thing I ever knew would get him running was the smell of death. But the bastard would be running straight *towards* it.'

40.

Things dried up, and Joe was nowhere to be found. I didn't have the time or resources for a cross-country manhunt. I had a new life to live.

At the end of the day, all I had him for was using a firearm against a law enforcement officer. Peanuts. Most of the rest was conjecture, and there'd be nothing to stop him running again once he'd served the wet bus ticket he'd get for aiming his rifle at me.

But he'd held me at gunpoint for a reason. He'd legged it for a reason.

Brent's team was working tirelessly to gather enough evidence to convince the Crown solicitor Joe was good for Gus's murder. But they weren't there yet.

But is that why he ran?

Everything else I'd recently learned about Joe suggested he'd legged it in order to put something down.

What are you chasing? Tell me.

Doubt you'd believe me if I did.

***

Anna and I had got a bit more serious. We'd done the Queenstown gondola, skied The Remarkables and soaked in the private spas at Onsen, overlooking the Shotover River. She'd added to her Instagram; I'd just sat back and considered myself to be bloody lucky.

We were sharing a lunch and a wine tasting at the Gibbston Valley vineyard when she smacked me out of my daze. 'You were in the army too, weren't you?'

I hadn't even mentioned it. At least I didn't think I had. 'What do you mean, too?'

'I was thinking about Joe. Not just any village idiot can make it into the SAS.'

'Right? Sergeant at arms of Epitaph *and* a corporal in the SAS? Fuck, man, leave some for the rest of us, I say.'

'I meant there's so much I don't know about *you*. Did you deploy?' She even had the lingo down.

'I made it to Timor, in the early days of that. It wasn't exactly a war zone, but it certainly had its moments. We lost men.'

She cut some soft cheese. 'Death is something you're used to.' I nodded silently. She smiled sweetly, apologetically, and reached out for my hand. 'I'm sorry that's the case.'

'Well, you know, between Timor, my wife, a couple of mates and then the job itself, I didn't really get the opportunity to ignore it.'

She stared at me with her mouth open. 'Shit, Matt, I didn't know . . .' She came around to my side of the table and sat next to me on the bench.

'Hey, it's okay, I'll tell you all the full details at some stage, honesty being the best policy and all.'

She looked at me as if I was some wounded, dying animal. 'You don't have to tell me anything. I like you. I like whatever you are or do or say. But if you did want to, I'd love to hear about it. Bet you bottled a lot up.'

'It was over a long period of time. Guess you could say I got used to it. Used to bottling it, anyway.' *Then uncorking it in brutal, spectacular fashion.* 'I'm better now. Hence the verbal diarrhoea.'

She grinned. 'Better that way.'

'Definitely.'

As we began the drive back north to Hāwea, I said, 'Hey, I've been meaning to say, I'm doing the PCT tomorrow. The physical training instructor is setting it up locally for me. I spoke to Sheryl and Tara's gonna do it too, since she seems set on joining up one day. Keen to join?'

'Sure. What's the PCT?'

'Bring your yoga gear.'

41.

Lungs burning, legs aching, arms swinging, I turned the corner, ducking under the hurdles, before heading for the open window frame. Hands placed, leg up, I shot through, across to and straight over the wall. On to the slumped seventy-kilogram dummy. I grasped it, raised it and walked backwards, constantly feeling that I was about to trip or fall, until the PTI screamed at me to drop it.

Then I sprinted for the high wire fence, grabbing bits here and there and swinging myself over. I don't remember using the right technique, but I hit the ground on the other side and dashed to the finish.

'One fifty-nine!' yelled the PTI as I hunched over, tasting copper and shrieking with every breath. 'Too much beer, Buchanan. You could get that down to one fifty, no trouble, if you took a good look at yourself.'

'Better men than me have tried.' I wheezed. *Also, get fucked, mate. Under two minutes is a solid effort.*

We had to do it every two years. It wasn't hard, and you could get away with doing little physical exercise and then having a go. I had almost three minutes to complete it, and I was doing it nearly a minute under time.

I heard clapping. 'Woo! Yeah! Don't quit the beer, Matt. Maybe it made all the difference. Nice!' Anna was taking the piss, and Tara was laughing.

Sheryl couldn't help herself either. 'Imagine what your time could be if you also laid off the doughnuts and hot dogs at the Craypot?'

Still bent over, holding my knees, I couldn't talk, so just raised my middle finger. Catching my breath, I tried a short sentence. 'Stuff the lot of you. Remind me why I brought an audience?'

The PTI was going to give Tara and Anna a basic run-through, then let them run it, untimed, so as not to push any injuries. That would be all we needed, a health and safety investigation.

'So she's actually pretty keen?' I asked Sheryl as the other two were led around the course.

'Dead set. She was always community minded – sports, Guides. She was weighing up something in health because she's quite outgoing and she's been nailing science. But for the last year or so she's been reading and watching everything crime.'

'She should still go to uni or do the OE thing. Or both.'

'Try telling her that. Go, Tara, dig it in!' she yelled as her daughter flew past.

I'd been the same: I'd headed straight for the army recruitment office out of school. Didn't need that tertiary shit, I'd told myself. And I'd done the same when I was thinking about the police. 'Take a break,' they said. 'Study.' But I'd walked in and signed up.

Sheryl eyed me. 'So how long you gonna be here for anyway?'

'Eh?'

'You're here by force, remember? When do you get to go somewhere else?'

'You know what? I have no idea. They said a year. It's been nearly two. Guess I haven't asked.'

'Rubbing off on you, then, the small town life?'

I grinned. 'Bugger off, the West Coast is still a shithole. Anyway, why do you ask?'

'Well, I don't know what I make of you, to be honest. Most foul-mouthed Aucklander I've ever met.'

'Fuck off, that's horse shit.'

She shook her head, smiling. Then her face was serious again. 'Tara needs to tell you something in confidence. She wouldn't tell me what but I guess anyone who gains the trust of my kid is somebody the town should probably try to keep hold of.'

I ignored the praise, but it felt good.

'Yeah, look it's just some minor stuff, I think involving her friends. Looks like she's developing a conscience with her new career goals. But anyway, just to give you a heads up.'

Darren came puffing up. 'Matt, phone call at the Antler – Wānaka station trying to get hold of you.'

***

A familiar voice, the Wānaka sergeant, Neil. 'Hey Matty, the guys and girls have been called out to a body.'

At times like this, I was glad not to be wearing a suit. Bodies were the domain of CIB and, at best, you only held the fort until they arrived. 'Bugger. Which side of the line?'

We always helped each other out, but I'd feel slightly more relaxed to know it was still theirs.

'Ours, but it's in the paddocks up past Hāwea in the flats, just before the boundary and the pass. Farmer found it.'

I went cold. Makarora.

Neil kept talking. 'Well and truly our side, mate, but it's suss. Very suss. Hands bound. Afraid our D's on leave, and Queenstown had a rape overnight, so they're busy. Dunedin CIB will arrive in the morning, but someone was saying you're more than capable of holding a scene, and it would be finite, mate, so I'm asking a favour . . .'

'No dramas, course I'm there. Have they got hold of ESR and the pathologist? May as well get them moving.'

'Yep, already done. Thanks, Matt. Let me just grab the deets.'

He rattled off the address, which I jotted down on some paper Darren pushed across to me. Plus the phone numbers for the constables holding the scene, though the cellphone numbers probably wouldn't connect, and the landline for the farmer who'd found the body.

When I dialled this, an older male voice answered. I explained who I was.

'Oh, of course. You're coming up this morning, I hear.'

'That's the one. Hey, look, I'm working out a plan. Can you talk me through where you've walked?'

I was trying to work out where the hell I was going to enter the scene from without fucking anything up.

Then I asked him to find one of the constables, who gave me the basics. I was about to hang up when he said, 'Matt, just prepping you . . . it's bad. It's pretty bad.'

42.

It wasn't too far from the Makarora Lodge, in the paddocks where the braided Wilkin River came out of the mountains to the west and joined the Makarora, before they both discharged into the top of Lake Wānaka. The Wilkin wasn't visible from the highway, but out beyond the farmland I could see the trees that must line its edge.

Crossing the centreline, but still facing south, I parked up in the high grass, well off the highway, and headed for the patrol car that was guarding the driveway.

An older constable greeted me. 'Matt? I'm Keith Nicholson. Cheers for helping out. We've left it well alone. Eammon and Pete are just taking basics inside. Give us a yell if you need anything.'

They'd taped it off at the driveway. The farmhouse was a good few hundred metres away. The body would have been even further out. You'd see anyone coming for miles. I shook my head. 'Wide cordons are all good, mate. Better safe than sorry.'

I'd be doing the most basic of recces, gathering enough to

brief ESR and whichever CIB office was going to do the actual scene examination with them. Where the driveway met the road was a cluster of sludge: mud, stone, grass and water. As an inner cordon, the uniforms had strung more tape from the house right out sideways to a fence that ran away from me into the distance, towards the river. At the house, one of the constables gave me a geographical rundown, with descriptions and some finger pointing.

I thought some more. The farmer had entered the scene from the far side, returning home after checking the fenceline. The constables, through no fault of their own, had come in from the driveway, but unfortunately that was probably the same direction used by whoever had dumped the body. There wasn't really another way in.

I walked the opposite side of the farmhouse to where the body was, following another trodden path into the tussock-like grass. I was a few hundred metres from the body, paralleling the track the constables had taken, just further away. I then boxed around behind the primary scene and came at it from the same direction the farmer had this morning.

As I drew near, I could see the body. It was hunched over, kneeling, propped up by the water trough near the fence. It was naked. It looked dried out. Flies were buzzing, and darker, purple lividity stood out around the back and the side I was looking at.

The hands were bound tightly behind, at the small of the back, with thin yellow tow rope. When I looked closer, it got even worse.

Jesus Christ.

Several fingers were missing. Only dark stumps remained. The hair was long, shoulder length and matted.

The smell hit me then. Not pleasant. Death, insects and the sun were doing their thing.

I paused and scanned the ground in front of me. I didn't want to trample anything. This would be the common approach path that the CIB crew behind me would use to place stepping plates. And I wasn't gowned up. There was no reason to check for signs of life ... this was a husk. And there was nothing else here – no weapon, no obvious stuff that this recce was supposed to pick up. I didn't want to go much further and risk unnecessary contamination.

A thought forced its way in. What Alec had mentioned, no questioned, about the devil. Pushing it to the side as I considered the scene, considered the next nine steps ahead so as not to balls them up.

But he was onto something. The hole, the intelligence gap. I needed to see. I walked to the fenceline, staying a good fifteen metres away from the body, but now at an angle that would allow me to see a bit of the face.

It was older than I was expecting. But it was just as I remembered.

I knelt in the paddock. To give my head time to catch up and process what this meant.

I've missed something. Something huge.

Because the bound, fingerless, tortured body wasn't a stranger. It was Joe.

43.

To say it hit me pretty hard was an understatement. I'd been kicked back to Haast after holding the scene, and Brent's team were about to ship out and co-locate in Wānaka with the crew from Dunedin who were investigating what happened to Joe.

I was sitting at my place in the Antler, bourbon in hand, Anna beside me, churning round an idea I'd been considering for a while. It wasn't one I liked, but it was an idea all the same.

I rang Ed Wilson, a clinical psychologist who'd long since left the Behavioural Science Unit up in Auckland, but who'd spent much of his career profiling offenders. We got on well and I could always count on him for telling it like it was.

He answered quickly, firing shots as soon as he recognised my voice. 'Let me guess, you're currently somewhere wet and cold, sipping shit coffee.'

'Hell, Ed, you should be working in sports betting. Clearly you've been keeping up with the times.'

'It's all over the news, but I must say I don't know more than the media does.'

'Look, I … I just had a query – a yes or no, really.'

'Bit more to it all than that, Matt.'

'I know. You know what I mean.'

I filled him in, then asked my question. 'What are the chances of a homicidal kid being able to kill both their parents and arrange their bodies?'

He paused. 'The daughter? How old was she?'

'Fifteen.'

There was silence for a bit. 'Well, it depends. On a lot of things.'

'It always does. But it's possible, right? She wasn't an infant.'

'Anything's *possible*, Matt, unless it required a lot of strength or was something a kid wouldn't be able to do physically. But mentally, anything's possible.'

'Right. And say that kid had done that back in 1978, and there's been a forty-plus-year gap and now they've killed again, once, maybe even twice … What sort of escalation … what would we be dealing with here? Right now, I mean.'

'If you're asking about the gap, I don't have enough to help you. If you're saying they killed back in the seventies, and they've killed now, well, you'd expect to see some kind of escalation. Something. Either taken out outwardly, like more violence, or inwardly: drugs, alcohol, suicide – that sort of thing. If there's been nothing, hell, still plenty of reasons why: imprisonment, life changes, health … But there's usually an explanation.'

'There's nothing. They were believed dead, no passport, no records. Never picked up anywhere.'

'Well, look again, because you'd expect to find something. That's odd. Odd to have such a huge intervening period without them doing something that would come to somebody's attention ... whether that's alcohol related, hospitalisation, mental health, violence. But, you know, if the murders are entirely separate circumstances, then they're essentially two separate events. You can't just come out and say they're predisposed to violence. Context is everything.'

'Right.'

'What's your gut saying, Matt?'

'I don't like that word.'

'Still.'

'My gut says this kid actually died, a while ago.'

And Joe's words. *They're both dead.*

I kept running with it. 'But let's say they didn't, and they have been ... escalating. Unchecked. What would I be dealing with *now*?'

Ed breathed in, long and slow. 'A familial double homicide, more than four decades ... well, let's just say I'd hope to God they weren't out there. That would be someone in need of a lot of intervention.'

* * *

When I repeated Ed's opinion to Anna, she thought for a moment. 'Joe, he was bled out like an animal?'

'Yeah, that's what the pathologist said. Drained from the femoral arteries.'

'Like a ritual.'

I gave her a look. 'More like a hunting trophy. But I've never seen that before either. People kill in anger, and the heat of the moment. I've never seen much thought go into it. That's the domain of TV.'

'Wasn't Joe looking into witchcraft?'

Her words stopped me cold. 'Uh, no, he was reading classical mythology. About Greek gods. Legends. The quiet life, nature and all that.'

'So paganism, rather.'

'What? This isn't satanic, Anna.'

'The pagans weren't devil worshippers, Matt. That's Christianity messing with history. Pagans worshipped the earth and the sky. The Greeks did too. You're right, satanism is TV bollocks. But putting that aside, isn't it weird that Joe was looking into myth, and then turns up dead, like some sort of –?'

'So you mean someone's fucking with us. With the police.'

'Maybe. Why was Joe looking into that stuff anyway? That seems key.'

Again, my mind turned back to my last conversation with him. *Doubt you'd believe me.*

'I don't know. But if he was talking to Nadine Ruyer in 1991, then whatever he was looking into has got to be something to do with either her or Casey, right? Or …'

Anna finished the thought for me. 'Or both.'

We locked eyes. 'I need to see that Ruyer file.'

44.

I was shattered, and soaked, but I rapped on Sheryl's door anyway. I'd made the records request to Otago HQ, and while I waited for confirmation, I wanted to use the time to speak to the locals in more depth.

I'd been here before with a case. A few pieces of the jigsaw, some of which might not even be relevant, and no clear direction. Brent's team on Gus, and the Otago team on Joe, were both confident that the scene examinations, forensics and vehicle checks would create a break shortly. And they ought to be confident. Homicides were marathons. Eventually, with enough mileage, the break usually came.

But I couldn't shake the chill. I hadn't felt it for a few years. Crawling up my back, telling me there was something lurking just out of reach.

Tara answered the door. 'You look like shit, Matt.'

'Fair. Shouldn't you be several towns away at school?'

'It's holidays again.'

'Tara, just let him in!' The yell came from further inside. I followed her into the lounge, removing my jacket and trying not to drip water everywhere. 'Whoa, you look like shit.' Sheryl started to chuckle, then must have taken in my look, my clothes, my general vibe. Her voice changed. 'Matt, what do you need?'

I dropped onto their couch, stared at the floor. I tried to get it into short sentences. 'I want to know about back then. About Casey. What sort of kid she was. Start where you like.'

'Wait here. I'm gonna put the jug on.' Sheryl disappeared into the kitchen while Tara took a seat on the couch opposite. Just before I opened my mouth to say something along the lines of 'Can you bugger off maybe?', she shook her head, sending me a clear message: I'm listening to this.

The fire was on and the rain hosed the windows. Sheryl returned, coffees in hand. 'You look like you're in physical pain, man. You should stop.'

I sipped the coffee, coughed – brandy.

She saw my questioning look. 'You look like you need it.' She sat down next to Tara, then pointed at her daughter and raised her eyebrows. I just lifted my hand in acceptance. 'Casey was smart. She knew herself. But she was also . . . sad. It was like an underlying sadness, I guess. But hindsight can be dangerous – we talked about that, *you* talked about that. Especially now, knowing her dad was abusive. And my memory may not be so accurate any more.'

I wanted to get some reassurance out. 'True. But all that aside, sometimes it's all we've got. Just have to sift the facts from the rest.'

'Right. Have you read my old statement? I don't remember it.'

'I have it here.' I opened my daypack and passed it over, all three pages of it, which was on the light side. It covered Casey's schooling, and some moments Sheryl had remembered with her, and not much else.

She read it over and sighed. 'You know how you don't mention things 'cause you think others might instead? Or you think you're wasting someone's time? That was how I felt. Like it wasn't important enough to go bothering anyone.'

'I figured as much. You were what, fifteen, when you gave that statement? All sorts of nuances and decisions and thoughts and feelings. And Casey was only *missing* in your head then – no suggestion she might be dead.' I took the pages back. 'I don't think this is a reflection of your integrity.'

'Nothing seems important until it is.'

I watched her face. 'What's bothering you?'

'Bothering me? It's not that, Matt. I'm wondering, what the hell is bothering *you*? Look, you're pretty much like family, but you came in here looking like you'd just run the fifteen hundred metres. Something's lit a fuse under your arse. The only thing I know that's happened, is a body being found up in the flats. The news said jack shit about that, and no one round here knows anything, but you got called away from that fitness session. What's going on?'

I shut my eyes briefly, sought some clarity.

'I ... I'm sorry.' I stood. 'I didn't mean to crash in, I just –' I pinched the bridge of my nose with thumb and forefinger.

Sheryl guided me back onto the couch. 'Sit, Matt, sit down.' My arse hit the cushions and I opened my eyes. She asked again. 'Just tell me. Who the hell was it?'

'It was Joe.'

'Bloody hell.' She sank onto the floor. 'Bloody hell, Matt.'

I told her there was something left undone. Something missed. I voiced my thoughts about Casey – and about Nadine,

Gus, Liam, Joe. All circling, twisting, colliding around a bigger mystery – something bad. I shivered. Got my thoughts in order. 'Casey and Liam, they were both tree huggers? Lefties.'

Sheryl nodded. 'We all were back then. So would you have been.'

'Did it go further than that?'

'What, the tree hugging?'

'Did they … what was Casey into? Did it include any … beliefs?'

'What sort? You mean, religious?'

'Not necessarily. You know, crystals, talismans, that sort of thing.'

She got up and headed down the hall. 'Stay here, I'm gonna try and find something.' She returned with a photo album, big thick cream cover, like the one I remembered my baby pictures being in when I was a kid. 'I keep this because there's nothing else. And there isn't much of this. Do you remember photos of yourself when you were in your early teens?'

I didn't. 'No, as a younger kid, maybe, ones my parents took. And as an older teenager, taken by mates. Not around fifteen, fourteen, no.'

'Exactly. Hit twelve and all of a sudden your parents stop taking photos, probably 'cause you're screaming at them that it isn't cool anymore.' Tara rolled her eyes and grinned. 'You don't think about it yourself until a few years later. So sorry, there aren't many here.' She was turning leaves slowly, carefully, not wanting to damage anything. Somewhere around the middle of the album she stopped, set it down to face me on the coffee table. She pointed to a photo. 'That's us. I'm not a hundred per cent, but I don't think that was long before they left, summer of '77 probably.'

Two happy, laughing girls were sitting against the side of a bed, a bright window behind them. There was some sort of game or book on the floor but the colour fading made it hard to see. I looked from the photo to Sheryl. I couldn't tell who was who.

She smiled. 'Me ... Casey.'

Now that I thought about it, she did look a bit like Tara – the dark hair and the confident grin. Casey had lighter hair, slightly discoloured red by the lens or the fading. Her smile was big.

'You're both pretty happy.'

She sighed. 'I don't know. I think ... I think I've manufactured memories. I tell myself there had to have been something there, about her father. I tell myself she would have been unhappy a lot, and I just missed it. Missed it all.'

'But that may not be the case.'

'Maybe not. Maybe I'm harsh on myself.'

'If there *had* been something, you'll never be in as good a position to pick it up as you were back then. You were fifteen. If there was something to see, you'd have known.'

I peered closer at the photo, noted the stringed object dangling against the window. A dream catcher.

'Was this your room or hers?'

'It's her room.' She pointed at the wall beside the window. 'This is what I was trying to find. You asked about her being into anything.' It was a poster, but it was hard to make out. 'She had stuff like this, you know, fantasy stuff.'

I couldn't see much beyond some figure against a green backdrop. 'Tolkien?'

She nodded. 'She read a lot of that stuff.'

I'd been a C. S. Lewis and Tolkien fan, so Casey got some points from me. But Sheryl called it like she saw it. 'What's eating you here, Matt?'

'I don't know. If Casey survived. If she'd run. If she'd made it out, after her dad went nuts in the pass. And if, for some reason, she couldn't go back to Haast. Where would she go?'

'Why wouldn't she go back to Haast?' As soon as she said the words, she realised what I'd meant, and put her hands to her mouth. 'You think she killed her parents?' Tara touched her mother's arm.

I jumped on it quickly. 'No, no. The whole scenario makes no sense if she did. So not both of them. But maybe something happened, maybe her dad … Look. I have nothing, absolutely nothing, to suggest this – just go with me. Where would she go?'

Sheryl hugged herself. 'Her boyfriend. She'd have stuck with her boyfriend.'

'Who was?'

'Well, I thought it was –' She caught herself again, unsure.

'You see?' I said. 'So many unknowns. You don't know for sure it was Liam, right? Could it have been … nobody?'

'Nobody?'

'Didn't you ever talk about a crush or mention something that wasn't totally true? We've all been there, back when we were kids or early teenagers. The things I know now, the type of men Liam and Joe were –'

I'm finding it hard enough to believe they were involved with Epitaph and drugs. But an underage girl? No way.

'I don't think Liam or Joe were into her like that,' I continued. 'I think they stumbled across her being abused, and I think they were looking out for her.'

Tara sat still, watching and listening, eyes flicking from her mother to me, then back again.

Sheryl was absorbed. 'It … it's possible, I guess. Wait, you think they –'

I held my hand up again. 'Look, I have no idea. Somehow, I don't think we'll ever get all the answers. But what happened in the pass aside, there's something else, something left over, and it's been killing to keep things quiet.'

'Who?'

'I don't know. I saw it scare the shit out of Joe. And I'm pretty sure it scared the shit out of Liam.'

She started to look concerned, realising there was a monster lurking in the dark, and that she might have some distant link. 'And they were both –'

'They were tough men, yeah. I don't know what they stumbled across. But after seeing Gus, and the way Joe ended up –' I shook my head '– I'm not exaggerating when I say that it scares the shit outta me too.'

There was a brief silence before I offered a qualifier. 'Just to be clear, there's not even a whiff of circumstantial proof of anything. That's why I felt like such a dick, showing up here. But people here have the answers. Some of the answers. There are holes. That's all. Every case has them. When you look back there appear to be gaps, because things get lost and forgotten. But maybe there aren't. There's nothing, absolutely nothing, to say Casey didn't die in the pass with her family. Maybe Gus, and Joe, crossed someone unrelated to all this, maybe for a wholly different reason. But I have to look.'

Sheryl looked at me for a while, moving her head slightly as though she was checking for faults. The pause went on, but it wasn't uncomfortable. We were both confused, tired, hit from all directions. Time to leave.

But then Tara looked at her mother. 'Mum? Should I?' Sheryl nodded. Tara turned to me as I stood. 'If I knew something about someone, is there a way to keep them from getting in trouble?'

Time for straighter answers than I'd given Liam. 'Of course. Hit me.'

'You know Brooke, Vinnie's girlfriend?'

I didn't, but I remembered the couple all over each other by the fire. 'Vaguely. I know Vinnie. Why don't I know Brooke?'

'She doesn't live here, she's from Greymouth. We went to primary together, though, before her family moved.'

'Right, sorry.'

'She's getting fucked up and the other day she ended up in hospital.'

I blinked. 'Sorry, *fucked up*? You mean on gear? What sort?'

'Pills.'

My brain was adjusting to this changed direction. 'Right. Prescription or illegal?'

'E. Illegal.'

'Okay, shit. Is she okay?'

'Yeah.' Tara glanced at Sheryl, who gave an encouraging smile. 'She was kept in overnight but she's okay. I don't want to get her in trouble, but I need to do something for her.'

I chewed my lip. 'Ain't that the age-old problem? Well, let's start with her. Does she take them all the time?'

'No, just gigs and the odd party.'

'So just for fun, every now and then?'

'Yeah. It's not really her I'm ... it's who she gets them from. It's someone who shouldn't be doing that stuff. But I don't know who else gets them from him, so I don't want to drag Brooke into it.'

I sighed. 'Look the reality is, pill dealers will have plenty of customers. Can't be sure, but probably a safe bet. Who's the dealer?'

'It's her school counsellor. Guy called David.'

I froze. 'What?' I pulled my cell out. 'What's your wifi password?'

'Use mine.' She threw me her iPhone.

I brought up Google, punched in David's full name, found the school and a picture. 'That the guy?'

'Yeah. You know him?'

'I've met him before, in Reefton. Leave it with me. I'll sort it with a team that knows what they're doing.'

***

It was only then that I noticed Sheryl had zoned out and was staring at the wall behind me. Then her eyes met mine.

'Shit Matt, there *is* something circumstantial ... Did Helen not call you?'

'Helen? Call me about what? Liam?'

'That body over in the forest, in Christchurch, Liam –'

I interrupted. 'What body? What are you –'

It was her turn to cut me off. 'Shut up, Matt, listen. They found a skeleton, in Bottle Lake Forest Park, north of Christchurch. Didn't you see the news?'

I must have looked like a dumbarse trying hard to think of something smart to say.

She kept talking. 'The article was in the paper that morning, the morning Liam ... he'd been reading about it. It's a girl. Call your mates over in Canterbury.'

I was still doing my dickhead impression, my brain trying to catch up with what she was saying.

Sheryl shot out into the kitchen again, then returned with a copy of the *Herald*. 'Here.' She threw it at me.

I checked the date. The day I found Liam slumped in his

bathroom. I turned the pages. 'It's a couple in.' I got it: 'Body found at Bottle Lake.'

There was little information. The piece had been fluffed out with a police comment about making no comment. But I recognised the name: 'Detective Inspector Tom Gerard stated that a scene examination was under way and at this early stage would not be drawn on...'

I knew Tom. He'd delivered a number of senior courses I'd attended at the Police College. He ran Canterbury CIB without mercy. In a good way. If a member of your family was killed, you'd want him on the case.

The article was very brief. It mentioned the find by forestry workers, the fact it was a skeleton ... and that it was believed to be female. *Holy shit.*

'Helen said that the paper was folded, face up, on the bench, to that article. The day he died.'

45.

I was staring at the scene photos from Liam's place on my screen.

Desperate to figure out whether the Bottle Lake body theory held water, I didn't think too hard about David the drug-peddling counsellor. Brent was tied up on the murders. There was only one other detective sergeant up in Greymouth, and I passed the information on to her. The last I heard, she planned to act sooner rather than later, but I'd essentially all but purged it from my brain.

Helen had been onto something. Maybe she hadn't called because she didn't think police would see it that way. But there was an image I'd taken, of the newspaper on his bench, and there was the headline. He must have read the article, and then, sometime later, he'd hanged himself.

I drummed my fingers on the desk. What the fuck did it all mean? I stepped myself back. *Maybe* Liam had some knowledge about it. *Maybe* it had influenced his decision to end it all. But *maybe* he was always planning to do it that morning and this was a total coincidence. But . . .

It was time to talk to Tom Gerard. 'Sorry for the call out of nowhere, but Bottle Lake, any headway on ID, or age, or when they died?'

A brief silence, then, 'No, yes, and kind of. Female, late twenties, been there for more than ten years. That's the extent so far. We've just got bones. And nothing out of place.'

'So not even a whiff of identification?'

'Not yet. There are a few missing people who could fit the bill. Waiting on all that to come back, and then we'll head down the dental route. What have you got for me? Something related to your murders over there, I'm guessing?'

'Sort of. I might have a possible if you're wide open to suggestions.' I filled him in on the Fawkes deaths. 'Coroner ruled Casey died at the time. But I'm following a couple of lines suggesting that . . .'

I knew what I was trying to say, but it was struggling to come out.

'That what?'

'That maybe she didn't.'

'Fawkes. Okay. And how does that link in with your work?'

I explained about Gus and Liam.

'No shit.'

That was the most emotion you'd get out of Tom, but it meant he'd been blown sideways.

'And there's been another murder, sir. The plot thickens . . .'

'Ah yes,' said Tom, 'I saw the emails.'

'It's a shambles, sir. Very tightly wound, and everyone's dead.'

'Who's in charge?'

I explained about the Wānaka co-location. 'Quentin Jones from Dunedin, your golden boy back in the day, he's on Joe's murder, so I'd touch base with him or Brent.'

'Okay. And what are you doing? Seems like a waste of a detective having cups of tea with locals and investigating lost cats.'

'Someone's gotta do it, sir.'

'Sure, but not CIB. Keep in touch, Matt.'

As he hung up it felt as though a tiny little fire had been lit under my arse.

46.

I finally had the full contents of what remained from the 1991 missing persons file, but I wasn't going over it with a magnifying glass. I just wanted to know who Nadine Ruyer was, what had made her tick and what she'd been into. I wanted a picture of the girl from France who hadn't made it home. If I could put her in the same camp as Casey Fawkes, then a whole lot of shit would make a whole lot more sense.

I'd driven to Dunedin HQ, dumped the boxes of files in my wagon and was ready to head straight back across the width of the South Island towards home. But knowing Alec already had a version of this file from his OIA request, I decided to stop off in Queenstown to nut it out with him. And I didn't have too long with the file – the homicide team needed it.

He brought coffee as I pored over pages. 'Find anything helpful?'

'Yeah. Listen to this. "Nadine was an environmentalist. She loved hiking, tramping, had been studying yoga and alternative medicine before taking her gap year in New Zealand . . ." Sounding familiar?'

'Shit yeah, it is.'

I found other loose pages, newspaper clippings converted to PDFs, then printed. The TV and newspaper money shots, the smiling girl looking like every picture you'd see of a happy backpacking tourist. Hair blown across her smiling face in Mount Aspiring National Park. Braving a bungy above the Shotover River.

'Much in the statements from the family? Most of that was withheld from what they gave me.'

'I'm not surprised – pretty private. But most of the interesting stuff is from people who knew her in New Zealand, like this bit: "She was quite into the green, you know, and talked about how we were all fucking up the planet . . ."'

'A real tree hugger, then.'

'Yeah, like everyone else in this jigsaw.' I reread the statement. It was taken from a friend of Nadine's, a Kiwi girl living in Hāwea – Ursula Dwyer. 'Couldn't be . . .'

'An Ursula runs the holistic health place Anna goes to. Chances are . . . it's a small world, right?'

'How old is she?'

'Maybe forty? Fits.'

There was only one way to find out, and I didn't want to do it over the phone. Alec dived for his laptop and bag and I grabbed my car keys. We didn't speak another word as we chewed up the road through the gorge, leaving Queenstown behind. But the silence got to him and he tried to get in my head. 'You're sure there's a link between Ruyer and Casey.'

'There is. But not the link I thought. Joe didn't kill those girls. He was looking out for them.'

'What makes you think that? Nobody knows why he was killed. Maybe he's been picked off by a good guy.' I turned and stared at him as we flew on, doing a hundy. 'Matt, watch the road!'

I obeyed. 'A good guy? Who the fuck is that then? Do good guys chop fingers off, sit in the dark, out of reach?'

Alec was thinking hard. 'You're right, this isn't good.'

'It's far from good, mate. We're dealing with someone who's lost their grip on reality. I thought it could be Casey, but that doesn't make much sense, and the more I think about it, this is something else. This is someone delusional, someone ...' I couldn't quite find the word.

'Evil.'

'More or less. But I'm not a fan of that.'

'Of the word?'

'Of the concept. "The devil did it." Some people have mental health battles that they can't control. And other people do bad things by choice. But they have their reasons at the time, however skewed. It's just my opinion, but I reckon evil isn't a thing.'

We drove on in silence for a bit. Then Alec got fidgety, and I knew he wanted to say something. 'What?'

'Well, that's fair enough, Matt, you've seen a lot of shit.' He spoke softly, looking ahead. 'But what if you're wrong?'

47.

I could smell liquorice tea and pine oil as Alec and I stepped through the door.

Ursula smiled. 'Constable, good morning. Come for those classes after all?'

'Absolutely not.'

Her lips curved. 'How can I help?'

Alec introduced himself and I did the explaining. 'Look, I'm sorry to bother you again. You'll have heard a body was found, up in the flats.'

'Of course. They didn't live around . . .'

'No, they were from Haast.' She directed us into the office, poured what I assumed was green tea. I didn't really know how to broach the subject, so I just came out and said it. 'Back in 1991, a French tourist, Nadine Ruyer, went missing.'

She stopped blowing on her cup and stared at me. 'Of course. I gave a statement. We both went to one of the earlier centres, over the other side of the lake from here. That's where I met her.'

'Yeah, I've read your statement. I was hoping to ask you about her.'

'This . . . this is to do with the body up in Makarora, though?'

I paused before answering. 'Maybe, yeah. That body is that of a man who I think spoke with Nadine back in '91. That's the only connection at the moment.'

She frowned. 'As in . . . he was responsible for her going missing, or, or . . .'

'I don't know. There are threads, but we're missing a lot. All we know for sure is that there's a murderer out there *now*.' Her eyes were darting between Alec and me, and I could see the anxiety rising. 'There's a much wider homicide investigation running, looking into all that, Ursula. It's getting the full treatment. But they're looking at the present, and working from there. Alec and I, we're chasing the past. We reckon that's where some of the answers are.'

She paused, came to terms with it. 'Okay, what can I say . . . Nadine was a lovely girl, there was just something about her . . .' Ursula's eyes lit up and I glanced at Alec, realising when he didn't react that he didn't know what Anna had told me. 'She was full of life, wanted to experience it all – that's why she'd taken a study break to come here. She embraced this country, and made an impression on everyone who met her. I don't know why she'd go hiking alone when she had so many friends – there was always a group around her.'

Alec was taking a few notes, but I kept my attention on Ursula. 'This may be an offensive question, but did she dabble in the occult at all? Don't get me wrong, I don't mean . . . I mean nature, incense burning, dancing in the forest, that kind of thing.'

I was never great at respecting things I thought were nonsense.

Ursula was obviously trying to stifle a smile. 'Yes, she had her moments. Yes and no, to answer your question. We were out near the lake one morning and we went skinny dipping. She was a regular but for me that was pretty spontaneous. She loved being one with nature, but I can't really explain it better than that. It wasn't anything weird. Call it spiritual.'

I shook my head. 'And sorry, I do a terrible job explaining myself at the best of times. Did she *believe* in anything?'

Ursula sipped her tea. 'I couldn't put a label on it, no. She collected stones and crystals, but was it a *belief system?* No, I don't think it was.'

'Right.'

I looked across at Alec, who piped up and explained how we'd come to be working together. 'But we're chasing ghosts, here, Ursula, and that's a hard task. What's your gut feeling about Nadine? About what happened?'

Her answer didn't need thought. 'I always felt someone had done something to her. Because she wouldn't go off alone. She loved people too much.'

I was looking at her as she talked and managed to get it out there. 'You were together.' I said it as a statement, not a question.

Ursula nodded. 'Yes, yes we were for a time. I . . . I didn't tell the police back in '91. I didn't think it mattered.'

'It didn't. But it's actually really helpful. You'd have had the best insight, you got to know her better than anyone. If anyone's gut should be listened to, it's yours.'

She continued. 'But I can't think who would want to hurt her. Sure, a bit of weed was passed around, but everyone was lovely. There were no weirdos, or not that I recall. Nothing worse than a bit of puff, from what I remember.' Her eyes filled and she looked at the floor.

I tried another angle. 'Did you know a Sandra Adams back then?'

She looked up. 'Yeah, yeah, Sandra hung around with a few of us. Did she ... ?'

'Yeah, she gave a statement too. She saw Nadine speaking with a gang member days before she went missing. Does that mean anything to you?'

Her brow furrowed. 'She was killed by a gang?'

'No', I replied. 'I don't think so. I reckon all that blurred the lines and it was a case of not seeing the wood for the trees. But the gang member, he's our Makarora body. So you see, anything you could tell us about Nadine, back then, any associates – we could make headway in the present.'

Ursula shook her head.

I needed new information. 'The wellness retreat, just north of here. What was it called?'

'You think that place had something to do with it all?'

I paused. 'It's gonna sound odd.'

'Try me.'

'I think ... I'm looking at the manipulation of good ideas. Nature and wellness ... morphed into something darker, something confused.'

'Well, I can't speak for it now – it doesn't exist. It was more of a community back then: backpackers could stay, anyone was welcome. But it suffered in the nineties and eventually the whole place upped and moved on.' Then she remembered my question. 'It was called Wellspring.'

Suddenly the smell from the back of that truck wafted over me, as real as it had been back then, on the Desert Road, twenty-odd years ago. I raced for the bathroom.

48.

We'd backtracked to Wānaka to drop off the Ruyer file and then, after filling up the tank, we were driving south again, back to Queenstown.

Alec was worried about me. 'You looked like you'd seen a ghost, Matt. And you reek of spew. You going to share?'

I thought about not telling him. It would be considered a break in the case, and he was a journalist. *Fuck it.*

'Back when I was a junior detective, early 2000s, we found a truck on the Desert Road. It was registered to Wellspring, like, a company . . . It didn't matter anyway, things kind of went nowhere.'

'How the hell do you remember that?'

'Well, it's a bit hard to forget. There were two guys in the cab, and my partner shot one of them in the head.'

'Holy shit.'

'The holiest.'

'Why?'

'Pulled a shotgun on him. We were stood down. They got

the driver for drugs, but the whole thing was so suss …'

'What was in the truck?'

'Drug lab equipment. A mattress, blood, shit, piss – all sorts. It was just filth. But there was death in there, mate. It smelt of death. Something horrific had gone on. It was like a body had been cut up. The local cops and CIB did an area search, but you know that place. Needle in a haystack. They found nothing. Driver did some time for the drug stuff and that was it.'

It was all I could tell him. The main thing I could remember was the boom of Shane's Glock, and the slick of blood hitting the windscreen. Apart from that, and the smell, things were hazy.

As we passed Arrowtown I voiced what we were both probably thinking by now. 'Why the hell didn't we take two cars?'

He shook his head, laughing. ''Cause we're dickheads.'

'You're the journo – you're supposed to be smarter than that.'

'You're a bloody detective.'

'*Was*.'

'Well, keep it up, I say. We're getting places.'

At Alec's we got straight back into his redacted version of the Ruyer file. I didn't want to lose momentum. We were starting to join some dots.

I needed people. People with memories, that was the key. Not paper, not words written down a long time ago. We trawled the file, spread the load with a few ring-binders each, looking for people who might have more to add with the passage of time.

About twenty minutes later, I found what I was looking for.

It was a jobsheet, dated 1 August 1991, from a cop who'd worked the disappearance. It had been relegated to the miscellaneous section, with some scrawled writing across it, obviously from the guy's supervisor. 'Opinion. Get rid of it. Attach the footage and state the facts.'

I started to read. 'From the bait camera positioned at the clearing, imagery was captured on the 4th July. I believe the imagery shows an obvious person of interest who requires locating.' I wrote down the officer's name: Xavier Hughes. I needed to track him down.

That thought was overridden by another in the same moment, and I pulled out my phone.

'Whatcha onto?' asked Alec.

'That shooting I mentioned. My partner.'

I looked him up in the personnel database, didn't give a rat's arse if he was in the office or not, dialled his number.

'Shane here.'

'You must be retiring soon, mate? Been at it too long.'

'Sounds like the full-of-shit voice of Matthew Buchanan. How the hell are you? You seem to have dropped off the radar.'

'Dropped is right. Sole charge at Haast. But we've been a tad unusually busy down here.'

'So I've seen on the news. What can I do you for?'

'Remember that guy you shot on the Desert Road?'

Shane was no shrinking violet, so he wasn't thinking about the abruptness of the question. He'd be thinking, What now? 'Oh yeah, that time you were fingering your arse writing in your notebook? What do you need?'

'That place the truck was registered to, there's a link to some killings down here. Loose link. But that's all I remember. I'm not at a terminal. Those two guys, do you remember their names?'

There wasn't even a pause. 'Owen Reynolds and Sebastian Foley. Foley was the younger one, the guy I had to drop.'

'Thanks. Now I can actually do some digging in NIA.'

'Things okay, Matt?'

'Yep, yeah ... Bit of a mess, a lot of conjecture, old cases and new all intertwining. Wellspring might be key to it all. If it's even the same place. Want me to keep you posted?'

'Bloody oath. I always felt for poor Seb. Young bastard had been brainwashed or something. That Reynolds, he was creepy, mate. You track him down, I'd love to know what he's up to now. He's the guy I blame for whatever the hell happened that day. Would have been his ecstasy lab and everything.'

'Ecstasy? I thought it was meth.'

'Yeah, we assumed it was meth. But nah, Clan Lab team confirmed later on. He'd been cooking MDMA.'

Next I tried a long shot: looked up Hughes in the phone's staff contacts list. And he was still in the job. A senior sergeant now, at Alexandra.

As soon as I mentioned the 1991 jobsheet, he knew. 'Ruyer. You're looking into Nadine Ruyer.'

'Yeah. Part of a wider attempt at answers. You mentioned some bait camera footage? What was all that about? It's not on the file, and your boss seemed to have an issue with it.'

He gave a low whistle. 'Best you come over, Matt. I'm in the station. I can show you.'

49.

Alexandra, sitting at the junction of two alpine rivers, nestled between tussock-covered mountains, seemed like a quiet little place that could be big when it wanted to. The population wasn't enormous, but the school took a lot of boarders, including Tara and her mates, so it had a younger demographic than a lot of Otago's smaller centres.

The drive had been easy, through the pass to Hāwea, keeping on for Queenstown but turning off early at Cromwell and Lake Dunstan, which had been formed back in the early nineties when they dammed the Clutha River. But after I'd passed the dam itself on my right, the Clutha returned in full force, to keep churning on through Alexandra and out to the sea between Dunedin and the Catlins. The station was on the right on the main drag, just before you crossed the metal bridge over the broad, alpine-blue river.

Xavier met me at the front door, ushering me in and shaking my hand at the same time. 'Matt, a pleasure. This is going to be an interesting conversation, I'm sure. I'd be lying if I said you haven't got my interest.' The white crowns indicating his rank stood out on the shoulder epaulettes of his pressed blue shirt. The pride was clear in a job that meant something to him.

As soon as we were seated in his office, so we wouldn't be disturbed, he leaned forward eagerly. 'So how can I help you? You don't have to share things you can't, I understand. But yeah, I've got something you need to see.'

There was no reason to withhold anything, as far as I could tell. He was the boss in a town that was part of the same district looking into Joe's murder. He'd know half the story anyway. 'I'll tell it in order, mate, so you know where I'm at.'

Bar some of the Haast detail, there weren't a lot of gaps I'd filled in Xavier's knowledge. 'Hell, Matt.'

He looked out the window. 'Wellspring. There's a bloody story. Sitting waiting for a journalist, or a royal commission even, that place.'

'How's that?'

'Gave me the creeps. Then again I've never smoked weed or sung around a campfire. Maybe I'm just allergic to the thought of eternal happiness.'

I knew the feeling. 'You must have turned the place over after Nadine's disappearance. What did you learn?'

'Massive search. Nothing solid. A couple of sightings, none of which gave us a direction to follow. Most of the information we came up with pointed towards misadventure out in the wilderness. There was nothing concrete enough to suggest anything to the contrary.'

'What about the Epitaph member seen talking to her?'

'A red herring. Well, that's just my own personal take on it. Why the hell would a gang member kill her? There'd have to be a reason for that, and we couldn't find any. She didn't have a hard drug habit, or debts, and nobody mentioned anything about any gang associations. Guy was probably trying to chat her up and that's all there was to it.'

I paid close attention, echoing what he was saying in my own head, though knowing who the guy had been, I didn't buy the chatting-up theory.

'The community didn't share much with us, Matt. They focused in on this gang member but I don't think he had anything to do with it. Wellspring held back more information than they gave. That was my opinion then, and it's my opinion now.'

'Yours and mine both. Talk me through it.'

'That place was all lovey-dovey on the outside. Couldn't fault them. They were helpful, they all gave statements, talked about Nadine, let us walk over their land – good as gold. But you know when you hit that? It's all a bit too easy, eh. You know what I mean?'

'Yeah. Most inquiries run into difficulty. At least questions, push-back.'

'Right. If only 'cause people are curious beasts. But Wellspring? Overly helpful. There didn't seem to be a hierarchy or anything, but if I had to describe the feeling I got, it was that there was something running beneath. The people we spoke to, at least the hardcore ones who lived at the place, they were vacant – gone.'

'That would have been the bong they passed around just before you arrived.'

He chuckled. 'No doubt. But you know what I mean? It went deeper than that.'

'I hear you. But I know what value the bosses would have put on your feeling.'

'Exactly. Anyway, there's my hunches, and then there's the thing I really wanted to show you. Take a squiz at this. I've watched it hundreds of times. Thirty years on it still gives me the willies.'

He hit the power button on a TV and an old VHS player sitting on a trolley that he'd obviously trundled in from the same decade as the case we were discussing. He fucked about with cables and buttons for a bit. Then the screen changed and the tape rolled.

It looked like a night-vision camera, infra-red probably. It was all bright whites and greys and black. It took me a minute to figure out that it was set up somewhere in the bush, watching a clearing. I glanced at Xavier. 'So this is the DOC camera?'

'Yeah. Part of their bait strategy to get rid of stoats and rats and give the native birds a chance. They set these up all over the place, even back in the nineties. They're sensor activated. When did you join up?'

''94?'

'Yeah, well then you'd know. Back then we didn't have the CCTV network we have today. There are cameras bloody everywhere now. But back then, no. So if we lost a tourist, around Hāwea, I mean, there was nothing. But then this guy in the office who was on Search and Rescue, he told us about these DOC cameras. We got onto them and there were a couple in the area. DOC were really good at getting the footage for us. We thought it was a ridiculous long shot. Just one of those things we needed to cover. You know, so that a review ten years down the track wouldn't criticise us for not doing it.'

'Fair enough.'

I kept watching. The scene didn't move for about thirty seconds, and then a dark, blurred figure entered the clearing carrying something. You couldn't make out much: it was just a bright grey silhouette, among blacks and whites. For a few minutes nothing happened. Then bright white erupted from the centre of the screen.

'A campfire?'

Xavier nodded. 'And the rest.' He hit the fast forward button. The figure stood there, shock still, as I watched the counter tick over ten, fifteen minutes. 'Think that's weird?' He hit play.

The figure dropped to its knees, then fell forward onto the ground, arms at its sides. Taking the hit on the chest and probably the face. Then it rose to its knees again, and repeated the performance – over and over.

I looked across at Xavier and raised my eyebrows. His went up in agreement and his lips tightened.

I shivered. The footage was bizarre. 'Can you rewind that? Back to when they enter the clearing?'

'Course.'

I was about as experienced a hunter as I was a cabaret dancer, but I couldn't make out a pack or any equipment.

'So they walked all the way in there, to … pray? Or whatever the hell that is?' My gaze was fixed on the screen.

'That's what I reckoned. But I couldn't put that in my jobsheets. Couldn't hand on heart tell what they were doing. Couldn't make assumptions. So it's nothing. That's what the record says about this: it's bloody nothing.'

I understood the direction from above when dealing with a missing person: you needed facts. But this was far from nothing.

'If this is a person just wandering about, then they need help …'

He pointed his forefinger at me as though I'd hit the jackpot. 'Yeah, exactly. Caught on camera, worshipping the flame, in the general area Nadine Ruyer was in when she went missing?' He threw up his hands. 'And nobody like this was ever mentioned, at all, by the hippies at that place.'

That got my attention too. 'This camera was near Wellspring?'

'Bloody oath it was. You said this person walked all the way in, but this camera was operating in the bush, not even a kilometre from their site.'

We sat in silence for a bit, staring at the TV screen. Then he asked me what I considered a dumb question – for anyone who's ever been a cop. 'You ever think the department had it wrong about something?'

You have no idea, mate.

'Plenty. But that's the world we operate in, isn't it? We have to deal with absolutes. The law and the courts demand it.'

'Very true. And I had two young kids then, Matt. I needed the police. I couldn't make too many waves. There was a bigger picture, and something had to give. And it was Nadine.'

I knew exactly what he meant.

'Matt, if there's anything else you need, you give me a call. Have you visited the old Wellspring site?'

'I haven't, I've been meaning to.'

'Take a ride out there. It'll scare the bejesus out of you. If this wasn't enough.'

The footage had arrived again at the flailing figure, and I couldn't shake the shiver that washed over me once more.

50.

The tyres dug into the mud as I stood on the brake. I stepped out into the old paddock at the end of the track. It was empty, silent. The wind whipped up off the lake, shaking the trees that closed in on all sides and ripping through the overgrowth that covered what was once home to a bunch of wanderers.

I'd taken the private road, heading east off the highway, from The Neck, where the lakes were at their closest point to each other. The road wove around the north-western shores of Lake Hāwea, quickly giving way to several kilometres of gravel, a series of farm gates and then a muddied, overgrown track that terminated here.

The lake was just visible through the trees, grey and moody, and wind was slicing through my duty jacket as I stepped away from the wagon. I looked around as drizzly rain fell gently. I could see the remains of a number of buildings that had either been partially knocked down or simply given up to nature. The spaces where some had collapsed were filled with long grass and rubble. Some fencing and farm posts remained, but in a shit state.

I pulled my Glock from its holster, and carried it low by my right thigh. I wasn't expecting anyone here, but I'd taken a chance with Joe and I didn't want to be caught out again.

There were two buildings that still had four walls, and I approached the first, tried the door, which was either locked or rusted fast.

I picked up an ancient hoe and smashed the window, raking the glass out and then scanning the darkness beyond with my torch. Meeting nothing startling, I pocketed the torch, holstered the Glock, carefully placed my hands and climbed over the window frame into the gloom.

With the torch flicked on again, I could see that the place was empty. Old chairs and tables filled the space and there was nowhere to hide. It looked like it may have been the kitchen and dining building. Long, with lots of room. There was some plumbing down one side.

I went out the way I'd gone in, as the door wouldn't budge from this side either. As I walked across the scrub-covered space to the second building, my ears strained and I breathed in deeply through my nose. I pulled the Glock from its holster again.

Then my stomach tensed up.

This was something I did uncontrollably when I expected to be shot at. I'd first encountered it in the army, on training exercises, when you were closing with the enemy party and you knew you were going to take some blank fire. It was all simulated, but some subconscious part of me way back then had been thinking about the real event. I'd later experienced it both in Timor, and on the job with the police, when entering the unknown.

Now I understood my body's reaction a bit more generally. It wanted information. Because what it was getting wasn't enough to silence the emotion that was bubbling up – fear. Fear of the unknown, and what it might bring with it.

But I didn't slow, or move tactically. I figured if someone knew I was here and wanted a crack I was stuffed either way. They would've heard the car a long way off.

The door to this building pushed open. It was lighter in here, the room was smaller and there were more windows. Or at least there used to be. Rotting mattresses were stacked up at one end but there wasn't much else besides a bathroom, its internal walls falling apart.

Every documentary I'd seen about communes in the States flooded my brain, the conditions some people lived in, to achieve ascendance, or some other rubbish. I didn't want to think too hard about it, but it was difficult when every sense was on edge, and my brain was building the jigsaw all on its own.

I backtracked to the wagon and scanned again in every direction, examining the surroundings. The more I looked, the more I saw where other buildings, like the dormitory I'd just been in, must once have stood. Moss- and vine-covered walls, fallen masonry overgrown, rectangular areas within the growing tussock and scrub indicating foundations.

Stuff it. Let's do this properly. I picked a start point at the last gate I'd driven through and decided to do my own grid search, alone, across the whole area.

Among the strangulation of nature, I found remnants of a wash house, and a couple of solid-looking buildings with full plumbing that were totally bare inside, except for old basic kitchens with built-in vents and extractor fans. There were brown stains up the walls and on the partial ceilings. The old labs.

So it was true. They'd manufactured E on site. Flicked it to

Epitaph in return for their weed. Weed down, pills back.

But cooking E wasn't a simple reaction. Harder than cooking meth. And growing weed was a piece of piss. It didn't make sense as a pure business arrangement.

Unless they had other uses for it too.

The sparse trees around the old compound merged before clothing the foothills, where they eventually joined the beech forest. I walked in that direction, no objective in mind. Soaking up the atmosphere of the place. Just putting one foot in front of the other.

I emerged into a cleared area. At the edge was a huge old fallen trunk with a heap of natural rocks piled in front of it. Curious, I stepped up and got down on one knee. They weren't chiselled, just larger stones straight off the mountains, taken out of the lake or the braided rivers that criss-cross this part of the country. But they hadn't ended up here on their own.

Some of the rocks, where they formed a grotto or depression in the rest, were blackened. A fire pit.

The sharp bell notes of a tui rang out, and I jumped, but there was nothing here. None of it had been disturbed for years. This place was well and truly dead.

* * *

My heart just about stopped when I got back within sight of the wagon and saw a male figure slumped beside it. Boots, cargo shorts, Swanndri and beanie.

He yelled out when I was still some distance away. 'Morning, officer! Quite the day!'

After I'd introduced myself he asked, 'What brings you to this old dump?'

'Questions. Had to see it for myself.'

'Nothing been here for a long time.'

'You're obviously a neighbour?'

He waved down the track. 'Yeah, back down there. Saw your wagon – bit hard to miss the coppers round here. Curiosity got the better of me.'

'Fair enough, it's your neighbourhood. When did this place give up the ghost?'

He sucked air in through his teeth. 'Been a while, probably in the nineties even. Never used to be any trouble from up here. I'm so far away and they never bothered me. Cars sometimes trundled past, the odd bike, nothin' worth complaining about.'

'Nothing recently?'

'No. Owner hasn't been round here much.'

'Look, something might have happened here, back in the nineties, maybe even further back too.'

He eyed me warily. 'Nothing to do with the cadaver they found recently, by any chance?'

'Possibly.'

'Shit, well Ivan's your man. Owned this place a long time. Probably still does – reckon anyone else wouldn't leave this crap here.'

My brain jumped. 'Do you mean Ivan Chambers? From the Makarora Lodge?'

'That's the one. Nice guy.'

After I'd taken his name and details and was about to leave, he indicated for me to drop the window of the wagon, then leaned in as it slid down. 'Sorry, officer. Should I be worried about anything here?'

I looked back at the abandoned community, the foliage taking everything back. 'No. Not here, mate. Not anymore.'

51.

The lodge was lit, but it was dark, and it was pissing down. I pulled up my collar. I'd thought hard. This was an older couple, who'd lived out their lives, maybe, struggling with some atonement they couldn't reach. I'd been wrong before, and I'd be wrong again, but this, I felt okay with. I knew he'd have something. And if I didn't push, I wouldn't get.

I knocked twice before Marilyn opened up.

'Matthew, come in, it's pouring. What can I help you with?'

'Marilyn, I need to talk to you about Wellspring.'

I said it with the confidence I'd felt a thousand times, that moment when the future was in most ways predicted, and the only changes would be the responses or reactions from the players.

She took in my face, my voice. 'You want to talk to Ivan too?' I inclined my head slightly. This was a long play. It was all about human behaviour, but it would only work for me if I got my facts right first.

It was a good five minutes before she returned with her husband, who was frowning. 'Matt?'

'Hi there, Ivan. I was just saying to Marilyn, I'd like to speak to you both about Wellspring – and the death of Casey Fawkes.'

Marilyn put her hand to her mouth as she realised what this was, or maybe more accurately, what it could be.

I held up my hand. I was talking to Marilyn, but watching her husband, whose eyes had bulged. 'Marilyn, nobody's under arrest. This isn't that, not that at all. I'd like to speak with you both about what you can remember. Whether you do or not is your choice.'

Ivan spoke, his voice shaking. 'We don't know anything about all that. Mari, I swear I don't know anything about that, and neither do you. Why are ...'

'Ivan, you're both going to be okay. We aren't going anywhere. This isn't a trick. I've got a lot of questions. I have some answers. But I don't have them all.'

I was testing the relationship. If I was wrong, he wouldn't care. If I was right, he'd be upset.

He began to cry, the tears falling silently down his face. 'Mari ...'

She took his hands. 'We're going to help the law, and we'll be all right. You go and make a cuppa.' She led me into a room behind the reception desk, where she sat on a couch, indicated I should take the chair. There was a coffee table between us, and not much else in the room bar a bookshelf and some art. I sat in silence, letting her choose to talk if she wanted. 'I'd do anything to help the police, Matthew. But I don't think I know anything about what you think I do.'

'I know.'

She frowned, fidgeting with her hands. 'If he's done something, we'll both ... I'll get him to help.'

'Thank you.'

'He didn't tell you what happened with us, did he?'

'With you two?'

'We split. Late eighties, we separated. As Wellspring ... started to ebb.'

'You left him?'

'I left, yes. Things had gone – I don't think *wayward* is the word, more disbelieving. It wasn't so much about acceptance anymore, as about conformity.' She shook her head. 'And when that French girl went missing, I got hold of Ivan. I demanded he assure me that nothing had happened to her. He swore, but it had all changed for him too. He'd seen it and he left it behind. He came back to me. We opened this business, forgot all about Wellspring and its leftovers.'

'He won't like talking about it then.'

'It's hard to admit that something you helped to build went awry.'

We sat in silence until Ivan returned with three mugs. 'Forgive me, Matthew. While I doubt we can answer what you need, I can't say I'm surprised you're here. Not after what's been happening around these parts lately.'

'What do you know? Tell me everything.'

***

It was part biography, part explanation. He began with his family and growing up in the Otago Lakes. He'd married Marilyn young, and they'd always been spiritual, but rejected the hard line of the church around about the summer of '69.

'A new wave of holistic healing and belief swept the world around then, you know.'

I did. 'Everyone was looking for something.'

'That they were. We started a small community on the shores of Lake Hāwea. We called it Wellspring, and it was open, it was inclusive. It wasn't a cult, let me be clear. It was about happiness, it was about the people in it, not about – well initially, not about – beliefs and traditions and the like.' There was a pause. I made a note but didn't say anything. 'We were there, right up and through the seventies. The family you're talking about, I remember that vividly, but there's some other things I need to talk about.'

'Absolutely. Tell me in the order you think is important.'

'We had visitors, regular visitors. There were others at the community that . . . it evolved, over time, you see. I owned the land, I set the place up, but I didn't *run* it – Marilyn and I didn't run it. It was supposed to be inclusive, a flat structure, you understand. But it changed.'

'At some point you left it?'

'Yes, yes. By the time it was actually abandoned, we pretty much had nothing to do with the community and it had all but disappeared.'

I was watching him as I made a couple more notes. I hoped I was right. Here was a man who had the best defence imaginable: time. Forty-three years of it. Time altered, warped and shifted everything. People, places, memories, events, alliances. Friendships. No amount of fancy interview technique, or playing hardball, was going to make this man tell me anything he didn't want to. He was safe. Which was why I'd played the witness card first. If he was culpable of anything, I'd deal with that if and when it showed up.

He'd got to the end of his chronology. It was time to focus on what mattered. 'You mentioned visitors. Some of them were gang members, Ivan. Tell me what you know about them.' I said it like I knew all about it. I didn't want him thinking he could hold back. But he kept his mouth shut, unsure. I made the bridge for him. 'Epitaph had a monopoly in parts of the country back then. They did business with Wellspring, didn't they.'

Marilyn was still but Ivan finally gave a small nod.

I tried to put them at ease. 'Look it was a long time ago. You're not going to be in trouble now for some drugs peddled back in the seventies. Look at me. You understand?'

He looked up, his eyes wetter now. 'I ... I don't know much. Those guys dropped the green off, regularly, but it was never more than a transaction. And it wasn't my responsibility. I was just aware of it.'

'Whose responsibility was it?'

'There ... there were a few newcomers, they always ... When are we talking?'

'Whenever you like.'

'Well, yeah, they'd drop it off. Initially it wasn't a big deal. They caused us no problems, they were even nice. We paid them. Money from a bit of a whip-round, you know. We made sure we had the price, before they turned up, so there were never any issues.'

I decided to leave the ecstasy manufacture for later. That would require some rights first. 'Okay. These guys. I know who two of them were, I'd like you to tell me about them. Liam Goodhue and Joseph Kranz.'

When I dropped two old photos on the table, something triggered inside him, and he started shaking. 'I ... I didn't know their names ... but ... yeah, they look like two of the guys who used to come by. But those names are familiar.'

'That's because they were both locals, Ivan, and they're both dead. You can't *not* know them.'

I put down two more recent photos. 'I knew them. They disappeared, right after … there was a huge gap, between them …'

He was struggling, and I held my hand up. 'It's the two events, either side of that gap, I want to know about, mate. Casey and Nadine.'

He went whiter, started shaking his head. 'I can't …'

'Try. Joe rode with Epitaph. Liam was involved. They did business with Wellspring, part of a business enterprise that stretched right back up to Nelson.'

Silence for a time. 'Okay. But what has that got to do with Casey Fawkes?'

'Everything.' I pulled out another news article and added a couple of photos I'd received from Canterbury. Bones protruded from the earth, string-lines made a grid; there was no mistaking the human remains.

This time they both went white.

I placed on the table the photo of Casey that Sheryl had given me. I couldn't tell them the skeleton was Casey. There was no confirmation, and I wasn't expecting it. Either they knew, or they didn't. And I was betting on the former.

'In 1978, Casey, Michael and Lynn went missing. Lynn was strangled, Michael blew his brains out. But –' I tapped the photos from Canterbury '– she lived, didn't she? She made it out of the pass. Somehow. And she went somewhere. This skeleton died in the nineties. She lived somewhere, for years, never found, yet the whole area was searched. She was somewhere totally off grid, totally cut off from the world.' I flattened a map of the Haast Pass and Hāwea onto the table. 'Here's the pass –' I traced my finger along the highway, then moved it sideways '– right here is where they found the bodies –' and back to the road '– here's where the Fawkes car was found abandoned . . . and here was Wellspring. Just around the corner.'

Ivan mumbled, 'That's like a half-hour drive.'

'In this part of the country, that's the bloody definition of round the corner.'

Marilyn and Ivan looked at each other for a long time. I needed to strike while the iron was hot. I threw down photos of Gus's body by the river. And Joe's body out in the field. They both recoiled. Ivan crossed himself. 'Gus, poor Gus. My God.'

I leaned in. 'I'm not doing this for drama. I need you both to see how important this is. Because Joe was involved with Casey Fawkes, right back in the seventies. I think he was killed because he was getting close to something. And Gus, he was looking into the Fawkes killings too. Casey is the key. What happened with her holds the answers. If there's anything, *anything*, you know, you need to tell me. And you need to tell me right now.'

Ivan broke down. Marilyn had her arm around his shoulders and was whispering to him. 'It's okay, it'll be okay.' I gave them a moment. Marilyn kept talking to him. 'Love, life, sometimes just gets totally out of control. It made sense back then, we were helping her. We can't undo it, but you aren't a bad person. I love you.' Ivan was wiping his eyes and I stuffed some tissues from the box on the coffee table into his hands. His wife said what he needed to hear. 'Tell Matthew the truth. Just tell him everything.'

Eventually he sat up and looked at me. He took a deep breath in, then let it out, long and loud. 'Okay Matthew. Casey Fawkes arrived at Wellspring one rainy night, in '78. With the two bikers.'

52.

I'd decided something this big should be dealt with a bit more professionally. We'd called ahead and Brent was waiting as we pulled up outside the Wānaka station. Ivan politely followed him through to an interview room.

I peeled off in search of coffee but Brent cornered me not a minute later. 'You're up, big guy.'

'Eh?'

I'd figured the homicide teams would want this. It crossed over both their cases, could be the break they needed.

'You found and started this, let him continue talking to you, it makes sense. Quentin and I'll monitor.'

'Sure. Hell, that's gracious of you, mate.'

'We aren't like you Jafas, Matt. No egos here. Right person for the right job, that's what matters.'

I liked the South Island way of doing things. It made sense to me. They didn't fuck about with niceties or taking turns, or what *looked* right. They just did what *was* right.

After I'd explained to Ivan that the interview was being

recorded and monitored, but reiterated that he was being spoken to as a witness and was free to leave at any time, he cut right to the chase. He talked over the top of his mug of tea, his hands clasped around it, made eye contact all the time. 'So Casey arrived one rainy night, with the two bikers, like I said. Those two you showed me, Joe and Liam. All three of them looked shocked, haggard – even those two, who I'd never seen fazed by anything before.'

'Liam was a biker?'

'Sorry no, I don't know, I lumped him in with the rest. But he was part of that business absolutely.' I let him go on. 'I don't remember much from that night. The three of them arrived – I didn't see how. I wasn't the first to get to them, others were already helping them. They dropped Casey off. She was cold, her clothes were bloody and soaked, and my wife and I ran her a bath and got her some dry things. She was in shock, didn't say anything for a long time. I can still picture her face, white, shaken. I was in a bit of shock myself. It was unexpected and we weren't told much.'

'What *did* you get told?'

He thought back. Closed his eyes. Made an effort. 'Nothing. The bikers told us she needed to be protected. They said she needed looking after and that she had nowhere else to go. They told us not to go to the police.'

'And you went along with that?'

'We didn't have a –' A glance up at me, then a correction. 'It made more sense after we heard the news reports. Her parents were dead and she could have been in serious trouble if we'd turned her in. She'd have been thrown in juvenile detention or worse – we were supposed to look after her.'

'She backed this up, this wish?'

'Yes, eventually she talked, she came around, and she lived with us at Wellspring for a long time. She was always grateful. She was a good kid, a good person.'

We sat in silence for a bit, the obvious question floating in and out of my head. The one Brent and Quentin would be asking next door right now. 'So why do you think she'd have been in trouble, if the police had found her?'

He scanned the wall above my head, chewed his lip. 'I was never told why.'

'But what did you *think*?'

'I'd be guessing. Talking about what I guessed.'

'Yes, but you're the closest we've come to any sort of answers. Your opinion matters. Maybe not evidentially, maybe not in a formal statement submitted to a court, but it certainly matters investigatively. Because we're in the dark.'

He made up his mind. 'I believed she'd had something to do with her parents' deaths. What Liam and Joe had said about not going to the police ... yeah, I thought she'd killed them.'

'The conclusion was her mother was strangled and her father shot himself.'

Although with Liam's rifle that's bloody unlikely.

He held out his hands, palms up. 'You asked. Why else would she need to be hidden away? I deduced it, from the behaviour of those guys, and her, and how much of a mess she was when they dropped her off.'

'But you just went along with this? What hold did Epitaph have over you? You wouldn't have done this for just anyone. You would have seen the news reports and called the police. So why? Why did you believe what they said? Why did you go along with it? You could have been arrested as an accessory, if you're right about it all.'

Ivan frowned. 'Well, I guess I felt she wasn't culpable. Either she'd defended herself or maybe she'd defended her mother, killed the father. I don't know. What I do know is that the girl we took in was no monster. She was scared and vulnerable.' He looked down at his hands on the desk, his face creasing in pain. 'And I can't . . . I can't actually say that I *wouldn't* have done it for just anyone, Matthew. In fact, I probably would have. It was an odd time. Wellspring was all about new starts, about forgiveness, about atonement – making peace with yourself, being okay with yourself and moving forward. So who were we to turn away this girl who needed our help? And she never made us regret the choice.'

'And if the police had raided Wellspring, found her, let's say she had done something, you'd have risked prison?'

'We would have accepted it as the course we took, yes.'

What the fuck had actually happened in the pass? Could Liam, or Joe, have killed Michael? It made more sense. The rifle and all. But if that was the case, then Casey wouldn't have had to be hidden away, other than as convenient cover for them. But Casey was never a suspect. And how had Joe and Liam entered the whole scene in the first place? Luck?

My brain was racing away and I fought to come back to reality as Ivan kept speaking. 'I'll say one thing, Epitaph had no *hold* on us. That was a small business relationship – Wellspring made its own decisions. Don't tar Wellspring with the gang brush. It wasn't the case.'

'Well, tell me all about Wellspring then.'

We went for about an hour, and the length of the interview alone told me that at least some of what Ivan was saying must be as he remembered it. He didn't have much to say about the intervening years, after Casey arrived. Wellspring cracked on. They sang, danced, smoked the nights away.

'But if I'd known what was going to happen later, if I'd known I'd have driven Casey to the police the night she arrived. For her own sake. For that, I'll probably never forgive myself.'

***

I decided to give him his rights. This was verging on culpable territory and I'd be slammed later if I didn't. If he coughed to anything now it would get tossed out of court.

I read them to him, word for word. 'Do you understand?'

'Yes, of course.'

'Would you like to talk to a lawyer, like I just said?'

'No, I don't need one. This is about other people.'

'Okay. You'll need to help me here, Ivan, help me understand something. You held a leadership role at Wellspring, you and Marilyn. Is that right?'

'Yes, of a sort, from an admin perspective. We owned the land.' He squinted slightly. 'We didn't have a leader as such. Not then.'

'So how does business become a motorcycle gang showing up one night and offloading a potential juvenile murderer, and you have nothing to do with it all?'

He didn't say anything for several seconds. 'I can't really put it in words. It was something that happened. People were into all sorts. It was the seventies. I don't even know how we came to do business with Epitaph. Members had their connections. It just happened, it made sense, for a lot of the community, and it became something that just was. It didn't have the stigma it does now. They gave us weed. That's the long and short of it, as far as we were concerned back then. We didn't see a dark side to that gang business.'

You're missing something at the edges here. What the fuck is it? Grip it, dickhead.

'I need to know about ecstasy consumption at Wellspring too, Ivan. Tell me everything. As I've said, there's no liability for mention of controlled drug offending here.'

So he told me about personal use, and then the group therapy sessions, and then about the free love and partner-swapping that went with the vibe of the time in just such places as Wellspring, all over the world. It wasn't a breaking story. It made sense.

But as I probed, as I pushed, as I nudged the edges of certain parts of his recollection, I began to get that old feeling of something cold inching its way down my spine. Ivan was avoiding something. There was a lurking omission in every tale, every memory, hanging just out of reach because he hung it there, deliberately or mistakenly.

We'd had enough background. I could come back to it later. He'd settled into storytelling mode and it was time to pull him back to reality and the magnitude of this interview. 'Ivan, how did Casey die?'

His head snapped up.

'Tell me what you know.'

'It was '90, '91, sometime round then. It was pissing with rain that night, loud, a storm, because I didn't hear the knocks for a long time. Some of our members were at the door and they had the bikers with them.'

'You mean ...'

'The same two, yes. They all piled into my house. I had a car, you see, and they asked me for it. Amid all the confusion, someone said that Casey was dead.'

Joe wasn't Epitaph anymore. He'd raced down from Papakura.

'Did they have their patches on?'

'I can't remember. It was dark and it was chaos. But they wanted the car keys, and they were armed, and they said they were going to sort everything out. I remember saying I'd go with them. I didn't even know what was happening, but I'd been responsible for that girl and I needed to help. I wasn't going to have them spirit her away and that be it, for the police to raid us the next day and be put in jail for something I didn't understand.'

'You think they killed her?'

'I don't know. I didn't get that feeling initially, but something else had happened to Liam and Joe. They looked at each other ... I remember it clearly, that look between them, and somehow they just decided that yes, I could come. I hadn't seen it before, they were always so staunch.'

'Seen *it* before?'

'If nothing else, Matthew, those two men, they weren't what you think they are. They were two men trapped in a crazy series of events ...' His eyes drifted off. 'They weren't the crooks they might appear to be.'

'What happened, Ivan?'

'We got in my car. I drove. They told me we were going to Christchurch, so to settle in. One of them sat in front next to me, Liam, I think – yeah, Joe was in the back. There was a pile of stuff in the seat next to him. I assumed Casey was – I assumed the body was in the boot – but I didn't see anything. And then as I pulled out, all the way out onto the main road and picked up speed, that's when ... that's when I heard it.' He started to weep, his head and upper body shaking.

I reached over and put a hand on his shoulder. 'Heard what, mate?'

'The baby. It started crying.'

53.

I'd taken a pause so I could get my shit together. I grabbed a coffee and went outside, taking in the air and the light. Then I phoned Tom.

'Hi Matt, how are things over in Haast?'

'I've crossed the border, sir. I'm technically in Otago.'

'Working murders, and not the theft of fruit, I'm hoping?'

'Seems to be that way. We picked up a witness for this cluster over here. Seems like they could help with your Bottle Lake identification.' I gave him the short version of Ivan's account so far, focusing on the child.

'Hell, that's pretty concrete. I can't remember pathology mentioning that but let me look into it and I'll get back to you. Keep me posted. I'm guessing you aren't finished.'

'Not even close, sir.'

Inside I found Brent casually chatting away to Ivan about Otago life. When we'd resumed our positions, I invited Ivan to pick up where he'd left off.

'We drove and drove. I remember looking into the back of

the car a lot. Joe fed the baby, looked after it, changed it on the roadside a few times.'

'Joe did?'

'Yes. Liam was still in front with me. He didn't seem to know what to do, but Joe did.'

My pre-formed ideas, much as I knew to ignore them, were constantly changing. I was questioning every line I'd taken. And I could see Joe's face as he aimed that rifle at me. *Some things worth protectin'.*

'We got to Christchurch, I was told where to go, I don't remember knowing any of it. We parked up in a place they knew, holed up, waited for the next night.'

'Where?'

'I couldn't tell you if I tried.'

'Right.'

'Night-time we drove again. Into a pine forest. I know now that it must have been Bottle Lake.'

'You didn't know back then?'

'No, I had no idea. They didn't tell me.'

'Okay. It's important to make that distinction. And you think it was Bottle Lake now, because ...'

'The skeleton. The news.'

'But you aren't certain.'

'No.'

'Okay. What happened there?'

'They told me to hold the baby. I did. They opened the boot, dragged and lifted something, I had nothing to do with it.' The tears came again. 'I asked them ... I said ... will you make it right, you know, not a, not a shallow thing where it'd ...' He hung his head and went silent.

'I get it, mate. Even in the circumstances, a fitting resting place.'

'They just nodded and told me to stay put. The looks on their faces, I'd never seen such . . .' He was really trying to find the right words. 'Their demeanour. They were galvanised. They were angry. They were on a mission, Matthew, and they were doing their best to keep me removed from it.'

'As in, it wasn't your place?'

'No, I don't think so at all. I think it was more that they didn't want to burden me. They were saving me from something. From knowing about something.' He kept thinking, eyes on the desk now, not on me. 'They were gone a long, long time. Made use of the night. I guess they must have done a good job of the grave. They got back to the car, jumped in and told me to head back south along the coast. We ended up in a swampy area not too far from the sea. I just remember the ocean sound and the salty smell of the rotting vegetation. They left me there. Kicked me out and drove away with the baby.'

'Okay, mate. I need to know more about this bit.'

He rubbed his eyes. 'I'm trying. They told me they had something to do, told me to wait where I was. I didn't believe them – I thought I was getting ditched. For a second I thought they were going to kill me too, but I realised then that I was the patsy. My car. I was there. For all of it.'

'Tough spot to be in.'

'Damn right. Who would have believed me, two versus one? That's if I made it out alive after telling anyone anything. So they left in my car, with the baby. I never even knew its name. I never even knew if it was a boy or a girl.' He broke down again. 'That was the last I saw of the tiny thing.'

Were Liam and Joe capable of that? There's so much I don't bloody know.

Ivan spoke again. 'But they came back. I don't know how

long. I was starting to freeze, but was just shit scared of going anywhere, and then they came back.'

'Just the two of them?'

'Just the two of them. They picked me up, I got in and this time Liam drove us all the way to Wellspring in one hit. Their faces when I climbed into the car, they were just saying, don't ask.'

***

The rest of his account closed off the return journey, a petrol stop, with a description of the station but no idea exactly where it was, and then we went back over everything, revisiting details, conversations, people, places – whatever Ivan could drag up.

I was checking through my notes when a scrawl jumped out at me.

'You said earlier that *initially* Wellspring wasn't about beliefs or traditions. What did you mean?'

'Well, the community changed, everyone sort of brought something, it morphed.'

'How so?'

'It was all along the same lines … one with nature, and all of that.'

'Paganism?'

'No, God no. More environmental. Kinship. A type of peace. But eventually it had changed so much that it wasn't what Marilyn and I felt we needed anymore. We left. We still owned the place, but we left. It wasn't us.'

'Did Casey's death have something to do with that?'

'Of course. But …' He was going to say something else but fell silent.

Then I placed the photo of Nadine Ruyer in front of him. He picked it up, looked at it closely. 'This girl. I remember her, just after . . .'

'Just after Casey died?'

'Yeah. How did you . . .?'

'She was into the hippie lifestyle too. And Joe was seen talking to her. Before she went missing.' He went white again. 'No, no, he wouldn't have.'

'Convince me otherwise.'

'He was a dead man walking, during that drive. He had this stare on, he was going to do something, to whoever was responsible. This girl, she was hanging around Wellspring, she was on her OE, there's no way Joe would've . . .'

'Killed her?'

'No. If anything he would've been telling her to keep away.'

'Away from what?'

He breathed in slowly. 'When I said Wellspring didn't have a leader in the early days, well, that had sort of changed by then. A leader of sorts emerged. Solomon. I don't even know if that was his real name. He took on the role of leading sessions, and really driving the one-with-nature thing. It got a bit . . .'

'Batshit crazy?'

He laughed through his drawn expression. 'No, just purer. The place had a meaning then, rather than just a place anyone was welcome. He also drove the drugs more. I lied to you before, Matthew. When I said I didn't know much about the pills. I'm sorry. I wasn't sure . . .'

I held up my hand. 'Signed off, remember.'

'Wellspring cooked E on site. I saw your face when I lied to you. I knew that you knew.'

'I did, but it wasn't the time to press it.'

'I didn't have anything to do with it. Solomon drove it all. Marilyn and I had decided we wanted out by then.'

'Okay. Can you remember what he looked like?'

His eyes met mine. 'Yeah, of course. If there was a . . .'

I showed him the 2002 arrest photo of Owen Reynolds. His eyes went wide. 'Yeah, that's him.'

Finally. *We have him.*

54.

Same as always, things were graciously taken off my plate and I returned to my normal duties. I'd become quite fixated, had certainly overstepped the requirements of the Haast sole-charge role, but the CIB skillset didn't fade too easy.

I thought about Cascy. Living through whatever nightmare had unfolded in the Haast Pass, coming out the other side and into God knows what at Wellspring.

On the one hand I hoped Tom confirmed her as the body at Bottle Lake. It would close the loop, provide some certainty that she was no longer missing. On the other hand, to know she'd died at Wellspring in uncertain circumstances, and then been shovelled into dirt beneath a forest, wasn't exactly a pleasing thought. *Fucking arseholes.*

As I sat in the cafe, watching the world go by, I was grateful that at least there were two well-supported teams over in Otago running with Ivan's statement, following all the leads that spilled out of it, and hunting Owen Reynolds.

'Matt!' Sheryl yelled from behind the counter. 'Tara's calling from school, she needs to talk to you.'

I took the receiver. 'Hi Tara, how are you?'

'Hey Matt. I tried the station but you didn't pick up.'

'Sorry, you've got me now. What's up?'

'The cops in Greymouth arrested David Williams. Brooke told me. They've been at his place all day searching. He got taken away.'

Nice job.

'Is she okay? If she saw that she must have ...'

'She heard from someone else. I don't want to get her ...'

'Don't worry about that. They would've kept her well clear and found things out in other ways.'

'Okay. I just thought you'd want to know.'

'I did. Thanks. Hey, nice work.'

Back at the station I dialled Brent at Wānaka, knowing he'd know what his Greymouth offsiders had got up to today. One of the D's working on the killings told me he and a few of the team were on their way. 'He was trying to get hold of you – left about an hour ago. They were going to grab you.'

There was pounding on the door and I opened up to Brent, wearing his stab vest and fully kitted out. 'Hey, soldier. Grab your gear. It's on.'

'Didn't they just pick up a guy dealing to kids?'

'We've fucking got him, Matt.'

Then I realised. 'Wait ... he's talked?'

'Gave him up hook, line and sinker, the E cook himself ... Reynolds.' He slapped my shoulder. 'So grab your vest if you want to jump in, 'cause we have the guy who killed Gus.'

55.

Jacobs River is a tiny settlement an hour's drive north of Haast, just south of Fox Glacier. There are places like it dotted along the West Coast – settled in the early pioneering days, where a section of bush and swamp grass would have been cleared for farming beside one of the many rivers flowing down from the Alps and out into the Tasman. There was a memorial now where the church of Our Lady of the River had stood before it was blown away in a cyclone a few years back.

Things started out positively. Reynolds' place was up a cutting in the fields, well back off the road. Sitting up the front of Brent's Holden Commodore while he pushed the accelerator to the floor, I'd actioned the M4 rifle he'd passed me and gripped it, barrel down. We were second in the convoy of three cars. Chasing the lead vehicle up the drive, we hit the brakes at the same time they did. I'd been told to take the rear with the guys from the first car, so I was out fast and running with them behind the farmhouse, taking up a position sighting two sides of the place.

I heard pounding on the front door as Brent shouted. 'Police! Search warrant! Open the door!'

It was then that things began to deflate. You get bored very fast at warrants. If there isn't a bang and a crash in the first few seconds, or some running and yelling from inside, it's one of two things: either nobody's home, or it's going to be a cautious, deliberate entry into unknown territory.

One of the guys who'd taken the front door with Brent moved around into my sight and checked the back door. Locked. He returned to the front, where Brent, I assumed, would then be discussing a forced entry.

I looked around properly, now that the initial race onto the place had hit sand. And my interest died.

The grass was tall. As in brushing above my waist tall. The roof had huge holes in it. The windows were smashed in. There wasn't a single thing announcing life was present. No chickens. No rubbish bin. No clothes hanging. It was dead.

I heard the front door go in, and boots moving through the house. I waited in my spot, crouching among the scrub, with Brent's other guys over to my right doing the same, waiting for someone to call us in from the back door. Usually, until then, there was the smallest chance someone was hiding and could make a run for it.

But not here there wasn't.

Brent came out the back himself, his Glock protruding off his hip as he wandered up to the three of us, shaking his head. 'Place is long abandoned. If ya couldn't tell.'

'His vehicle registered here?'

Brent nodded. 'Yep. Nissan Patrol. To here, renewed early this year.'

It was always the safest bet, the transport authority

information. For finding regular people, anyway. People like Reynolds, however, liked to keep law enforcement guessing. We went through the motions, searched the place half-heartedly, in case anything jumped out that might point us in his actual direction. But it was barren.

Brent sent his other four guys to the collection of houses on the riverbank to find out what the locals knew about this place and who'd been seen here. Then he turned to me. 'Thoughts, Matt?'

'Nope. I mean he's a cook. His lab is somewhere. But we've got a lot of ground to play with. We know he's supplying into Greymouth. David, and whoever else he's supplying, they're the best place to get more. You're not gonna come across him by kicking stones, not in this part of the country. Place is too big.'

He was nodding. 'Bloody oath. Need that counsellor to help pull him in.'

'Yeah, slap him round a bit. Guy dealt to some kids down my way. Having a bit of sense knocked into him would be good.'

'Ah well,' said Brent. 'Let's hit the road. Unless the boys have dug up some gold.'

They hadn't. The place had been deserted for decades, according to the neighbours. A shaggy-haired man sometimes bashed back the grass and scrub, but that seemed to be all. As Brent suggested, 'Obviously keeps it just alive enough so the council doesn't rip the place down.'

I unloaded the M4 and dropped it on the rear seat of the car. Brent removed his Glock from the holster attachment, then threw it behind him. 'Let's get outta here.' We'd pack things up properly back down the road, hopefully over a coffee somewhere.

* * *

As we drove south, I rested my left arm on the window sill and watched the scenery go by.

'So damn close, Matt. We would've had him. For Gus.'

'You're on the right track, though, mate. Back at the start you didn't even know who you were looking for.'

'That's now all thanks to you, Senior Constable.' He chuckled. 'Why didn't you ask to go to CIB after a few months? The boss would've jumped to have you. Like, they sent you to Haast, but that doesn't mean you couldn't apply for local jobs, or be rotated somewhere.'

'You know what,' I replied, 'I didn't even think about it. I guess I was just enjoying the quieter life. It's a good town, it's a good job. Well, it was until ...'

As we passed the Knights Point lookout, not too far from home, a silver four-wheel drive flashed past us. I didn't give it a thought, but Brent had swung his head around and I realised: Four-wheel drive. A compact one. Nissan Patrol.

Brent stood on the brake, jerked the Holden over to the left, spun it around and put his foot on the gas, the vehicle straining and then lurching as the mechanics caught up with his intentions.

'Got the first two letters of the rego.' His face was tight as adrenaline flooded his body. He pushed the Holden back past the lookout and down the hill, throwing it through the twists and turns of the highway, bush crowding in on all sides. 'That's fucking him. That's his fucking vehicle, Matt.'

Brent crossed the centreline where he could, to eat up the road quicker. Over a bridge, through more bush. We planned as we hunted him, and I got to work loading and checking both weapons.

'Straightforward high-risk 3T – that work, Matty?'

'Sure.' I slapped the bolt release on the M4, chambering a round, and placed it in the footwell. Then I reached for Brent's Glock, dropping in a mag and working the slide. 'And if he doesn't stop, we let him go?' I knew Brent had been AOS at one stage, but I couldn't remember if he was still on the Tasman squad.

Brent nodded. 'Couldn't expect you to pick up the nuances of a non-compliant stop in the heat of the moment now, could I?'

AOS were trained to bring a car to a stop by forcing it off the road, the person sitting where I was training their firearm on the driver from a mere arm's length away through the open window. Not really something I was confident in pulling off.

'Bless you, Brent, and apologies for my lack of knowledge.' I held the Glock in my hand, finger outside the trigger guard, pointing at the floor. I was going to hand it to Brent as soon as – well, if – we stopped. We closed the gap further, as the road opened onto a straight, skirting the edges of Lake Moeraki. 'But don't worry. He'll stop.' I flicked the lights and siren on, and after a moment's hesitation, the vehicle in front slowed and started to pull over.

I quickly turned in my seat. The two other cars in our convoy had caught up to us, after spinning around up near the lookout. They were ready to back us.

Brent brought our Holden to a stop behind Reynolds, angled slightly to let us use the roof pillars as cover.

Eyes on the driver seat of the Nissan in front of me, I passed Brent the Glock, gripped the M4 rifle and stepped out of the car, moving back, back behind the rear left pillar. Brent appeared beside me, leaning over the rear right side.

I was aware another Holden had stopped alongside us, and the sounds of boots and doors slamming told me the rest of

Brent's team had done the same. We now had at least four, maybe five or six, firearms trained on Reynolds.

I was looking across the top of the red dot sight, keeping a wide awareness picture, staring at him through his headrest, mindful that if cars came the other way, we didn't really want a whole lot of rifle and pistol rounds firing off all over the place. Hopefully any vehicles coming up our arse would see the cop cars blocking the road and think twice before trying to get around us.

Brent did the yelling. 'Driver of the vehicle, put your hands out through the window where I can see them!'

Movement in the Nissan. The window came down and two arms emerged.

'With one hand, remove the keys and throw them out the window.'

Reynolds obeyed. A hand disappeared, then reappeared, dropping the keys onto the ground.

'Slowly remove your seatbelt and step out of the car! Hands on your head!'

Brent was doing a sterling job – clear, concise commands. Reynolds got out, and I looked into the face of a ghost from the past.

The truck on the Desert Road flashed before my eyes. The long, dark, greasy hair. The frown on his face. The jittering shape of Seb Foley in the seat next to him. I blinked, shook my head.

Reynolds was older. His hair was lighter and shaggier. But the face was the same. Solomon. If he was our guy, then not only had he killed Gus and Joe, but he'd had something to do with Casey, and Nadine.

Lost in my thoughts, I missed it. Missed the indication Reynolds gave.

Brent had called him forward, ready to get him to kneel down before we moved in to handcuff him. Reynolds was walking, doing as he was told. But his eyes darted to his right, which was my left, toward the verge. He was eyeing up where he was going to go. I saw it, saw his eyes move, but I didn't process it.

Reynolds reached behind his back and in the same movement darted across the arse end of his wagon, backing up on its left-hand side. He'd put the solid metal pillars of his Nissan between himself and our colleagues off to my right, halving the danger from several armed cops to two. In the same movement he'd pulled the pistol from his trousers and had it out and up.

I should have dropped him as soon as I saw that pistol leave his pants. But I was reacting, not acting. And thinking too much. Too slow.

As I settled the red dot sight on his chest, I could see the barrel of his pistol and knew he'd arrived in the aim first, would squeeze the trigger first…

And that I'd die first.

I was deafened as three loud booms erupted, so close together it almost sounded like one long explosion. Reynolds crumpled to the ground and I tracked his fall through the sight, watching him hit the grass, the pistol drop from his hand. He rolled a little down the sloping verge and came to a stop, very still.

I smelled cordite, but I hadn't operated my weapon. Brent had fired first, and had saved my life. I moved up with him, shoulder to shoulder, our weapons trained on the body on the ground.

Owen Reynolds, denim shirt soaked dark red, stared up at us from lifeless eyes.

56.

Three months later
Christchurch

The flat, pleasant city I'd visited but never lived in, Christchurch was an easy place to be. Five minutes outside the CBD was rural fringe. And between the Port Hills, Akaroa, the coastline and the skifields – it had everything you wanted. Unless you looked hard and had memories of the place, you'd never guess that its heart had been ripped out by two major earthquakes and the deadliest terrorist attack in the southern hemisphere.

The Uber driver took the main from the airport, then skirted the edge of Hagley Park, where dogs were walked, joggers and cyclists got over that burger from last night and Tinder dates got to know each other better. We crossed the river to reach the justice and emergency services precinct, the big, new, concrete and glass behemoth that housed police headquarters, the courts, Civil Defence and so on.

A familiar face met me at the door as I got to the top of the stairs. 'Matt, how's it, mate?' The dark flop of hair and huge grin plastered across his mug were the same as ever. After Reynolds' death, Quentin had wound up the homicide case into Joe's killing, all evidence pointing to the same motivation as for Gus's murder. One of his team had remained in Wānaka to manage the file for the coroner, but that was it. Quentin had returned to Dunedin, until Tom had called him up here for my visit.

'Matt, great to see you again.' Tom extended his hand, then pointed me to a swivel chair. Quentin took another next to me. 'The news is good: we're pretty certain it's her.'

'Sir?'

'Casey. The account from Ivan, his account of the baby – I think it's enough to circumstantially ID her. The pathologist said the person had given birth, at some stage. Couldn't say when.'

So there definitely was a child.

'But as for a full positive, we're struggling.'

'No DNA?'

'Turns out both Casey's parents were cremated. We thought the father hadn't been. So there's nothing to compare. Nothing to exhume. Then there's the rest. You need to keep this tight. If it makes it outside the investigation, it'll sink anything in the future. A suspect would have no need to confess.'

'What do . . .'

'There's no cause of death, Matt. None. Good bone is all we've got. Whether she died from a drug overdose, from strangulation, from bleeding out after a muscular or organ wound . . .'

'Or childbirth?'

'Or childbirth, we'll never know.'

57.

Quentin drove. It was a few minutes north-east from the city centre, though some locals would call it 'way out', and just a few k's north of the pier at New Brighton. It was a state forestry block that had some time ago been allowed dual use as a public recreation area, so there were still areas off limits, where I assumed guys in Swanndris swung their axes, but part of it now had mountain biking, horse riding and jogging trails, and a carpark. We cut straight through that and took one of the main forestry roads. When the body had been found, scene guards had blocked off all the vehicle access points, but now there was nobody. No constable in a fluoro raincoat to wave us past. Nothing.

I'd lost my sense of direction a bit after leaving the city, but knew we must have been nearing the coastline as we got deeper into the pines. After we'd parked, Quentin headed under the trees and up a pine-needle-covered slope, then down the other side. Halfway down he pointed ahead to a large depression. 'It was like an archeological dig with tents and every man and his dog, but now you wouldn't notice. It was back-filled and the pine needles have kept dropping.'

I couldn't imagine Joe and Liam, shovels digging, about to bury Casey here. It made no sense. They didn't have to. They could have taken her to the police. To a hospital. Dealt with it properly. Why had they hidden her?

They didn't kill her. I was certain of it. It had happened at Wellspring, and they'd arrived to sort it out.

I tried to snap out of it. I was over beating myself up and ending up with mere conjecture. I felt I should listen to myself more. Was this really even a murder?

And Reynolds was dead.

Nobody had turned out to be who I thought they were. Nothing had been what I thought it was. And there was a chance I'd find out nothing more about any of it.

I followed Quentin down the slope, treading on the soft carpet of sand, earth and pine needles. He used his arms to give an indication of the size of the dig.

'How deep?'

'The full six feet apparently.'

I looked around. Pine trees and dead lower branches in all directions. Needles covering the ground. The ocean, somewhere out past it all. How would I do it, if I was hiding a body? Probably come in from the beach, do it, then back out, wash myself in the waves.

But they hadn't done that. Not according to Ivan. It was like they didn't care. Didn't care if they were caught. Yet they'd still ordered him along as cover for them.

'What was this place like back then?'

'More forest, less recreation, but pretty much the same hereabouts.'

'But not somewhere the public would spend their time?'

'Not like today.'

Body dump research was pretty solid now. People dumped bodies in places they were familiar with. It was just how the brain worked when you panicked. You go, 'Where should I put it?' And the brain says, 'Here's a nice out of the way spot' – it knows, because it's been there. Everyone gets spooked by the unknown. There were plenty of exceptions and other factors going into things, but the research didn't lie.

'Liam was raised in this part of the country,' I said. 'Makes sense.'

As we rolled back out to the main I relaxed into my seat.

58.

I felt I should unburden my head. So after rolling out of Anna's bed in Hāwea, I wandered along to the nearest cafe, bought a couple of coffees and was back before she was up. I sipped, looking out at the lake from the back deck until I heard the door behind me and felt her arms reach around my neck.

'What are you thinking about? Talk to me.' She started on her coffee.

I gazed out over the water. 'I dunno. Just frustration. I won't get the answers.'

'Of course not. It's been decades. You never will. You told me that yourself.'

'I know, I get that bit. Casey. It'll forever be a question. Nah, I'm thinking about the guy Brent shot.'

'The Wellspring leader.'

'Yeah. Reynolds. I just don't quite get it. We dealt with him, years ago. Like I told you. But he was driving that truck . . . Shane said he was creeped out by him, but for me, he just seemed like a runaround, a guy who just got shit done. He didn't seem like a charismatic leader.'

Anna sighed. 'Well, it was a long time ago. That was a pretty tough situation and it went south really fast.'

I finished my flat white. 'Yeah. Thing is, Joe and Liam and Gus, they were hard men. Tough fellas. Joe in particular. It's crazy.'

'What is?'

'That he was shit-scared of what Reynolds was capable of.'

'You didn't know Reynolds, Matt. You saw him once, before a shooting quite a few years back. Then for a minute before he died. Give yourself a break – it wasn't much to go on.'

I shook my head. 'I know. But Joe atoned. He made it into the army. He excelled at it. But he left to fix something. Liam and him both. They joined up, together. Reynolds – it doesn't make sense. They had the opportunity to at least front him, find him, interrogate him . . . maybe kill him? He was nothing. An E cook maybe, that's it. But Joe told me . . . whatever he was going after, that I wouldn't believe him if he told me the truth.'

Anna stared out over the water. 'So you're asking what was Joe hunting Reynolds down for all these years later? Why would Reynolds kill him?'

'Yeah, that's what I'm struggling with.'

'Not a revenge killing.'

'I can't see it. It was a spectacle. A message. *Don't come knocking.* Very clear. Joe was a protector, Anna, not a killer. We don't have the chronology down, but I guarantee he left the SAS in '91 because Liam told him something was happening with Casey, or that she'd died. He disappeared to bury her, remove the child . . .'

' . . . to safety?'

'Exactly. He said to me once that some things are worth protecting. That kid was placed somewhere safe. I know it.'

'So you think the kid is what brought out all this, these killings, now?'

'It's the only thing that makes any sense. The only leftover thread.'

She turned to face me. 'So what are you going to do? What is there to do?'

I shrugged. 'Nothing. Canterbury aren't trying to track the child down. They think it was killed too, and shit, I mean where do you start? Hospital records or something, maybe even police records, 1991, found babies – records aren't gonna be friendly there. But it might be possible.'

'Matt, it's only been months, but I know you. The guy you were, that you've told me you were, when you worked murders, do you really want him back?'

I shrugged again. 'Seems working murders is the thing I can't shake.'

Anna sighed. 'Maybe. So why don't you stoke the fire a bit?'

'How so?'

'Well, you can look into whatever Joe was hunting Reynolds for. This many years on. Might help cement it all in your head.'

'I guess a starting point would be ...' I caught myself before finishing, stared at Anna. 'The warrant at his place.'

She was nodding too. 'Right after he ambushed you. What happens to all that stuff?'

'Knowing the police, it'll still be sitting in the property store at Greymouth.'

I stood and so did she. As I disappeared inside to use her phone, I couldn't shake the thought, not for a second: Joe wouldn't be scared of a man like Reynolds.

59.

'Most of it's up for return. To who now, though, I just don't know. He didn't have a will, estate, relatives – nothing.'

The property officer at the Greymouth station had gone above and beyond. We'd been given a small barren room off the main storeroom, and he'd even helped carry half of the items taken from Joe's shack through for us.

Brent had given his blessing for both Alec and Anna to join me. I'd said that we were looking for the now-abandoned labs, but this wasn't an evidential piece in the hunt. He'd agreed pretty quickly. It was an open line of inquiry, but he didn't have the manpower. And anyway it was all only heading for the coroner, who would want to know how everyone had died, but couldn't give two shits about some labs sitting idle in the Haast wilderness.

Most of Joe's stuff was books, memorabilia and a couple of journals. There was nothing electronic, no phone, no laptop. Which wasn't a big surprise.

Starting with the familiar, I began thumbing the *Classical Myth* text again, and noticed that apart from text and photos relating to Pan, nothing else in the book was annotated or underlined. He'd picked the strangest Greek deity and decided to read about him. *Pastoral tradition. Pan, the Feeder.*

One photo showed a statue with three figures. I read the caption: 'Aphrodite, Eros and Pan. National Archaeological Museum, Athens.' Joe had circled Aphrodite and written 'His Morning Star'.

I showed it to the others but they shook their heads. Joe seemed well-read – Anna and Alec picked up book after book: *Moby Dick. The Count of Monte Cristo. The Aeneid.* Most of the non-fiction was books relating to the psychology of killing, and PTSD. So far, so Joe. The man, the enigma. Like a cruel joke.

Alec suddenly went quiet and held up a journal containing Sellotaped-in newspaper cuttings and other printouts. 'Matt, check this out.'

The page he indicated was a 1984 *New Zealand Herald* article about satanism. It explored New Zealand's own witchcraft history, and the groups involved in worshipping the occult. Long story short, there wasn't much to talk about, and the article was heavily fluffed up. The US had been barking up the wrong tree and it didn't look like New Zealand had much to be concerned about either. It did mention Otago and West Auckland, not as hotbeds of devil worship, but as hippie nests where people enjoyed dancing naked among the trees.

Witchcraft. Bollocks.

But the image of Joe's bound and bled body rose in front of me. And I remembered Billy's words, about the children murdered by the invading tribe back in the 1800s. Right in that same area.

I started to feel nauseous. I held my guts and stared at the ground, trying to hold it in.

'Matt? You okay?'

I rested my mouth on my fist, rested that on my knee. 'Yep, yep, just might need a coffee.'

We took a break and discussed our progress so far. 'So he liked reading. Full credit to him. What the hell else was he gonna do with his time?' Anna was on the fence.

'The notes in the books are significant because they're few and far between.' Alec zeroed in on the things Joe had obviously wanted to revisit.

'Yeah, I agree. There's something in Pan, the farming, nature, that links in with the whole movement, into Wellspring.'

'Nature loving?'

'Yeah,' I replied. 'But according to that book Pan was a bit of a soft cock. He was the forest god, the wholesome keeper of the trees, protector of flocks.'

'Not really something that's worth hiding. Environmentalism.'

'No. It doesn't really make sense. It's the cooking ecstasy that would've been what got anyone into trouble. But then, if that's the case, and the drugs were the worst of it, why was Joe researching all this other shit?'

We decided just to keep going. I continued flicking through the journal, deciphering Joe's scrawl, staring at the articles.

'Matt!'

I didn't even notice them trying to get my attention. When I looked up, Anna and Alec were both staring at me questioningly. 'What?'

'We just lost you, for like ... a whole minute there, mate.'

I shook my head. Joe *had* researched the ecstasy angle. And he'd made a connection that I hadn't. A connection that suggested maybe there was more to the ecstasy labs than simply making some cash. Within an article about drug production, I'd stumbled on a reference to something I did know a bit about. And Joe had underlined it: Centrepoint.

It was what had frozen me. It was what gave the average person on Auckland's North Shore, back in the day, reason to lock their doors at night. The Centrepoint commune was set up in the late seventies, continued through the eighties under the eye of the law, and in the early nineties, far too late, was raided by the CIB. There had been convictions for offending that straddled both drug manufacture and child sexual abuse.

As I kept turning the pages of Joe's journal, I saw more articles and notes: 'Reports from ex-members described the community as a place where free sexuality was encouraged, including among the children.' 'Allegations of MDMA manufacture are potentially the first known clandestine drug laboratories in New Zealand.' When I was at Police College, as a trainee in '94, we'd been delivered a presentation on the raids.

The cold feeling in my spine was back.

Joe had been chasing this for years. A comparison, a way to try and understand. Weed down, pills back. But sexual abuse of children? The consequences of *that* getting out would be worth killing over. Worth it all the way. It lifted the risk to Wellspring's leadership from nil to lengthy imprisonment for rape.

Gus had been pushing around the edges. Too close for comfort from a former police officer. Joe had known where to look but hadn't made it out. Had Nadine Ruyer threatened to tell police something? Way back then? The image of the figure from the bait camera loomed in my memory.

I needed guidance. Something had gone on at Wellspring. And there was no doubt in my mind that it was something far darker than some pot, some singing and a bit of guitar.

60.

Carl Liggins was an old friend and Associate Professor of Classical Studies at Otago University in Dunedin. We'd been through high school together, and all I'd done was give him shit in class for being so in love with the past. I'd said that if he studied classics at uni, there was only one option for him, teaching it.

So I felt like he owed me, for crystal-balling his future. But then again, I probably owed him for dragging my arse through school and getting enough passes so as not to seem entirely repulsive to the police.

I turned up my coat and dodged the throngs of students who'd managed to roll out of bed without a hangover that morning. The stone towers and walls were an impressive ode to Scottish architecture. And then there was the little river flowing through the middle of the campus. If it wasn't for the empty Woodstock cans and the group in front of me in Highlanders jerseys, it could've been somewhere in the mother country.

There was personal nostalgia here for me, as I'd never been

a student, but I'd visited mates who were, and had fond memories of drunken nights, drunken afternoons ... and drunken mornings.

I found the building, the floor and then Carl's office. I pushed the door open without knocking, took in the dark wood, the awards, the drinks cabinet and the books. 'Well, fuck me, you've done well, mate. I take it all back.'

He stepped from behind the polished desk, dressed like a knob in a maroon cardigan and corduroys, and lifted, then immediately dropped, his outstretched hand, opting for a solid hug instead. 'Matty B. Still with the mouth of a trooper. You don't look any different.'

His sideburns met his beard, but he had no moustache. 'Yeah, well, you look like a twat.'

He burst out laughing, then walked over to the cabinet and pulled a bottle from the shelf, grabbing two glasses. 'This is delicious. Single malt, but aged in Caribbean rum barrels. Quite the mix, and a bit better tasting than the twenty-five-dollar stuff we used to knock back.'

'Wouldn't anything be?'

We sat and talked shit, caught up on life and family. We'd kept in touch over the years, which is why I was confident he would come to the party with the answers I needed. His wife was an astronomer, now splitting her time between gazing at star data and lecturing. Their boys were about to head out into the bright blue yonder. I was stoked to hear that both had been accepted into the two fairer branches of the Defence Force.

Carl pointed his finger. 'And that's your fault. I used to tell them how much fun you had in the military.'

I was offended. 'Stuff off. You must have told them lies, so that's on you. At least as officers they'll be sipping tea in their number ones, not standing to while taking a shit, having to cut it off and aiming out into the night with their pants around their ankles.'

He laughed again. 'How's Hailey? And any love in your life again yet?'

Carl and his wife had both known Kate, but that was a long time ago.

'Hailey's with MFAT in Wellington. She's doing really well, loving it there. As for the rest … well, maybe. There's this girl over my way, we met at the bar.'

'Serious?'

'Probably ballpark serious. It's been a few months.'

'That's great. What's the poor girl's name?'

'Anna, she's from these parts. And yeah, she's great. A reminder there's something decent in an otherwise pretty standard world of shite.'

He was genuinely happy for me. 'It's good to see you smiling, mate. Now, you mentioned Greek myth, some case you're working on?'

I was up and pouring two more. 'Don't know if I've got the terminology right. Religion might be more accurate?'

He was interested. 'Often one and the same. Go on.'

I returned to my seat, handed him his drink. 'I want to know what I'm looking for. Whether they might be standard drug manufacturing crooks, or whether there's something darker at play.'

'Try me.'

'There were a few murders over in Haast last year – you may remember the news.'

'I was following, yeah. Terrible stuff.'

'Both the men that were killed were looking into … hell,

what even *were* they looking into?'

I filled Carl in. 'And it all collides in a community located between Wānaka and Haast, where people gathered and sang and smoked.'

'Hippies.'

'Yeah, basically. But a recurring theme is that a few of the key players were either into, or trying to learn about, Pan.'

'Pan?'

'Yeah, ugly guy with horns, about yay big?' I held my hand off the floor at chair seat height. 'The one that fucks all the nymphs.'

'Yes, yes, I can tell you all about Pan, but I need context. Classical myth isn't a science. Everything's open to interpretation.'

'Okay. One of the guys was bound. Tortured. His fingers were cut off … and he had his femorals slit open. He bled out real quick. I can't see a reason to do that. Except maybe to collect the blood.'

Carl coughed into his glass. 'Jesus Christ.' He wiped his face, gestured for me to continue.

'He'd been looking for someone, someone linked to the Fawkes murder–suicide, but he'd been reading up on Pan and his links with the pastoral tradition. Something about the totality of nature? About it being misinterpreted, like a bending of the truth. He was trying to get a bead on whatever this community was actually up to.'

Carl sat back, frowning. 'Bending of truth is what religion is based upon. You know what the Christians did, right?'

A trick question, surely. 'Was there anything they *didn't* do?'

'Fair call. No, I mean to Pan, to all the old gods.'

'Not familiar, no.'

'Pan was unique. He was Greek, right, lived in Arcadia and slept in trees and played his flute and chased nymphs, like you said. He was laughter, he was mischief, but he was supposed to be good.'

'Right.'

'But out of all those ancient deities, he was the only one that made it across to England, into paganism. The pagans worshipped the gods of the earth and Pan transitioned quite well.'

Carl savoured a sip of his drink. 'Have you heard of the Green Man?'

'I've read some Lovecraft, yeah.'

'Well, he's more ... you said totality of nature ... that's more the Green Man's domain. He and Pan aren't the same, but they have a few things in common – both environmental guardians, the cycle of growth – you know, birth, death, rebirth, everything connected and all that. Some reckon he bridged the gap between paganism and Christianity. His face appeared on many medieval churches. The record isn't great at answering why.'

I was processing what he was saying. 'The environmental stuff isn't an issue. It's whatever else there might have been.'

'Well, there is another side to it. A darker side.' He finished his drink, handed the glass to me with a grin.

'Hell, no lectures today? This'll put you over.'

'Not today, no. You've got me interested, but I might be about to upset you.'

'Go on then.'

'It sounds like this place you're talking about was a hybrid. Old paganism wasn't even a religion. Not the way we see it. They just lived their lives, and there was ritual to life. But they didn't believe in things the way modern Christians or Muslims or anyone else does. They were farmers. Peasants. Simple people.'

'There's the pastoral link.'

'Yeah. But it's not until neo-paganism, that it gets darker. And that's very modern stuff. Worshipping the earth, Wicca, all that's very new, and has little to do with the ancient origins.'

'Is drug-taking condoned?'

'Absolutely. An altered state of consciousness is often the aim. Plenty of drugs that can help that on its way. And while Pan doesn't feature in the new stuff, a bloke called the Horned God sure does, and he bears a resemblance. Have you heard of Baphomet?'

'I can't remember. Sounds like something from *The Exorcist*.'

'Close.' He went to a shelf, pulled out a volume. I couldn't see the title. He checked the contents, then flicked through the pages. 'Here.' He dropped it into my lap. I was looking into a goat's face. Black, with a beard, the horns and the pentagon carved into its head.

I looked up at Carl. 'A bit dramatic.' I was joking because I'd shivered involuntarily.

'That's Baphomet for you. But he was probably a Christian fabrication. A false-flag job to discredit the competition. They came up against the pagans, against other lifestyles and belief systems, and they needed to grip them. They turned Pan into this. They turned the old gods into devils. It was an easy way to eradicate the non-believers.'

'Pan became Satan?'

'More or less. They made him out to be the embodiment of him, at least.'

I was frowning now.

'Because Pan, even in his original form, wasn't exactly innocent, Matt. Remember *The Wind in the Willows*? The Piper at the Gates of Dawn? That's him in all his innocence. But when you look at the stories, the way he sometimes dealt with his needs, through the lens of today, he was a murderer and a rapist . . .'

I was thinking, dragging all the threads together.

'And the word "panic" has its origins for a reason. That feeling when you're alone in the woods, and something's closing in on you, creeping up, you feel claustrophobic, despite being outdoors, that's *pan*ic, and it isn't a good feeling.'

'So this is some pretty dark stuff I'm looking at.'

'You're the detective, aren't you? You said they tortured and bled a man out, for fuck's sake. Of course this must be dark – you didn't need me to tell you that. I'd tread carefully, mate. Classics lectures aside, when you boil it all down, and all of the varied interpretations and bastardisations are up for grabs –' he gestured at the books lined up on his shelves '– whether your killer channels Pan, or channels the devil –'

I knew what he was going to say.

'– what's the bloody difference?'

61.

Between my regular duties, and time off with Anna, I ran a side inquiry. Chipped away at it every shift, poring over maps and statements from the past and from the recent murders, dredging my memory.

Reynolds could have well been the only person with knowledge of his bolthole, wherever he'd been cooking E, after Wellspring closed down. The way people spoke of the person he was, Solomon, he'd surely have kept something going. A place, a retreat, a location – something more than a lab in a garage.

I was focused on the ecstasy manufacture because of the hazards involved. You didn't want the chemicals and equipment lying derelict for some unsuspecting person to stumble across in the future. But at the back of my brain, I knew what was really driving me. There might be bodies there. More than just Nadine Ruyer.

Christ knows what else had gone on at the place. I had to search. The break only came after I spent a while getting nowhere. Nowhere through land records for the entire region, for Reynolds, or Foley, who at the time he was shot in 2002 must have been living with Reynolds at the new Wellspring site.

Then I'd phoned Phil at Westland Helicopters.

'Matt, pleasure to hear your voice. Hopefully nothing we've done wrong?'

I put him at ease. 'Far from it, mate. I actually need your help.' Their chopper base was over in Makarora, but he had a job this morning and said he'd be on the ground in Haast at nine.

At the small airfield, which sat across the road from where Gus's body had been found by the river, I heard the familiar sound of a Squirrel's engine and rotors thumping, long before I saw it appear through the grey clouds hugging the land today. It flared and settled on the grass, and I waited until Phil had the rotors winding down and was striding towards me with a flight bag in hand before I stepped forward.

'Thanks for taking the time, I know time is money when you're operating something like that ...' I thumbed at the Squirrel.

He grinned. 'Always have time for the boys in blue. You wanted to know about construction jobs?'

'Yeah. In connection with the murders. Gus and old Joe were both in different ways on the hunt for a community site, probably in the middle of nowhere. Huts, power – likely a container or two. But strictly in this region – Haast, Makarora.'

He seemed to know exactly what I was talking about. He started opening up the local VNC, the charts pilots use. Then he paused. 'Matt, has this got anything to do with Liam Goodhue?'

'Yeah, a little. He was looking into the same thing. Did ...?'

Phil made a face that told me he was pissed off with himself. 'Shit, sorry Matt. This makes so much sense now, I should have mentioned it when you were on the phone. He asked me last year if I'd worked any long-line jobs, burying shipping containers anywhere, in the last few decades.'

'And you had?'

'Not recently, but there was a job years back: I dropped three containers on a site up the Wilkin River.' He stared at the map for another second, then pointed. 'In here, that's where I dropped them.'

'What did Liam say about that?'

'Not much. He just said it was DOC related, a contract he was looking into. They needed to use a powered site, or find a powered site, or something. For track building. He just wanted to know where it was. But the original job was for a guy, for a company – I'll dig out the record for you. Liam wanted to fly up the Wilkin and check it out. We never got up there, though, because that was the day we had the power failure and came down.'

Liam found it. Alec had said something after he died, about him maybe wanting to confess. But that hadn't been it at all. *He'd bloody found it.*

Phil said he'd get me the details. 'I can't remember the guy even. I think we dealt over the phone, met once …'

'No problem. His name was Owen Reynolds. He was the guy shot by police up near Knights Point last year. I'd be interested to know if he used a company name.' Then I moved on to legalities. 'Mate, this site may have some derelict drug labs. If this works out, the cops will be executing a warrant up there. We're going to need your information. Are you okay with that? It'll only be on the application for our warrant. Not a court witness or anything.'

'Matt, I'll do whatever you need me to do. You think this is the place? It's what you're looking for?'

'If Liam thought it was, well then yeah, so do I.'

But there were still knowledge gaps I needed to fill. I wasn't walking blind into the devil's den.

62.

I was sitting at one of the picnic tables that lined Lake Wānaka's shore, the bars and shops over the road behind me. I pulled my puffer jacket tighter. The ash trees hung silent, their tendrils reaching to the ground. The water mirrored the clear sky, and snow-covered Mount Aspiring was visible at the far end of the lake.

He arrived an hour late. But I'd waited anyway because I knew it'd be a miracle if he showed at all. But eventually he sauntered up, beanie on, hair down to his shoulders. He had half a cigarette between his teeth and sucked air in as he popped the question. 'Excuse me, sir, you wouldn't be Officer Matthew, would you?' He looked around as he said it, as if the families playing with their kids and the couples lunching were hostile.

I knew he was in his early forties, but he was wrinkled and aged beyond his years. He had a few days' growth on most of his face, and a well-on-the-way goatee at the bottom.

I stood and shook his hand. 'Yes indeed. Matt, please. It's a pleasure to meet you, Cyrus.'

He gingerly took a seat, not opposite but next to me. He fiddled with his pocket, pulled out a plastic bag of buds and started rolling up a joint. He gestured casually at me. 'You obviously won't mind this, given what it is you're actually askin'. Now I need this, you realise? After everything you guys in blue have done, it's the least you can do, so I don't personally care whatcha think.' He got eye to eye with me, stopped rolling. 'No offence.'

I shook my head. 'None taken.' I left him to it and gazed out at the water.

Alec had identified him from the Ruyer file, a mention in another person's statement. A young guy who had embraced the Wellspring vision and probably knew a few things, but had also fallen a bit hard in the direction of the mind-altering practices. It had taken me a few days to track him down through my Otago colleagues, but it turned out the local Wānaka cops dealt with Cyrus regularly for disorder, wilful damage, minor drug possession. He was a guy lost, battling a few issues, and he hadn't received the help he needed.

He lit the joint. The smell wafted over me, but it was one I didn't mind. He spoke first. 'I'm a victim, and I need to know what I'm getting.'

'Of course you're a victim. That's what I'd like to talk about.'

'I'm a victim of the system, Matt. A victim of the state. I needed some help way back then, and all that's happened since is I get picked on. If it isn't you lot it's Work and Income cutting my benefit. If it's not them, it's fucking Oranga Tamariki telling me to stay away from my kids. I need something from you – you're the one asking the favour after all.'

I sighed. There wasn't much I could offer him. Informant payments were so low that it made money a shitty reason to grass. It wouldn't be worth it to him. Beyond that I could show him the door to some support, but he'd have to walk through it. 'What do you want?'

He laughed. 'Money, bro. That's what I need.'

'There's not much I can give. It wouldn't be worth it.'

'How much you talking?'

'A hundred at the most is all the bosses would pay. And that's for top-tier stuff. It would be an insult to you, Cyrus, and I didn't come here to insult you, mate.'

'Well, how much you got on ya? Let's do this old school. Bit of money, that's a start. I don't care where it comes from.'

I did have several twenties in my wallet, but this was well off script. 'What else do you need a hand with?'

He drew in some smoke and held it, closed his eyes, then let it drift off with the breeze. When he opened his eyes he looked at me, drawn, angry. 'Can you get my kids back for me? Can you get my *life* back for me? No? Didn't think so. There's *nothing* you can help me with, *officer*. I've been round that bush for years. Just get dicked around by everyone. If you can't help with any of that, then get your wallet out. Sometimes you just need something to make it through the day.'

I wasn't going to leap to the defence of various government departments. Most of what he was feeling was probably fair enough. And he was right. There wasn't much I could do. 'Look, you've got me. I'm part of that system. A cop, programmed to do what he's told. But this, why I'd like to chat, isn't part of my day job, mate. It's more than that – it's because nobody else is doing it. I'm looking for answers to some old riddles, and maybe, just maybe, there'll be some justice meted out along the way. But hey, I wouldn't want to get in the way of a busy afternoon.'

He grinned at that and his eyes brightened. 'Smartarse. Okay.

Tell you what. Pass us some coin for the trouble. Not for the chat. Expenses.'

'Expenses? You walked here.'

'Look, do you wanna draw up a bloody contract? Just pay the man. Then I'll hear you out, see if it takes my fancy and I'll try share some of what I know.'

I pulled out my wallet and passed him three twenties. 'You'll get beaten up for that in your circles, Cyrus.'

He pulled one shoe off, then his sock. I wrinkled my nose. He rolled up one note and stuffed it into his sock, then put them back on. He shoved another note down his jocks – a bit too far down, I thought. Then he put the other in his jacket pocket and zipped it up. He grinned at me. 'Not my first dance, officer.' He placed his arms on the wooden table, leaned over them, then opened one palm in acceptance. 'Okay. Interest me.'

I couldn't work out whether I liked him or not. But I respected his hustle. I let him get comfortable. God knows how he'd slept last night. I focused on the mountains over the lake, allowing him to rest without having to look at me.

'I'm looking into some murders from way back. One of them, may have been around the time you were at Wellspring.' A groan came from his throat, but he didn't say anything. 'There's a wider picture here. A man was killed in Makarora, another was shot over in Haast. He was the cop there before I was. Anyway, the guy responsible, you'd know him as Solomon.'

Cyrus sat up, straight. He stared ahead, didn't look at me. 'Did … did you get him?'

'We did. He confronted us, further north, when we tried to arrest him. He was shot dead on the highway.'

'You got Solomon?'

'Yeah, you haven't seen the news?'

He coughed and spluttered. 'The only news I get is from the bloody judge when he slaps on some new bail conditions. Do I look like I can afford a phone? Fuck's sake.'

'Sorry.'

'But you got him?'

'Yes, mate. He's out of the picture. I'm guessing that won't come as any great loss to you.'

He shook his head. 'That fucking ... he's the one, officer. It all started with him. Shit, I'm sorry, I didn't mean anything personal, you know, before, hassling the cops, I just ... I know you guys do a good job – sometimes.' He looked at me from the corner of his eye and the smallest grin crossed his lips. 'Nah, Solomon, he was a different kettle o' fish. Where it all started.'

'The drugs?'

'And the rest.'

I could only imagine. 'You want to tell me what happened to you?'

He breathed weed smoke out between his teeth. 'Nope. Not really. But you seem like a smart fella. I'm sure you've seen the gist of it during your career, can fill in the gaps.'

'Okay. I think I know what you mean.'

'So if he's toast, what's the story now?'

'I'm looking further back.' I told him about Casey and Nadine.

A long slow breath came out his mouth and he buried his head in his arms. I waited. Like him, I had all afternoon. He finally spoke. 'I don't know any Casey. When was she there?'

'I think from about 1978 through to the early nineties. Maybe. Initially willingly, then later on, not so much.'

'That's how they played it. They sucked us in, hooked us – and they used us.'

'Wellspring?'

'Yes, sir.'

'I thought it was all-in-this-together type stuff.'

'Fuck no. Maybe way back. Not when I was there. Solomon, he ran the ship. His way or the highway. I … I welcomed the drugs, officer, fucking welcomed them toward the end. Helped me forget. Helped me forget all the –' his voice went up several notches '– shit he did to me and …' He smashed his fist into the table. A bloke sitting on a blanket with his girlfriend a bit further away turned and stared at us. 'What's that prick looking at?'

'Don't let him wind you up, Cyrus. Let it out, no one's gonna stop you doing that while I'm here.'

There was silence for a while as Cyrus battled his demons. Then he just stood up and started walking away.

'Oi, mate …' I jogged up and touched his arm.

I wasn't prepared for the reaction. He swung his other fist and caught me on the jaw, knocking me sideways into the grass. 'I'm not your fucking mate. Piss off.'

The couple stood, the girl first, the guy less sure, but concerned. I waved them away, 'All good, my fault.'

I got to my feet. He was angry, though not at me. But did that matter?

I held up my hands, then felt my jaw. 'Cyrus, I didn't want to talk to you today to cause you grief. I'm looking for answers about those girls. Lots of people have died. I want to make sure there are no leftovers.'

He stood there, breathing heavily, calming himself. 'They're dead. That French girl, he saw her coming a mile off. Did his thing. She didn't stand a chance. Now piss off.'

'Where did Wellspring move to after that?'

He came at me again, lifting his fist, his eyes darting all over the place. I stepped out of his way, came at him from the side. As he turned to face me again, I struck my palm into the bottom of his nose, sending his head backwards. As he toppled, I guided him into a controlled fall, then sat on top of him, locking his arm back near his arse.

'Come on, Cyrus, where did they move? That's all I need, where did they move to?'

He didn't say anything, just lay there.

'Nadine, Cyrus – and any others. So we can find them. There were others too, I take it.'

He spat. 'Yeah, there were others. But you know what? I don't want a bar of it. Good luck, officer. I don't know where Wellspring moved to, I fucking legged it soon as shit went down with the French girl and the cops moved in asking questions. I don't know and I don't care. If they moved, follow the drugs. Must have kept that going, it's how he got shit done.'

'Right. Any pointers there?'

'No. But ...' he coughed. 'You might be a bit healthier than I am but if I were you I'd go carefully now. Those folks ran that place, they were so fucked up they'd make the devil himself look sideways at 'em.' He spat. 'Now get the fuck off me.'

I released him and he leapt up, dusting himself off, shaking himself down. Then he locked eyes with me, turned and ambled away.

He gave me the finger over his shoulder.

63.

Follow the drugs I did. I'd hassled Brent to put a good word in with the other detective sergeant at Greymouth, convince her I wasn't going to stuff her case up.

And David Williams had been positive about catching up with me. He'd obviously been helpful already when it came to Reynolds, and had had his sentence reduced to home detention as a result. Just before I left home, the phone rang. It was Phil.

'Matt, I have those details for you. Got a pen?'

I wrote down the job number, the cost and the coordinates for the location of the drop.

'Thanks, mate. This is what I've been after. You're a legend.'

'No worries. I'll get the hard copy of the invoice to you somehow.'

Anna could see I was stoked. 'Good news?'

'Got the location. Wellspring version two. Where they moved. Should be able to find the labs – and maybe anything else we haven't found.'

She beamed. 'This is good, this is bloody good ...'

'Here's hoping. Look, I've gotta go. David might have a bit more on it. May have even been to the place, if he'd been buying drugs off Reynolds for as long as we think he had.'

I kissed her goodbye and drove north to Greymouth.

* * *

He met me at the door, the same cheese-cutter sitting proud on his head. 'Well, here we are, full circle, Senior Constable.' He gave a short smile, clearly still dealing with the fallout of his wrongdoing.

I thanked him for what he'd done already. 'That supplier, he was responsible for a lot of really bad shit, David. Despite the way he was taken out ... look, bringing an end to that, was a good thing.'

'Doesn't excuse what I did. I just got carried away. First for cash, then I actually convinced myself I was doing a good thing, helping those kids have a good time. Can you bloody believe that? I actually thought I was doing something that wasn't so bad.'

I inclined my head in understanding. 'We only do them 'cause it makes sense at the time. I get what you mean – I've been there before. I haven't sold drugs to teenagers, mind, but I've done a fair few things I thought were right, that in the cold light of day were pretty bloody bad.'

He looked up, but I wasn't going to elaborate. 'What else do you guys need to know?'

I handed him a photo of Reynolds. 'How many times did you meet him? I think you told the Greymouth guys it was every month?'

'Yeah, yeah. Sometimes he came up, sometimes I went down.'

'Did you ever meet at his place?'

'No. Never. He never talked about it. Fair enough, too. You don't exactly tell all to street-level dealers, they're the ones who roll on you. And look, here we are.'

I moved on to Makarora, the connection to Wellspring. 'Did he ever talk about a community like that, a retreat?'

'I gave all I knew to the local guys … I think they did a warrant on a house down at Jacobs River …'

I stopped him. 'I know, I was there. Sorry, I know you've covered a lot of this before. Did he mention the environment, or birth, rebirth, life cycles, anything like that? Anything you'd call spiritual?'

He looked confused by my question. 'No, I'd describe him as having a straightforward sort of attitude, I didn't get any sort of hippie vibes, no. Nothing like that.'

This was what was confusing me. Nothing about Reynolds so far screamed charisma. Nothing suggested he had the people-power to pull Wellspring off.

'Did you ever know him by his other name, by Solomon?'

David's eyes came up and met mine, a frown deepening between them. 'Solomon?'

'Yeah. That was another name he went by, at this retreat.'

David shook his head. My blood went cold. 'Nah, that's not right. Where did you hear that?'

My face felt warm. 'It's …' and I had to stop myself. Where the fuck *had* I heard that?

'I think you guys have been getting muddled. See I met Solomon, once. He came to a resupply. With Reynolds.'

You knew there was something wrong. With all of it.

As he described Solomon, my heart began thumping. I started shaking, or at least had that feeling where you think you're shaking but it's actually adrenaline and shock rippling through your body.

You knew this. You fucking knew. But you didn't back yourself on it.

He'd played me from the start.

Of course he had. Someone like Solomon would have to be pretty good at that.

I pulled out my work phone – Greymouth had cell reception, of course – pulled up a photo and showed it to David.

'That's him. That's Solomon.'

I thanked him, grabbed my keys and sprinted for the door. Brent's cell went straight to voicemail. *Shit.* I left him a message.

I pushed the wagon, doing an easy one twenty most of the way. *Bloody should have called more people. Now you're in zero phone coverage, you dumbarse.* The hours ticked by and the wheels hummed below me, as I mentally beat myself to a pulp.

***

As soon as I got to Haast, I started to spread the word. He was a local and any sighting was important. Darren at the Antler hadn't seen him, but he said he'd ask around, get some people onto it. Next door at the cafe I got a different response. As Sheryl digested what I was telling her, she actually grabbed my forearm. 'Matt, he was just here, looking for you.'

'For me?'

'Jesus, Matt, he said he'd ...'

'What?'

'He said he'd wait at yours ...'

Leaving Sheryl with her eyes wide, I tore around the corner and immediately spied the muddy tracks on the driveway.

No, fuck, Anna ...

I almost broke my own door down, Glock drawn, yelling as I went in like a steamroller. 'Anna! Armed police! Anna, are you here?'

Two chairs were turned over. There was glass on the kitchen floor.

Blood on the kitchen bench. Anna's phone, screen shattered, was lying on the stovetop where it had been thrown against the splashback.

64.

I called comms from my landline, gave the operator the rundown and handed on Phil's coordinates. I did the maths. I was going to get there long before anyone else. She said back-up would be dispatched to my place, and asked me to hold the crime scene until they arrived. I politely told her fuck no, the scene could hold itself. I wasn't hanging around for a catch-up.

I got thinking and phoned Alec too, left another message. Maybe he could write a story about it all if I didn't make it back.

I was outside at my wagon, actioning the M4 rifle, checking the chamber when Tara came running up the drive. 'Matt? What's happening? Mum said you . . .'

I cut in. 'Anna's been abducted – she's probably out in Makarora somewhere. Possibly up the Wilkin. Go home and wait out, tell your mum it'll be fine. Back-up's on the way.'

She processed it all. 'What? No, I'll . . .'

'Bullshit you will.'

'Your back-up is miles away, and they'll come here first

anyway, won't they? To the scene? They won't meet you wherever you're going.'

'I told them where I was going.'

'Well, I bet that's off script.' Her look was accusing. 'They won't charge on after you. They'll secure this scene first.'

She was completely right, but I couldn't deal with her concern. I held her upper arms. 'Tara, I need to get moving. Wait here, hold this scene for whoever turns up. Don't go inside. Nobody in or out. Can you do that?' She eyed the semi-automatic rifle as I rechecked the chamber, then placed the weapon on the passenger seat of the wagon. She nodded, and without a word, retreated down the drive.

The look she cast me as I reversed past her gave me pause. She wasn't angry. Or upset. She was scared. Scared for *me.*

***

Tyres burning, I left Haast behind and climbed into the Alps on the pass road. I went over the movements I'd make, trying to put some sort of plan into action. I'd ford the Makarora, then head up the Wilkin River valley as far as the wagon would take me.

I didn't even notice the darkness of the trees as the forest closed over when I crested the pass. I was head forward, focused on the road, brain racing ahead, thinking through where I'd try to cross the river.

You're a mess. If you'd bottomed all this out at the start, Anna would be safe. You've killed her. You've bloody killed her.

As I left the beech forest of Haast Pass behind and came out into the flats, I saw the river flowing to my right. Somewhere up ahead and further right, the Wilkin joined it. I went on almost to the head of Lake Wānaka, before turning off to the right, into an appropriate-looking private drive. Another farmer's place. I chewed up the gravel all the way to the front door, stopping in a cloud of dust. Out, rifle slung and one hand keeping it held behind me, I was met by a shocked young couple, shielding a kid.

I explained I was police. 'Folks, I need to cross the Makarora, get to the other side and up the Wilkin valley. I need to do it now.'

The guy recovered slightly, looked at my wagon. 'Well, you aren't gonna do it in that.' He went inside briefly, then threw me some keys and indicated his Ford Ranger. 'Take it. It'll get you across.' He pointed behind the house, out to the river. 'Go in down there – you'll see a track we've made. Head straight for that bank of stones. When you're there, you head straight for the tallest tree on the far side. You'll make it fine. The banks between the braids in the river are your friend. Keep the foot light, but not too light, or you might get pushed along.'

'Thanks.' The cavalry would be coming at some stage and I didn't want to remove transport options, so I left the keys on the wagon's roof. Then I started up the Ranger and gave it shit.

I hit the water a bit too fast, kicking a wave up the front and over the windscreen. I kept on, the water shoving up against the vehicle, rocking it as it bounced along the riverbed on the huge tyres. I crested the stony bank midway, straight up and over, got eyes on the tree he'd described and hit the water on the other side.

More bouncing, more rocking. But I didn't care about the vehicle. Or myself. If I got stuck, I'd be out the door, I'd swim my arse off and walk the bloody rest.

But the vehicle made it out and on the banks of the Wilkin I drove as fast as I dared. Sometimes I was on the rocky riverbed, bouncing and shifting and grinding, knocking myself about as the truck did its thing. Sometimes I was on grassy scrub that had taken root on the sand, the tyres digging in in protest and then jolting forward, losing traction, then gripping, losing then gripping, as I kept my foot down. Occasionally I was on solid land, but the kind that was forever changing as it was ripped, torn and shaped by the river that had been carrying shreds of mountain down with it for millennia.

Keeping the main flow of water on my right, moving up the valley, peaks on both sides, I left the Makarora valley, and civilisation, behind.

I had the Google satellite images in my brain, and knew that when the river bent around to the south-west, up ahead to my left somewhere, was where Phil had dropped the shipping containers. There were big open flat areas of land there, alluvial grassland between the rugged bush-clad slopes and the water. I wished the vehicle on, bouncing, rolling on the uneven ground, knocking it with every rotation of the tyres. I kept an eye on the M4 rifle stuck beside me, not wanting that thing bouncing around the cab and maybe the safety coming off.

What are you doing? He's unhinged. Put himself on a pedestal like a god. Thinks he's the sum of all things. Are you equipped for this?

But all I could think about was Anna.

* * *

I must have done several kilometres. My arse hurt, and so did my head and shoulders. They'd taken a couple of good cracks as I hit the uneven ground too hard, too fast. As I neared the huge, sweeping bend in the river, I slowed, stopped, grabbed the rifle and leapt out.

Into silence.

The first thing I did was move well away from the truck. Into the tree-line. I got on my stomach, and leopard-crawled a good few hundred metres further on into the bush, heart thumping, getting a nose full of soil and leaf litter. If someone had spotted me the last thing I needed was to be slotted by some high-powered hunting rifle before I'd even started. I waited in the bush for ten, fifteen, twenty minutes. It was agony. The feeling of wasted time. Every second counting for Anna. But I told myself I was no good to her dead.

But Anna's running out of time. She could already be dead.

Remaining in the beech trees, I kept the water out on my right, moving upriver, looking for the area that Wellspring version two would have called home.

About a kilometre on, it was easy to pick. The riverbed flattened out wide, around the bend. Towering snow-capped peaks were visible on the other side, and on this side, a huge, flat area opened out in the crest of the river bend. There was a collection of small buildings, and the hum of a generator.

I tried to calm my breathing, to make use of every sense I had. I was only going to get one shot here.

I waited, breathing, trying to slow my heart rate. There was no movement. But I couldn't see any shipping containers. They must have been buried.

I decided to box around the whole place, get a feel for it. I stayed in the trees, moving left, thinking through every step with big, exaggerated movements so that I didn't trip while keeping my eyes out where it mattered. I caught a whiff of chemicals on the air. Acetone.

There was something else too. Smoke. Charring.

A clearing opened up in the bush behind me and to my left. Backing up to it, I took a final look out at the shacks, then turned my attention to the little open space among the beech where the trees had been felled and the stumps removed. The far end ran into the base of a rocky cliff, which rose above me, the feet of the mountain range that overshadowed the whole place.

The smell of charred wood grew stronger.

Rifle ready, thumb playing with the safety, I stepped towards a depression in the rock ahead. As I drew closer, it was clear a fire had been lit here, how long ago I didn't know.

I saw burnt wood and charcoal, then stopped cold. Blinked.

What had once been a goat or a sheep's head, scarred horrifically, teeth glaring, had been burnt in this pit. What the fuck had gone on here? I touched the edges of the rocks and immediately pulled my hand back in surprise. *Jesus, that's hot.*

And, sitting near the edge of the pit I spied a wooden bowl. It held something black and viscous. I touched the liquid, lifted my finger, rubbed it between finger and thumb. It was a familiar sensation. I gave it a sniff. Blood.

My senses shut down, focused on keeping my own blood pumping, on preventing me from freezing out of some sort of fear paralysis. But it meant all external sounds overlapped each other, and I was too slow to react.

Wind blew through the clearing, rustling the beech trees at the edges. My hearing had tuned out the sounds of the bush, the birds, the odd branch falling in the wind. Everything merged together, lowering my awareness.

Fast, determined footsteps trudging across the grass.

Before I could turn, before I could bring the M4 up into the aim, something heavy smashed into the back of my head. My vision exploded into slivers of silver and red and I pitched forward.

It all went dark before pain even registered.

65.

I was hurting badly. A full body ache that terminated at the back of my head, blurring my thought processes and leaving me reeling, disorientated, confused.

It took me a while to set things in some kind of order. I was sitting – in a chair of some sort. I couldn't be bothered looking around. My eyes hurt. I couldn't be bothered thinking.

'What the fuck.' I spat the words out, to myself, to try and get some brain cells going and make some sense of what was going on.

Night? Day? Who knew.

It was dark. I couldn't see anything. The blackness closed in, suffocated me. I tried to use what I had. Strained my ears. I was pretty sure I was inside, because I couldn't hear a thing.

When I shifted, trying to reach up to my head, pain shot across my arms and back. I realised I was bound by my arms to something below and behind me. *Shit.* Then I remembered. And knew I wouldn't be working anything else out right now.

I started opening my eyes wide, trying to absorb any speck

of light, looking around for something to focus on, a different shade of black or a sign my vision might be adjusting to the dark. I tried twisting my head left and right, but achieved little other than firing sharp pains down my neck with every move. I was thirsty.

I could now see that there was a lighter, greyer area in front of me. Maybe a door. I lifted my foot and dropped it hard, checking the ground. It clanged with a dull sound, but something dragged on my boot. Plastic sheets? But definitely a hard surface beneath. I stamped on it again. Metallic.

I did it again, then moved my foot around on the surface. Learned nothing else. I looked left and right again, but I couldn't really see anything. So I gave in.

I sat there, waiting. I felt like I'd give it a few hours, then start yelling. This wasn't the movies. Panic needn't set in immediately, and if he'd put me in here, like this, he was obviously coming back. And if not, if I was to be left, then a few hours probably wouldn't hurt me either way.

Breathe. Use this time to try and get your shit together.

It felt like it wasn't a very long wait. The sound rang out ahead of me, someone dropping down metallic rungs or steps. Then silence. Then a harsh twisting, pulling, clanging.

Of course, you idiot. You're in a shipping container. You're underground.

There was, too, that chemical smell I'd caught a whiff of in the trees.

The door screeched open and light poured in from outside, giving me a glimpse of a ladder that climbed out to somewhere above. I saw gumboots, somebody backlit and in shadow, dragging something behind them. I heard grinding and the door closed again.

I knew it was him. The way he moved, his footsteps on the container floor. Another light was switched on, blinding me, the bulb somewhere near my face. I couldn't see anything, but I didn't have to.

Ivan's voice croaked by my ear. 'Thanks for joining us, Matthew.'

66.

He was carrying my M4 rifle, slung down his side.

I'd always thought it'd be something out of my control if I left this life early. A car accident. Shot during a traffic stop, or a warrant gone wrong. Maybe a freak medical event – a ruptured aorta at forty-five, or something genetic, predisposed.

And now my life was up. I wasn't going to say goodbye to Hailey. I wasn't even going to get to apologise to her, for chasing ghosts – the same thing that almost got us both killed a few years ago.

I looked up at the figure in front of me. Tried to lick my lips. 'What do you want?'

There was no movement, no recognition I'd spoken. Maybe I hadn't – my throat was paper dry. He lurched over to the side of the container, then behind me, fucking about with something back there.

His voice croaked again, drifted over to me. 'Lose the fear, my friend. We're all in this together. Everything will still be here when it's over for you. And you'll be part of it all, again.'

Jesus Christ, I'm going to be delivered a sermon by a nutcase in my final moments.

'They took something from me, all those years ago. Men who believed they were the keepers of the law, despite their ... extracurricular activities. Men who had a different standard of right and wrong – hypocrisy, at its purest.' He was moving about, pulling something, something that slowly squeaked along on wheels. 'The morning star. When she was thrust upon us years ago, I knew I had to stay with her ...'

I closed my eyes.

The voice kept echoing around the container. 'When her time came, it ended and began in the same moment. The fire didn't burn out, it transferred, and then before I could even step in, those men took her from me again. Stole her from me.'

He pushed a trolley, with a flat, bench-like top, out in front of me. On it were a series of plasticuffs threaded through holes in the centre. There was also a solid-looking, rubber-coated mallet. And a steel chisel.

He came closer. His bald head was glistening with sweat, and his eyes were bloodshot. 'You know where she is, now, don't you, Matthew?' He held up the mallet, checking its weight, then placed it back on the trolley. He cut the plasticuff holding my left arm to the chair, slid the trolley beside me, and secured my arm to that instead. I was fixed to the trolley and there was nothing I could do about it. His eyebrows went up. 'You need to tell me, my friend.'

I was thinking fast, too fast, my heart rate skyrocketing, the blood starting to pound in my ears. I stared at my left hand.

I licked my lips again. 'Liam and Joe took the baby, you told me ... they probably buried ... her, over in Canterbury

... from what you described, probably in the swamps behind New Brighton ...'

'You're like a dog with a damned bone, Matthew. I'll be honest with you: you're going to die here. But you can speed up that painful journey if you're straight with me too. I know you've found her. Share that with me. Please.'

I'd made inquiries, sure. Hospitals in Canterbury. Old birth records. Foster parents with long memories. No description, just a feeling, just a time, and just a huge part of the country.

He picked up the chisel. I shivered as he lined up the cold heavy steel at the base of my forefinger. He paused, then I felt the chisel lifting, being replaced in the same position on my ring finger.

I shut my eyes. *Give him an alternative. Anything.*

'I can help you, Ivan. There's a way to sort this out. Let me help you.'

He glanced at me, saw the panic rising and shook his head. 'There's only one way and I'm waiting.'

The blood was pumping, fast, through my heart, feeling like it was going to burst out my pulsing ears.

The cold metal lifted off my finger again. Fast breaths, in and out.

'No, I'm not an animal, Matthew. Here.' He moved away and I felt my heart rate come down a few clicks. But then I tasted salt and hide, as a leather strap was forced into my mouth. 'Bite. Honestly, you'll want to.'

Some cloth was tightened around my face, tied off behind my head.

'It's for the saliva. Goes everywhere, unfortunately.'

I began to shake. My body warmed all over, as I lost control.

My metabolism was trying to take over, to deal with what was about to happen.

He picked up the chisel again, and I looked away. Stared at the floor of the container. At the plastic sheeting.

I felt the steel against the base of my ring finger again.

I groaned, as my body tried to shut down, to escape, to switch off. The nausea burst up my throat and I hurled into the gag, the mess hitting the cloth and spilling out the edges, warm chunks spreading down my face. The smell of bile hit me. Silent tears streamed down, joining the vomit.

Not like this.

He raised the mallet, but kept his eyes on the chisel. I vomited again, bucking, shaking, sick pouring down my chin and chest, struggling to breathe through the thick, chunky mess in the cloth.

I bit the leather strap hard.

The mallet dropped fast.

And I screamed.

67.

I opened my eyes to pain.

It was radiating all over me, head, heart, chest, arms … I couldn't identify it, it consumed me. Helpless, I was moaning, the pitch rising steadily. I smelled sick, I smelled piss, I smelled copper.

Then the pain receptors sorted themselves out, and I screamed.

My finger. My fucking finger.

My left hand was bandaged tightly. I couldn't see the stump, but I saw the blood seeping through.

He appeared in front of me, expressionless. 'Can't have you bleeding out on me, Matthew. I need to keep some control. But you're one down, nine to go. How long, do you think?'

I couldn't arrange any thoughts through the pain. The agony swept my whole body in waves, constant, spreading. My breathing was ragged, and fuck knows what my heart was doing.

I registered a stronger odour of spew, realised the gag had been removed.

Did he just say something? Or had I made that up?

My head was swimming. There was no way I'd last ten fingers.

Fuck this. Hailey would understand. Better I went quicker than her hearing I'd suffered for days.

How could I end this? I was tied down. Couldn't move. I tried to think. Maybe I could piss him off, get him angry, make him lash out. But he didn't seem like the type of person whose skin I could get under. Not now. Not in my condition.

'You want this over quicker? Tell me where to go. To find her. Whatever you can give me, I promise I'll speed this up.'

Fuck you.

'If not, I've got all the time in the world.'

My head was rolling from side to side.

'Fine. Your choice.'

I blocked him out, focused my thoughts on family, on Hailey, on the pointless way I'd ended my life, chasing a creature who'd offed people with no effort. Why the hell hadn't I waited?

And Anna. Where the hell was Anna?

I needed to know, before I went, I just needed to know: Would she have a chance before the cavalry arrived? I gritted my teeth. 'Is Anna ... what's happened to ...'

'Just concentrate on ending your pain, my friend.'

The words got to me. My eyes flew open and I spat vomit in his direction. He didn't flinch. Just wiped the bile off his face, then fixed his blazing eyes on my finger.

I felt the chisel again, this time against my middle finger. I knew I couldn't last. My body wouldn't hold up to much more of this. It would be over pretty quickly after this one, I was sure of it. The mallet rose again. I forced my teeth together but kept my eyes open – and waited.

Then I heard a sharp, piercing beeping.

The mallet clanged on the trolley. I heard his boots pounding on the container floor, the door being wrenched open.

He'd disappeared in a panic.

68.

I wasn't getting another chance. I was going to die anyway. There was no reason to sit back and wait.

Move. Move, you fuck.

I tensed, gritted my teeth, breathed in and forced my body up and backwards. The chair tipped and I hauled on my left arm, pulling the trolley with me. The bloody stump of my finger shot pain right up into my chest. I went over backwards and hit the container floor hard.

As my eyes darted around, I spied the bench at the back. Saw the black sliding stock and the pistol grip. The moulded handguard. My rifle.

I shoved with my legs, moved my one good arm, strained, groaned, pulled myself along the floor. It was only a couple of metres, but I was dragging a trolley with me, and a chair, the plasticuffs biting the whole way up my arms.

The graunching of metal on metal was going to bring him back.

Move. Move faster. Or you're dead.

I wormed my way to the bench, taking the furniture with me. But I couldn't stand. I swivelled on the floor as best I could and used my feet to kick the M4 off the benchtop above me. It clattered to the ground, and I knew my time was up.

Feet stamped down a ladder and I pulled the M4 around with my good hand, aiming it in the general direction of the container door. The gun wobbled like fuck, all over the place.

Ivan came steaming in, then slowed and pulled up as he took in the sight of me, bleeding on the floor, trolley and chair still attached, aiming a rifle his way. He turned on a dime and rushed back for the door.

I dropped the safety with my thumb, but had to tilt the rifle up as I did it, to stop the weight dropping it forward out of my grip. As the barrel came back down, I fired off some rounds at his retreating shape.

But he was gone.

I couldn't think of any other way to do it. I needed freedom from the shit hanging off me, but couldn't get eye level with the benchtop to see if there was anything that would cut.

I rested the muzzle of the rifle against the plasticuff connecting me to the trolley. I checked the clearance, tried to keep the firing line away from the hard metal bits. But I was in a bloody shipping container. With jacketed hollow-point rounds. Even if it wasn't going to ricochet, pieces of hot rounds were going to spit everywhere. Chances were high I was about to hurt myself even more.

I squinted and squeezed the trigger.

The boom popped my ears and I felt the exhaust gases blast my face. But I immediately felt release on my fucked hand and arm, as the plasticuff split apart.

I could push myself up now, to bench height, attached only

to the flimsy chair. I grabbed some pliers, struggled with my throbbing, mutilated left hand to slip them beneath the plasticuff on my right arm. Got them under. Squeezed and twisted and yanked. It snapped.

I slung the M4 and stumbled for the door.

69.

I heard the storm before I came up the ladder into it. I rolled over the top onto wet grass, cold rain smashing over me. I got my breath, spitting water out with every exhalation.

My whole arm burned with pain. I'd got the blood pumping, and the pain in the stump of my finger had exploded right up to my shoulder. As I sucked air through my teeth, I heard engine noise. Powerful headlights washed over me. I rolled onto my stomach and tried to aim the rifle at the vehicle, before slumping and clutching my hand.

'Matt! Matt!'

Tara?

'Let's get him in. Come on!'

Another voice. *Alec.*

The tension in my chest slipped away as relief flooded in.

They gripped me under the arms.

'Matt . . .' Tara's voice was small and broken now, taking it all in, seeing how busted up I actually was.

Alec froze too. 'Holy shit.'

Then I held up my left hand.

'Let's get you in the car. We gotta move. He's somewhere here? Or . . .' Alec left the alternative unsaid.

I shook my head. 'He's moving around.' I coughed. 'And Anna's here. Somewhere. He's got some sort of monitor on her, she must be in a shit state. Are there other containers?'

I moved with them, balling my butchered hand under my right armpit, balancing the rifle across me, grunting through my teeth as we searched through the pouring rain. It was daytime, but the darkness of the storm had killed all visibility.

Alec, on his knees, ripped open another hatch. He dropped down the ladder, twisting open the container door. Light flooded out from inside. But so did the stench of acetone. Even up at the top of the ladder it burned my nostrils and made my head swim. Peering down, I could see a gas mask hanging beside the door.

He yelled up. 'There's no one in here, Matt. Just cooking pots, fans . . .'

'Get back up here, mate. It's a drug lab! Come on, those fumes will knock you down.'

He clambered back up the ladder and the three of us moved to the next one.

I was hoping, praying to fuck knows who, that we'd find her. *Please.* But I wasn't prepared for how.

Tara got to work on the final hatch, then repeated what Alec had done. No smell. But this time the silence told me all I needed to know. I practically fell down the ladder, staggered through the door.

Anna was lying on a mattress, cuffed to strops fixed at the corners of the container. She was out of it, juiced up on something.

There were trolleys against the wall. Full of pill containers and syringes.

I stepped forward slowly, watching for signs of life – begging for signs of life – then saw the blood-stained bandages wrapped around her arms. I felt the anger surge.

She was hooked up to some sort of heart-rate monitor, with various pads stuck to her and wires sprouting from them.

Alec had come down behind me. While I stood there, frozen, broken and useless, he and Tara got Anna free, ripping off the wires, but sliding the IV lines out a lot more carefully.

They didn't fuck about. They knew time wasn't something we had. Between them they managed to haul and carry her up the ladder, Tara pulling from above and Alec lifting her in a fireman's carry.

I followed them up, my hand now experiencing a new burn, a cold one, and the throbbing felt like it was going to explode.

They laid Anna down, then each gripped her under an arm and hauled her over the grass to the headlights. They pushed her in across the rear seats. Alec stayed in the back with her.

Tara stood in the rain, hair plastered down her face, looking at me.

I gestured at the driver's seat. 'Jump in. You're the one with two hands.'

But that's not what her body language meant. She knew I was leaving them. Her eyes were wide. 'Matt, let's go, now.'

Alec yelled from the back seat. 'Oi, Matt, get in the fucking wagon, let's go!'

The rain was loud, but not loud enough to drown out the cracks. Shots slammed into the vehicle, harsh thumps as they punched through metal.

Shit.

I turned, tried to raise the rifle. My left hand wouldn't grip it, so I balanced the barrel across my left forearm, and squeezed off several rounds into the grey murk where his shots had come from. Then I dropped the M4 on its sling, crossed the gap to the wagon and pushed Tara into the driver's seat with my good arm. 'Go! Take Anna, get her back to the farmhouse.'

'No . . .'

I cut her off, spitting water. 'You got me? You guys are it for her, got it? Go!'

'We're not . . .'

More rounds punched through the metal of the vehicle's body. One shattered the rear windscreen. I slammed the driver's door on her, pounded my palm against the window. 'Go! Bloody go!' I made circles with my finger, fast, egging her on. She revved the engine and put her foot down.

I fired back, then moved offline, away from the disappearing wagon, low, as fast as I could. I covered several metres and then knelt, peering into the rain. I couldn't move my arm. It was both frozen and on fire. I'd lost a lot more blood – it was seeping through the cloth.

I cradled the M4 again, thumb resting on the safety, and eyes searching ahead, stole into the storm.

70.

Water drenched me as I moved. My crotch was rubbing and my upper body was starting to freeze. The pain in my hand and arm was getting duller, but the thumping was increasing. That wasn't a good sign when the blood was flowing out.

I was trying to remember the land from the satellite images. He couldn't cross the river. Too cold.

He had a choice of left, upriver into the mountains, which was doubtful. He could go right, downriver, the way I'd arrived, but he'd run into whoever came to help us out if Tara made it back. His only other choices were forward and back. Back into the beech forest, but he certainly couldn't scale the mountains behind.

He could hunker down under the canopy, wait till we left. But if I'd hit him, he'd be bleeding solidly, and the cold would soon kill him. No, he needed to leave and he must have had other transport. I'd remembered a vehicle as I'd come in, sitting out towards the river by the shacks and the generator.

I ran forward about ten metres, then moved offline again, running, diving into the dirt.

But no shots came.

I stared ahead, got my bearings and headed for the river. I found the vehicle, an old white Toyota Hilux, and cleared it. No sign of him.

I ran forward another few metres, about to move offline again, but this time I'd seen him.

With rain streaming down my face, my left hand throbbing, spew and blood trickling away down my front, I closed in on the figure hunched in a ball, down near the river.

Ivan tried to crouch and raised something long up from the ground. I squeezed three shots at him, rifle waving about, hoping they would at least make him put his head back down.

He dropped to the ground and I approached him from the side, gave him a kick. He rolled over onto his back, groaning.

I pointed my rifle at his face, but it swung wildly, jerking, uncontrolled.

Then I spied his, lying just out of his reach where he'd dropped it. I stepped sideways towards it, keeping my rifle moving over him, until I could put a foot on it. It was some sort of automatic .22 with a wooden stock. Either he'd run dry or he was too fucked to bother anymore.

Keeping my foot on his rifle, I looked closer at him, over the top of my M4.

He was a miserable picture – eyes squeezed shut, soaked through, hammered by rain. His bald head was white and he wasn't looking good.

The hate rose. I let it. A sense of calm moved over me.

Letting the M4 hang on its sling, I grasped his collar with my right hand. He made a gurgling sound and I realised one of my rounds had actually hit him. He was on his way out, unless he got some medical attention fast, but I didn't start looking for and plugging his wounds.

I spat through the rain. 'I never knew there was a child. Until you told me in the interview. You gave me something to undo.'

He tried a laugh, but he choked on blood and water. 'I gave that to you on a plate … when I thought you'd lead me to her.' He spat again. 'After they stole her from me.'

I dropped him, levelled the M4 at his face. 'Those men …' But I checked my reaction. Felt the rise, and let it pass.

'Nadine Ruyer. Where's her body?'

He shook his head. 'Don't know. That was a job for … you killed up … up on the highway. That girl was with us for years, she lasted until –' he coughed and spat again, '– until the drugs … I don't know. But help me, get me help, and I'll do my best, help you look … 'Cause I told him … I told him, up off the Desert Road, they'd never find her …'

I kept the rifle moving over him. He was in a shit state. I figured he needed pressure on at least two wounds, and he'd lost a lot of blood. The exposure out here wasn't helping his chances. If I got him out to the farmhouse, got an ambulance heading there, or a chopper, he might have a chance. But he needed pressure on that bleeding.

I watched him, saw him pleading, willing me to gift him a way to survive. I kept the M4 moving over his chest. Then I dropped it slightly, so I could talk over it. 'We're all in this together, isn't that right? You'll be part of it again. That's what you're all about, isn't it?'

My left hand throbbed and I felt dizzy. Grey flecks were closing in at the edges of my vision.

He frowned, not quite grasping what I was saying.

I was becoming aware of the man I'd been, and who I now was. Joe had had better insight than I did myself. *Some of the guy you used to be.*

I gave Ivan a final look, let the M4 drop on its sling beside me, then walked away into the storm. He called out through the rain. But I didn't turn back.

71.

With the passing of decades, the chances of getting all the answers diminishes quickly. We didn't find Nadine Ruyer. The land surrounding the Desert Road is a very, very big place.

I was feet up at home and Anna was going overboard looking after me. It was only a finger. I'd live. It was still wrapped up, and needed dressing changes, but it was looking okay. But she was feeding me, keeping an eye on me – and, if I'm completely honest, ensuring I didn't hit the bottle too hard.

She'd recovered pretty well. Physically anyway. Psychologically, she would probably never mend. Morph, change maybe. But fix? Not sure that's truly possible, not after trauma like that.

We'd just farewelled Darren and Alec, who'd arrived together to share a beer. Darren had been subdued, not his normal piss-taking self. I think the reality of the events swirling around Haast had hit him pretty hard.

Alec had just blamed himself for ever giving me any information, not quite knowing, as he'd said, how far I would end up taking it and running with it.

Anna was passing me a cup of coffee as there was another knock at the door. She turned but I grabbed her arm. 'Hey, it's okay, I'll get it.'

It was Brent.

'Mate, good to see you!'

'Hey, Matt. Got some stuff you're most likely keen on seeing.'

Anna eyed us nervously but Brent reassured her it would be okay. He passed me a stapled series of pages, a statement and a small brown paper bag. I checked the statement first: 'My full name is Marilyn Susan Chambers . . .'

I glanced up at Brent. 'She rolled?'

'She's gonna do some serious time. For what she was a party to. But yeah, she rolled. In a sense. There obviously won't be a trial for him, but it helps clear things up for the coroner.'

After the events up the Wilkin, a team from Otago had entered the new Wellspring site, completed a full clearance. They'd found Ivan's body out near the river. His death was the result of excessive bleeding from the gunshot wounds. Exacerbated by exposure.

I read Marilyn's statement, remembering to take it with a grain of salt. But it was revealing in places.

I didn't agree with any of it, when it all changed. I didn't agree with the representation, having a leader, any of it. Ivan said they needed controlling, they needed help to achieve what they were hoping to. It happened slowly, not overnight, and when I realised that he'd essentially brainwashed people, and drugged them, and turned them well off the path they'd arrived to find, I . . . I panicked. But I was scared. There was nothing . . . I didn't think anyone would believe me. He had total control. And I knew what he was capable of.

I wondered how much she knew about Casey's death. I soon

found out.

That poor girl was drugged up to make her forget. She told me when I bathed her that first night. She'd killed her father, you know. The parents had fought in the car. The father strangled her mother, and Casey had found a golf club in the boot.

I looked up at Brent, then at Anna, my mouth open. Brent gestured for me to keep reading.

I guessed that the bikies had helped her, had cleaned things up, used the rifle, had made it look different, to protect her, but they never said anything about that to me.

I reached into the paper bag, pulled out an old, light leather journal. The yellowed pages were pretty flimsy, but it had obviously been well preserved.

'Mate, is this . . . ?'

'Yeah, that's hers. There aren't any belters in it, but I thought, you know, you might like to read what's there. For closure.'

I held Casey's diary in my hand, feeling the weight of it, then returned it to its bag. Something for later.

EPILOGUE

Dunedin

I gently touched my left hand, pushed against the scar tissue on my finger. It wasn't the same, I'd never get full movement back. And it still throbbed. But it had been months, and the dressings were gone.

I got my head in the game, pushed open the door of the cafe. I took off the coat in which I'd shielded myself from the winter, placed it on one of the stools at the leaner. Sat down on the other. I'd planned this, rehearsed it. Thought about the impact on her life. Tried to figure out if there was a better way to do it. I just didn't want to do it at her flat, or interrupt a lecture she had to attend, or make it any worse than it would probably already be.

I'd phoned her two hours ago. Yes, I'd got through to Hannah. Yes, absolutely she'd be happy to meet with a police officer, and help in any way she could. Of course, she knew she wasn't in trouble, but was intrigued all the same.

I was early, and my brain was racing, wondering how this was going to go.

Then the door swung open, and though I'd never seen a picture, I knew it was her.

She had that same in-love-with-life look I'd seen before, captured in the briefest moment in time. In an old photograph of her mother.

When her eye fell on me in my suit pants and collar, she smiled questioningly, then walked towards me. Complete and utter trust, confidence in the goodness of the world.

ACKNOWLEDGEMENTS

I am incredibly grateful to Juliet Rogers and Diana Hill from Echo Publishing, for putting their faith in me and guiding me all the way.

Special thanks to my agent Nadine Rubin-Nathan at High Spot Literary. Ever since that early encouragement and positive feedback, I've known I was in safe hands.

Thanks to editor Anna Rogers for being fully invested and understanding what I was trying to say. And to early test-dummies Hamish Hood, Martin Coutts and Daniel Blake, whose first impressions and suggestions were crucial. Thanks, gents.

To my wife Emma, thanks for what have been the best years of my life. Your all-in support and constant encouragement got this one off the ground and back to earth again. And of course my two favourite comedians, Ellia and Archer. You are the greatest inspirations, and also the reason for my putting pen to paper. Fingers crossed I'll now be able to spend even more time with you both.

And finally Craig Sisterson, trumpeter of Kiwi crime authors far and wide, from Invercargill to Scotland and everywhere in between. The most heartfelt thanks to you, mate, for seeing something right at the start, and for believing in Matt Buchanan.